NICE GUYS
FINISH DEAD

The Hollywood Murder Mysteries

PETER S. FISCHER

THE GROVE POINT PRESS
Pacific Grove, California

Also by Peter S. Fischer
THE BLOOD OF TYRANTS
THE TERROR OF TYRANTS

The Hollywood Murder Mysteries
JEZEBEL IN BLUE SATIN
WE DON'T NEED NO STINKING BADGES
LOVE HAS NOTHING TO DO WITH IT
EVERYBODY WANTS AN OSCAR
THE UNKINDNESS OF STRANGERS

Nice Guys Finish Dead

Copyright © 2012 by Peter S. Fischer

ISBN 978-0-9846819-5-2

To Bob Swanson and Jim Vawter...
...first in war, first in peace and first to
suffer the indignities of my first drafts and
set me back on the path of righteousness...

CHAPTER ONE

There are two Wrigley Fields.

The real one, home base to the beloved Cubs, is located in Chicago on West Addison Street in the northwest part of the city. Built in 1925 it has a storied history. Within its ivied confines most of the great ball players of the 20th Century have performed their heroics. Unfortunately, the vast majority of these great players have played for other teams. Seven years ago the Cubs won the American League pennant but it has been 44 years since they have won a World Series. Even as the infatuation for their lovable losers continues, Chicago's citizenry grows impatient.

I am sitting in a box along the third base line at the other Wrigley Field, a lesser stadium also owned by chewing gum magnate William Wrigley Jr. who owns the Los Angeles Angels, a AAA ball club in the Pacific Coast League. Since it is early March, the season is at least five weeks away and so the studio for which I work as a publicity man, Warner Brothers, has leased the stadium to film several scenes for an upcoming picture starring Ronald Reagan and Doris Day. Am I excited? You bet.

I didn't just volunteer to ride herd on this picture, I jumped at the chance. My boss, Charlie Berger, head of publicity, wanted to hand it off to one of the junior juniors on staff because he knew, and so did I, that publicizing this picture was going to be trouble free. But I said no, this one's mine. As the number two man in the department I can usually wheedle Charlie into giving me what I want and this is one I really want.

It's not just that the cast features a couple of easy going stars. It doesn't get any better than working with Doris and Ronnie. The picture itself, "The Winning Team", is a warm-hearted, low-key biography of one of baseball's greatest pitchers, Grover Cleveland Alexander, and his loving wife Aimee. No violence, no infidelity, just a story of two likable people you can't help but root for. Pap? Not on your life. Alexander suffered from epilepsy which in mid-career drove him to drink. Labeled a hopeless drunk and washed up in baseball, Aimee convinces Rogers Hornsby of the St. Louis Cardinals (Frank Lovejoy) to give Alex another chance. He responds by delivering a winning season and in the 1926 World Series, he wins three games for the Cards, re-establishes himself as a genuine American hero, kisses his leading lady, fade to black. THE END, and everyone goes home feeling uplifted.

So why am I so anxious to be involved in this pleasant but far from extraordinary picture? Two words. Peanuts Lowery.

For those who never heard the name, Lowery is a top echelon professional ball player. He is one of a dozen or so major leaguers like Bob Lemon, Hank Sauer, Jerry Priddy, and George Metkowich who have roles in the film. When I saw that he had been signed, I could hardly contain myself. Peanuts has always been a special hero to me.

It goes back to the 1945 World Series which was being sent via shortwave to all the troops still in Europe. The war had been over for months but the Army moves slowly when it moves at all and I was stationed in Bonn writing insipid stories for 'Stars and Stripes' and wondering what four-star's butt I would have to kiss to get myself on a troop carrier going back to the U.S.A. Then came the Series. Purists scoff. They dismiss it as a seven game farce between Tall guys and Fat Guys. The "real" ballplayers like DiMaggio and Williams and Feller hadn't returned home yet so these were the wartime stars, the oldsters, the young kids and the 4Fs. It didn't matter to me or to my buddies. We huddled around the radio close to midnight reveling in the exploits of the Cubs and the Tigers. So maybe the aesthetics weren't there but the games were close and it went to a seventh game and for a week my pals and I could vicariously enjoy a little bit of home in the midst of a foreign land where "bitte" doesn't mean the opposite of sweet.

And it was then that I became fascinated with the exploits of Peanuts Lowery. Why, I don't know. Maybe it was his name but from that moment on I would make it my business to check the box scores to see how he was doing, even after I returned home, even after he got traded to the Reds and then to the Cards.

It's now Thursday morning, March 2nd, and as I said, I'm sitting in a box seat section along the third base line in Wrigley Field which is doubling for Sportsman's Park in St. Louis, Yankee Stadium in New York and several others. We had gotten in a half day's worth of footage on Monday before it started to pour. The rain continued Tuesday and Wednesday but today the air is clear, temperature brisk but not cold and director Lewis Seiler is getting a lot of film on Reagan, Lovejoy and the "real" ballplayers.

On Monday I'd showed up early to seek out Lowery and within thirty minutes, we were laughing and chatting like a couple of childhood friends who grew up in the same neighborhood. He's a good looking guy with a nice smile and at 35, he can still play but we both know he's coming to the end of the road. Even so he's looking forward to a terrific year with the Cards who have a top notch team and a new manager in Eddie Stanky, the scrappy second baseman from the post-war Dodgers.

"We got a great bunch of guys going for us this year, Joe," Peanuts said. "Leo Durocher has it all wrong. Nice guys don't finish last and we're going to prove it."

He became amused when I told him about our little gang of typewriter hacks huddled around the shortwave radio in Bonn for the '45 Series. He was less amused when I mentioned Hal Newhouser and Virgil Trucks, the Tigers' ace pitchers. He shook his head. "Unhittable," he said. "Absolutely unhittable". At that point, the assistant director called for the ballplayers and he had to leave. We shook hands, vowing to reconnect later.

Meanwhile Buddy Raskin, Warner's top photo guy was running all over, speed graphic in one hand and a couple of Argus 35mms hung around his neck, one for color and one for black and white and he's shooting everything in sight. The Pathe Newsreel team was also on hand and picking up footage of the ball players and of Reagan in a vintage Phillies uniform, doing windups. To tell the truth I've seen better form on a department store mannequin and if the real Alexander had pitched that way, he wouldn't have made it through spring training.

It was just before noon with the storm clouds gathering when I looked over and saw Peanuts in an animated conversation with this skinny little blonde guy in civvies. I'd never seen him before but even as I was looking, Peanuts spotted me and and waved and the two of them started toward me.

"Joe," he said, "I want you to meet a pal of mine. Ned Sharkey. Ned, this is Joe Bernardi. He handles publicity for the picture."

Sharkey reached out and grabbed my hand firmly, a warm smile on his face. The guys complexion was olive, swarthy, maybe Italian or Greek, and his eyebrows thick and black but what I thought was blonde from a distance was a second rate bleach job that made him look a little silly.

"How y'doin', Joe. Nice to meet you." There was no disguising it, this was a big city boy. He had a ring with a big rock on the pinkie of each hand and he wore a flashy three-hundred dollar watch. If I'd had to guess, I'd have said he was a hundred per cent Chicago. A moment later Peanuts confirmed it.

"Ned used to hang around the ballpark all season back in the war days."

"Loved those guys. Loved 'em!" Ned grinned.

"Anything we wanted, Ned took care of it. Hockey tickets, comp meals at some nice restaurant, nylons----"

"Nylons. Wow," I said appreciatively.

"Yeah, they were tough to find but I had pals to help me, you know what I mean. Hey, nothin' was too good for my Cubbies, you know what I mean?"

I didn't know what he meant exactly but I could guess. Wartime was boom time for a lot of sharp characters and I guessed that Ned was one of them. But then who was he hurting? He was just giving it away to a bunch of his idols and what was wrong with that?

"So, Ned, what are you doing in town? Visiting?" I asked.

He shook his head. "Naw, I live here. Well, not here exactly but in Altadena. You know where that is?"

I said I did. It's a town of maybe 35,000 people nestled in the foothills of the mountains just north of Pasadena. It's about as far away as you can get from City Hall and still be part of greater Los Angeles.

"I gotta sports bar and grill up there. The End Zone. Well, not exactly just me. Me and my wife, Minerva. Well, she's not exactly my wife, you know what I mean?"

Yes, I knew what he meant.

"What is it with women, anyway?" he asked. "In the beginning she's great. Loves sports. It's her life. Can't get enough of it. A couple of years later, its like, sports. Yeah, sports is okay. So is this what we're gonna be doin' the rest of our lives, running this lousy sports bar? Two more years and it's 'I'm going out of my fucking mind in this bar and in this town. Let's get a life!'"

"She sounds like a peach," I smiled.

"Yeah, and she's been sitting in the fruit bowl too long. I tell you, Joe, I don't know what she's bitching about. We got the best damned sports bar in the L.A. area. Good food, good booze, lots of memorabilia. Hey," he grinned, "you know what it's worth?"

"No idea," I said.

"Two million bucks. That's what I got offered twice already by this guy in town, Jesse Hovack. Runs a real dump of a bar and grill down near the bus depot. Me? I've got the primo place in town and am I going to sell? Hell, no. I don't care what the old lady wants. So, anyway, whatadaysay, Joe? Come on up. On the house. Be proud to have you. And bring a lot of friends."

I thanked him for his generous offer and said I would take him up on it.

His eye fell on the craft services table with its collection of cakes and fruits and sandwiches and soda. "Hey, how about soda? You guys want a soda? Sit tight. I'll get 'em." And before we could reply he was hustling down the steps onto the field headed toward Maisie, the craft services girl, who was starting to pack things away because the ever darkening sky promised rain momentarily.

"Nice guy," Peanuts said.

"Seems to be," I concurred.

We watched as he scooped up three cold sodas and then tried to hand Maisie a bill. She shook him off but he laughed and refused to take no for an answer and finally ended up stuffing it in her shirt pocket. He laughed and blew her a kiss and started back. Maisie saw us watching and threw up her hands helplessly, smiling. We toast each other with the open bottles and drink deep. Ned starts to tell a story about Peanuts and some redhead in a bowling alley but he doesn't get far.

It was at that moment that the first raindrops started to fall. Not those itty-bitty drizzle drops but humungous globs that, if they hit you in the nose, could drown you within seconds. We ran like hell for the entranceway before we got totally soaked. Meanwhile pandemonium reigned on the ball field. The AD was hustling Reagan toward the dugout holding an umbrella over his head. Everyone else was getting soaked. Peanuts said he had to hook up with the crew and Ned went with him. I stood in the shelter of the passageway for at least ten minutes in the vain hope that the rain would abate. When it didn't I made a mad dash for my car in the parking lot. It was farther than I remembered and I squished loudly when I slipped behind the wheel.

At that moment I spotted Ned also making a mad dash for his car which was close by mine. I laughed watching him get as soaked as I was. He fumbled for his keys and finally climbed in. He was driving one of those odd 1950 Studebaker Starlight coupes, designed so it looked almost the same coming and going. It made quite a splash when it was first introduced.

He took off and I followed him to the gate where he turned left and I turned right.

Lucky for me, my adoring and adorable secretary, Glenda Mae, summa cum laude from Ole Miss and one-time Homecoming Queen, has an in with Men's Wardrobe and within thirty minutes of hitting my office, I found myself wearing a double-breasted suit worn by Gary Cooper in "Meet John Doe". It probably looked better on Coop but I didn't complain. It was dry.

At three-thirty I was hard at work at my typewriter cranking out press releases to be mailed out that night to the hundred major papers in all parts of the country. I'd hone in on a local angle if I got a chance: Hank Sauer, born in Pittsburgh, Gene Mauch raised in Los Angeles, Catfish Metkovitch, right fielder for Boston's pennant winning team of 1946. Aside from that they'd be pretty much the same but the photos from Buddy would be included. I anticipated a lot of press, mainly in the sports pages, but as the saying goes, any publicity is good publicity. Besides, I'm pretty sure that baseball junkies are going to like this picture.

The phone rang. It was Buddy. He had this picture of Peanuts Lowery and me and this kinda short guy in civvies having a laugh sitting in the stands toasting ourselves with Coke bottles. I told him the guy's name was Ned Sharkey and he owned a sports bar somewhere up north near Pasadena. He and Peanuts were good friends back in Chicago a few years back. That's all I remember. Buddy said no problem and hung up.

So like I said, now it's Thursday morning and I'm watching Peanuts take a few cuts with the bat while the camera is rolling. The box seats along the first base side are packed with maybe 150 extras who will scream and shout, wave banners and chew on crackerjack. After getting several hundred feet of footage, the second assistant director, a kid named Bud Aronson, will send them off to change wardrobe and then he will bring them back, rearrange the seating and start all over again. This will probably go on all day as Alexander had a long career and performed his heroics in a multitude of ballparks.

I look over to my right and spot Ned Sharkey coming toward me. He looks sharp in his cashmere sweater and a green plaid Irish cap and a suede leather jacket. In his hand he's holding a copy of yesterday's edition of the L.A. Times.

"Great story, Joe. Really great. Peanuts liked it too. So did the other guys."

"Thanks, Ned," I say.

"I had a bunch of the guys up to my place last night. On the house, of course. They loved it. Great bunch of guys."

"That's what I hear," I say.

He looks at the article prominently featured in the sports pages and smiles wistfully. "Sure wish I could write like you do, Joe. I got ideas, just can't get 'em down on paper."

"It's a knack, that's all. Some guys can take an engine apart and put it back together. Other guys can't sharpen a carving knife."

"Guess you're right," he says. "I'm pretty bright with The Racing Form but that's about it."

I smile. "You must spend a few hours out at Santa Anita then."

His face darkens and he looks away. "Once in a while but mostly I stay away from that place. I try to stick around home base. We got a guy in town handles the action. No problem." He pauses then looks at me with a sly smile. "I got one going today. Got a good feeling about him, Joe. Seventh at Santa Anita. Base on Balls. That's his name. I mean, look at what's going on here. How could I not bet him, right?" He's looking down toward the batters' box and he sits up straight, "Hey, look at that. The guy's underhanding lollipops into Peanuts and he's missing by a mile."

"He's supposed to. It's in the script."

Ned shakes his head. "Don't seem right," he says.

"It's called acting, Ned."

"You guys ought to let Peanuts do some real acting," he says. "Maybe give him some lines. This isn't the first time he's been in a movie, you know."

I look over at him, surprised, and see that he's not kidding.

Ned laughs. "You mean he never told you?"

"Told me what?"

"The Our Gang comedies. You remember?"

"Sure do."

"Peanuts was in a bunch of them. He was like ten or eleven."

"You're kidding," I say. It's the first I've heard of it.

Ned raises his right hand.

"Swear to God", he says. "Ask him."

"I will," I say, feeling like a dolt for not knowing about it and also feeling like a million bucks because if its true, I've got a great human interest angle to pursue.

Just then I see Bud Aronson jogging toward us. He greets me with a smile and then turns his attention to Ned.

"Excuse me, sir," he says, "but we need a few more people to fill in the spectators. Would you be interested?"

Ned waves him off with a smile. "No, thanks."

Aronson persists pleasantly. "Ten bucks for the day and a free lunch. You sure?"

Ned's face darkens imperceptibly. "Yeah, sonny, I'm sure and I can afford to buy my own lunch." His tone is sharp and edgy and out of character.

Aronson backs off, raising his hands defensively. "Sorry to bother you, sir," he says as he turns and hurries back to his gaggle of rooters.

"Some guys can't take no for an answer," Ned says.

I look over at him. The happy go lucky expression has been replaced by a look of annoyance. I see something new in his eyes but I don't know quite what it is.

Just then I look toward the field and I see that everyone is moving off. The A.D. has called lunch and everyone will be eating at the tables set up just inside the main entrance. I know the caterer, he's a good one, and the menu will probably include fried chicken, steak or pot roast and some kind of fish. You get 45 minutes to eat and then the whistle blows and it's back to work.

Ned gets up. "You eatin', Joe?" he asks.

"Not right now."

"I'm gonna catch up with Peanuts," he says.

I nod. "See you later."

I watch as he ambles down the steps and starts across the field to the lunch area. I decide that, despite that little flareup, Ned really is a nice guy.

After lunch the A.D. dismisses the ballplayers who have already been filmed and I watch as Peanuts and Ned leave the stadium. They both wave to me as they head out to the parking lot. I see Jerry Priddy standing alone near the batter's box and walk over to him. I want to know what it was like to play for the dreaded Yankees and how he liked being second base to Phil Rizzuto's shortstop. I am not surprised to find that he is a genial man, happy to reminisce. I decide he's worth a stand alone feature.

By now I'm getting a little hungry. Ollie Perkins, the caterer, and his crew are just cleaning up but Ollie's an old friend and he makes me up a plate of fried chicken and cole slaw with a Dr, Pepper on the side. I sit down to eat and open up yesterday's Times which Ned had left behind to check out Phineas Ogilvy's Hollywood gossip column which I had missed reading yesterday. Phineas is a flamboyant character who has a way with words that never fails to amuse. He's also a good friend.

I'm about halfway through the first paragraph when a shadow falls across my paper and I look up. There's a guy standing behind my left shoulder. He's big enough to block out the sun and the moon and the stars as well. I put him at about six-four and two-eighty minimum. He's wearing a dark blue suit with wide pinstripes, a yellow polka dot tie, and a pearl grey fedora. His huge nose is like a blob in the middle of his wide swarthy face and his cauliflower ears jut out at right angles from his head. I suspect at one time he might have been a fighter who lost too many fights. In his ham-like fist he is carrying a newspaper. He tries to smile at me. It's an effort. I think his brain is in first gear and likely to stay there.

"You Bernardi?" he asks.

"I am," I say hoping he's not a bill collector.

"Your people come from Calabria?" he asks.

"No, Newport, Rhode Island," I tell him. It's none of his business that I was an orphan raised by three different foster families.

His face screws up. It's obvious he's never heard of Newport. It's even money he may never have heard of Rhode Island.

"I knew a guy. Aldo Bernardi. His people came from Calabria."

"That's nice," I say.

"He almost married my sister."

"Even nicer."

"Good thing he didn't," the big guy says.

I'm not curious enough to ask why that was.

He thrusts the paper at me, holding it so I can see the story it is open to. The paper is the Chicago Sun-Times and next to the story, which I wrote, is the photo Buddy asked me about on the phone. Me and Peanuts and Ned toasting Coke bottles.

"This guy here, he's an old friend of mine. I'm trying to find him." A big sausage of a finger is pointing at Ned. The caption identifies him as a "local restaurateur".

"Ned," I say.

"Yeah. Ned," he says as if he doubts it. "I figure you must know where his place is, right?"

From the moment I looked at the big galoot I sensed there was something wrong with him. Amend that. A lot of somethings. I decide that a guy as nice as Ned really doesn't need a visit from this guy so I play dumb.

"No, actually he never told me the name of it. Just that it was down near the airport. That's all I know."

"Airport."

"Where the planes fly in."

He nods. "I was there this morning." He screws up his face again. "You sure he didn't mention no name?"

"Very sure, but in case I see him, who shall I say is looking for him?"

The big guy glowers. "Nobody. Tell him nobody is looking for him."

At that he turns and strides toward the parking lot. I don't think the stadium shook but I wouldn't swear to it. I try to finish my lunch but I've suddenly lost my appetite. I get up and head for the parking lot. I think maybe I'd better get in touch with Ned or Peanuts or maybe both and tell them that this big guy is on the prowl.

As I slip behind the wheel of my Ford I look in the rear view mirror and catch sight of this big black Cadillac across the way. Maybe it's my imagination but I think I see the big guy in pinstripes sitting in the driver's seat, watching me. I start the engine and back out and then as I drive by, I look intently at the Caddy. It must have been a momentary hallucination. The car is empty.

CHAPTER TWO

get back to my office around three and as soon as I walk into the anteroom I smell it.

"What the hell is that?" I say to Glenda Mae.

"A wild guess? I'd say Moo Goo Guy Pan," she says. "He's been waiting for forty minutes. For him that's a new world record."

"Who's been waiting?"

"Charlie Chan," she says. "Look for yourself."

I walk into my private office and Phineas Ogilvy is sitting at my desk, scooping Chinese food from a carton with a pair of chopsticks. A black and gold enamel tea pot I recognize from Glenda Mae's shelf is at his elbow. There are two empty white cartons in my waste paper basket.

"Come in, old top," he says with his mouth full, pointing to my visitor chair which apparently he wants me to sit in. "Missed lunch. Couldn't wait for din-din and it was imperative I speak with you this afternoon. Tea?" He smiles, gesturing to the pot. I shake my head.

Phineas is larger than life, outgoing and flamboyant. He is also larger than a hippopotamus. He and food have been life-long friends and weighing in at close to 300 pounds I am afraid his lifelong friend is some day going to kill him. Phineas knows it but he hasn't the will to cut back. His excuses are legion and for a man with a Mensa level I.Q. they are neither well thought out nor convincing. Those who do not know him believe him to be homosexual. An afternoon spent with any one of his three ex-wives is guaranteed to convince you otherwise.

"Before I get involved in whatever intrigue you have brought me, I need to make a couple of phone calls," I tell him.

"Of course," he says, making no move to get up, He turns the desk phone around and shoves it toward me.

I shake my head as he shovels more lichi nuts and pea pods down his gullet. I ask Glenda Mae to get me Peanuts Lowery. The unit manager has the number and after that a guy named Ned Sharkey who owns a sports bar called The End Zone in Altadena. I'm sure it's in the book.

"What do you hear about Reagan?" Phineas asks, peering at me over the rim of the food carton, loaded chopsticks hovering near his mouth.

"What do you mean, what do I hear?"

"What do you hear?" he repeats.

"I know he's thrilled about making this picture," I say.

"Good God," Phineas mutters in disgust.

"Okay. How's this? He's in his last year as President of the Screen Actors Guild. He's not going to win an Oscar anytime soon and he throws like a second string pitcher on a high school baseball team. Quote me on those last two and I'll put you on my shit list."

The intercom buzzes. I pick up the phone and listen. Peanuts is not answering at the number they have and Sharkey hasn't been at work all day and no one knows where he is. I tell her to keep trying and hang up.

Phineas is glowering at me.

"About Reagan?"

I shake my head. "I have no idea what you want me to tell you, Phineas."

He pounds his fist on my desk.

"Prevaricator! Dissembler!" he shouts.

"I don't think so," I say calmly. Phineas is a frustrated ham actor with a huge vocabulary. When he gets like this, I humor him.

"You cannot seriously sit there and tell me that you do not know that Reagan is getting married this weekend," he fumes.

He's got my attention. "Ridiculous," I say.

"I hardly think so."

"And how did you stumble upon this nonsensical piece of misinformation?"

"I will not reveal my source," he says huffily, "But it comes circuitously from Brenda Marshall."

"What's she got to do with it?"

Phineas's eyes start to pop as he raises both eyebrows. "Do with it? Do with it? She is going to be Nancy's Matron of Honor and her husband Bill is going to be Best Man! That's what she has to do with it! And thank you, my good friend, Joseph, for sharing the news with me!"

Suddenly I think Phineas has actually caught wind of something. Bill Holden, Best Man. Brenda Marshall, Matron of Honor. It's possible. Everyone in town knows that Ronnie proposed to Nancy a few weeks ago at Chasens but assumed a wedding was months away.

"When? Where?" I ask.

"When? Saturday. Time of day, unknown. Site of the nuptials, also unknown. This is all very hush hush, old top, and I demand to know why," Phineas tells me.

"It may be hush hush because that's the way they want it or it may be that someone has fed you a line of rancid limburger."

"A Hollywood wedding without cameras, without reporters, without an admiring throng at the church door? Ridiculous. These people are actors!"

"Calm yourself, Phineas. I'll check with Reagan and get back to you."

"Do that, old top, but if I don't hear from you by deadline, I am prepared to print the rumor. Tell that to the Gipper."

"I will. Meanwhile, do nothing until you hear from me."

"And can I trust you?"

"Haven't you always?" I ask.

"Reluctantly," he sighs.

When Phineas finally departs, leaving the smells of Shanghai behind, I ask Glenda Mae to track down Reagan for me. Six minutes later she lets me know he's in Men's Wardrobe picking out a robe and pajamas for Monday's shoot. It's the scene where he goes out to the back of the farmhouse in the dead of night and starts to pitch baseballs at a glove nailed to the barn wall. Its a short walk from my office so I amble over and when I get there Pinkie Weitz, the wardrobe guy, is showing Ron something in silk paisley. Reagan is unimpressed. Grover Cleveland Alexander is a farmboy, not Cole Porter.

Reagan grins when he sees me.

"Joe, how'd you like the shoot this morning?"

"Looked great, Ronnie. Seiler's moving right along."

"He's a decent guy, I guess. This picture may turn out okay," Reagan says. Pinkie shows him a plain colored wool robe, nothing fancy. "Better, Pinkie," he says slipping into it. It's a good fit. "It'll do," he says. Pinkie nods but he doesn't seem happy. I think he had his heart set on that paisley. Reagan hands it back to him and the two of us go to the door and step outside.

"So, Joe, what's new?" Reagan asks me.

"Not much," I say. "What's new with you and don't tell me

nothing, Ronnie. Any plans for the weekend? Like Saturday, maybe."

He stops short and eyes me cautiously.

"What do you hear?"

"I don't hear anything, but one of my boys does."

He grimaces and looks away, muttering, "Damn." He looks back at me. "Who?"

"Phineas."

"What does he know?"

"He knows that Bill Holden and Brenda Marshall are part of the package."

Now he's annoyed. "How the devil---?" He doesn't finish it.

"He didn't say. Is it true?"

Reagan nods.

"Nobody's supposed to know. It's just going to be the four of us. Low key, nice and quiet. And now---" He looks at me. "Can you keep this under wraps?"

"I'm not sure. Phineas is ready to print the rumor in tomorrow's edition. If he does, your secret's out." I hesitate. "I might be able to make a deal."

Reagan's listening. "Go on," he says.

"We give him the full story after the ceremony. He writes it up in the Sunday edition. I send Buddy Raskin to the site and he takes one photo of the happy bride and groom. Phineas has an exclusive for Sunday. Monday morning we tell the world."

"Will he go for it?" Reagan asks.

"Yes," I say with certainty.

Reagan hesitates, then says, "Make it happen."

We spend a few minutes going over the ground rules, what he can say, what he can't. The ceremony will take place at the Little Brown Church in Studio City in the Valley at 11 a.m. After that the happy couple will slip away from the city until Sunday evening. Even though it's Nancy's first marriage she wants no press, no hoopla. Reagan, once divorced, shares her feelings. I tell Reagan I'll put Phineas on a short leash. Not to worry. He thanks me and walks off.

I head back to my office rehearsing my speech to Phineas which may in the end include threats of bodily harm to his person. As I turn the corner and head for the building which houses the press unit, a man who apparently has been loitering nearby starts toward me.

"Mr. Bernardi!" he calls out.

I stop and turn toward him as he approaches, hand extended.

"Hi," he says. "Jack Cody, M-Milwaukee Journal."

I shake his hand a little warily. His name is not familiar.

"Did we have an appointment?" I ask.

He shakes his head. "No, I just thought I'd t-take a chance."

He's a young guy, clean cut, early twenties I imagine. Looks more like a copyboy than a reporter. Maybe that's because I'm getting older. I try to remember my early twenties. I was wearing khakis and trying to learn French from Berlitz, just in case I met a ma'amselle who didn't parlez Anglais.

Cody reaches into his wallet and extracts his business card. I give it the once over. Milwaukee Journal. John "Hat Trick" Cody, Sports Columnist. I smile at him.

"Hat Trick?"

He grins sheepishly. "It's a l-long story," he says.

I nod. "How'd you get on the lot?" I ask.

He shrugs. "Just walked on. T-told them I was here to see you. No p-problem."

This is a lie. The guys on the main gate make the Secret Service look like mind numbed slackers. No, there's something about this guy and it isn't just his mild stammer which at first I attributed to nerves but now I think is something else.

"You seem a little young to be a columnist, Jack," I say.

"Wartime," he replies. "I was too young for the service and the T-Trib needed ambitious would be sports reporters. I was sixteen when I started. In less than a year I was covering the C-Cubbies and the Black Hawks." He reaches in his pocket and takes out a cigarette. His hands seem to be shaking as he lights it. I start to get a little crawly feeling across my shoulder blades. It happens sometimes when someone's trying to bullshit me.

"If you've g-got a few minutes---" he says hopefully.

"Actually, I don't," I lie.

"It won't take long. We got your release with the photo of you and P-Peanuts Lowery and Ned Sharkey and since I had to fly out here anyway to see family, I thought I'd catch up with those two. M-Mid-40's my old man used to take me to Wrigley Field and he had an in to get into the locker room and even though I was still a k-kid these guys treated me real well and, heck, I'd just like to see them again."

The crawly feeling is getting crawlier.

I shrug. "Well, I'd like to help but---"

"The paper said Ned was running a local restaurant and I was w-wondering----"

"Press release," I say.

"What?"

"You said you got the press release. Now you say you saw it in the paper. Which is it?"

For a moment, he seems stumped. Then he says, "It was both. We got the release, we p-printed the story. It was in the p-paper."

"Right," I say, disbelieving.

"So if you could just tell me where Ned's restaurant is----"

I cut him off.

"I'm pretty busy right now, Mr. Cody. I suggest you call my office and set up an appointment."

"All I n-need is---"

"And next time you try to come on the lot, make sure your name is on the visitor list at the main gate. Okay? Nice meeting you."

I push past him and head for the staircase to my office. I sense he's following me and I turn, looking him square in the eye.

"You don't really want me to call security, do you?"

He hesitates for a moment and a hard look of anger flashes at me. Then he turns on his heel and walks away. I watch him go. This is the second guy in two hours that has come looking for Ned Sharkey. I am not amused.

As I enter my office I throw Glenda Mae a big smile and ask her to get Buddy Raskin on the phone for me. A couple of minutes later I'm at my desk sifting through my phone slips when Glenda Mae buzzes twice and I pick up.

"Buddy?"

"What's up, boss?" he asks.

"That picture of me and Peanuts Lowery and Ned Sharkey. Which papers got it?"

"The Chicago Trib and the Sun-Times," he says." Lowery and the restaurant guy gave it local interest."

"What about the Milwaukee Journal?"

I hear the pained disbelief in his voice. "Why would I send that picture to a Milwaukee newspaper?"

"Yeah, that's what I thought. Thanks, Buddy," I say as I hang up. I buzz Glenda Mae.

"A guy named Cody from the Milwaukee Journal may call for an appointment. Give him one and then make sure someone from security is nearby," I tell her. He may show, although

I doubt it, but if he does, I want to find out what he wants with Ned Sharkey. Somehow I doubt it's anything good.

"Will do," she says.

"Any luck tracking down Peanuts Lowery or Ned Sharkey?"

"Not so far," she says. "Shall I keep trying?"

"No, forget it," I say. "I'm going home."

And I do.

I live in a little two bedroom ranch in a pleasantly quiet neighborhood in the San Fernando Valley about fifteen minutes from the studio. It's been my home for four years and it fits me like an old shoe. I can afford better now but why bother? I'm not one for flaunting my success. Besides I like my neighbors and they like me.

I pull my almost new dark blue Ford Coupe into the driveway and park by the kitchen door at the side of the house. I don't pull into the garage because there is another car in there, a shabby 1938 Plymouth Coupe. I can't get rid of it because it isn't mine and the registered owner is out of town and has been for some time.

I can hear the phone ringing even before I open the door and I get to it before my caller hangs up.

"Hello."

"Joe, it's Lydia."

Lydia is my ex-wife. We had a short lousy marriage interrupted by a long lousy war. When she divorced me I thought my world had collapsed on top of me but I survived. We are now pretty good friends and she is married to one of my best guy-pals, Mick Clausen, a bailbondsman. They have one kid, a little boy, Patrick, age one and a half, and another on the way. Mick's older than she is but they act like teenagers in love. Lydia's found her life. She feels bad that I haven't found mine.

"Hey, Lyd, how are you doing?" I ask.

"Hangin' in here, Joe," she says.

"How's the kid?"

"Did you know that the Terrible Twos sometimes come early?"

"That bad?"

"I'll live," she says.

"How's the new one?"

"Judging by the way she's kicking, I'd say she's learning the conga."

"She, for sure?" I ask.

"We're hoping. Listen, Joe, Mick and I are going out for ribs at McMurphy's and we thought you might like to join us."

Uh-oh. Blind date alert.

"What's her name, Lyd?"

"Who?"

"You know who," I say.

"Joe----"

"Lydia."

I can hear her sigh.

"Okay, her name is Jillian. She writes children's books. She's cute and funny and sharp as they come. I think you'll love her."

"Great. And where did you find this paragon of womanhood?"

"Actually, Joe, Mick met her at the office."

"Oh, and which member of her family is the ax murderer?"

"Her nephew and it's only grand theft auto."

"Wonderful. This perfect lady comes from a family of car thieves."

"Now, Joe---"

"Now, Lydia, you are a dear and I know you only want the best for me but I'm fine, really. You don't have to fix me up."

She, of course, is convinced that she does and I suspect she has already dedicated her life to finding me a suitable mate. We dance around like this for a couple more minutes and finally, to get off the phone politely, I say I'll think about it. Maybe some other time. Maybe later in the week.

I go into the bedroom to get rid of the jacket and tie and my gaze falls on Bunny's mirrored vanity. By the mirror there's a mostly used up box of Kleenex next to a dried up mascara brush. They've been sitting there for well over a year, ever since Bunny walked out of my life to pursue a career in New York. I haven't the heart to get rid of them or even touch them. I'm a sucker for self delusion. I keep thinking that someday she'll walk through the door and things will be as they were. If I were rational I'd know better but a guy with a broken heart and a shattered brain stem never knows better. He's lucky if he knows anything.

I go into the kitchen and fix dinner if you can call scrambled eggs and bacon dinner. Usually I call it breakfast but I forgot to stop at the grocers so I make do. I uncap a bottle of Coors, my ration for the evening. Last year, pining over Bunny, I was putting away a six-pack every night and was in serious danger of needing a rescue by Alcoholics Anonymous. Sanity prevailed as I made a wise decision. I may be nuts but I'm not going to be nuts and drunk at the same time.

I plop down in front of the TV with my plate in my lap and watch as the masked rider of the plains and his faithful Indian companion come into view promising a thrill a minute. If I don't fall asleep Groucho's on at eight o'clock. Always good for a laugh. And if I doze off, well, it won't be the first time. Maybe I should have checked out this Jillian babe.

It's twelve-fifteen when the phone rings. I've fallen asleep on the sofa and I'm groggy but manage to get to my feet and into the kitchen to the phone before it stops ringing.

"Yeah?" I grunt into the receiver.

"It's Charlie, Joe. Are you awake?"

It's after midnight and my boss is on the line asking a really stupid question.

"No, Charlie, I'm sound asleep having wet dreams about Rita Hayworth."

"Need your help, Joe. Just got a call from the desk at Rampart Division. They're holding a few of your ballplayers."

"What's the beef?"

"Not sure. Disturbing the peace. Vandalism. I think the cop on duty said they tore apart a pool parlor."

"Nice."

"I'd go myself, Joe, but I've got nobody to watch the twins."

"I'm on it, Charlie. Don't give it another thought."

"Thanks, Joe."

"Forget it, boss. What are underlings for?"

It takes me a half hour to make myself presentable and drive over the hill to the Rampart Division headquarters in downtown L.A. When I get there I find Peanuts, Gene Mauch, Catfish Metkovitch and Bob Lemon crammed into a holding cell. Whatever hell they had been raising a couple of hours ago has evaporated. Now they are quiet and contrite. It takes me about forty five minutes to fill out all the paperwork but when I'm done, Warner Brothers has posted their bail and promised to pay for any and all damages to the pool parlor premises. There is no question Jack Warner will extract this from their paychecks. They are damned lucky they were spared the expense of hiring a lawyer.

When we finally get outside, it's one-thirty and exuberance has returned to three of my four no-longer-contrite charges.

Lemon, who was born and raised in the L.A. area, knows of an all night bar that operates beneath police radar. Mauch and Metkovitch are game but Peanuts just wants to get to sleep. Tomorrow at the ballpark is an "if needed" day. Technically all the footage involving the ballplayers has been shot but they have to report in case there was a problem with the film and retakes would be necessary. Otherwise, they're finished.

The three gay cabelleros, not quite sober, go off in search of more partying while I volunteer to take Peanuts back to his hotel. As we pull out of the headquarters parking lot, I ask the burning question.

"Okay. What the hell happened?"

Peanuts just shakes his head.

"Damned if I know," he says. "One minute we're tossing back beers and shooting pool and having a helluva time. Ned is throwing around money like he had it, paying for everything, but then he was always like that. Always the big shot, even when he was broke. I don't know. I thought he was being real goofy and I ask him if he's okay and he laughs and he says something like, you got no idea how good I feel. I was about to say something else when all of sudden this guy comes out of nowhere, climbs all over Ned's back and starts banging on him with his fists shouting,'Son of a bitch' and 'Bastard' and a lot worse. We try to drag him off Ned but the guy is strong even though he doesn't look it. He was kinda short and fat and I mean, really fat, like the fat guy in Laurel and Hardy. And he wore this toupee that came off in the fight, but I'm telling you, Joe, the guy was like a tiger. Gene and I are yanking at him and he's kicking Ned while he's down on the floor and then we all stumble into a table where this guy is sitting with his date and we knock 'em over, guy, date, table, chairs, pitcher of beer, everything. By now Ned's on his feet and he grabs a pool cue and he's coming after this guy and Lemon is trying to get the pool cue away from him. Ned gets away and head butts the guy who stumbles backwards, grabs a billiard ball and tosses it at Ned. It misses and flies right into the big mirror behind the bar. Now we've got the bartender pissed because he comes out from behind the bar carrying a Louisville Slugger. I guess that's when Ned ran for it. I see him heading out the front door and right away the fat guy is getting to his feet and going after him. That's when the bartender goes to the door and says nobody else is leaving even if he has to break a couple of heads to prove it."

I shake my head. "You ballplayers, you sure know how to have fun."

"Shit," Peanuts mutters. "I hate brawls, even on the ball field."

"And who was this fat guy?" I ask. "Any idea?"

"Never got a chance to ask and Ned didn't say." He points off to the right. "That's my hotel," he says.

I pull to the curb and he gets out.

"See you tomorrow at the ball park," I say.

"I've got a late call. Ten o'clock, I think. If I oversleep you know where to find me," he says. He gives me a little wave and walks into the hotel. I pull away from the curb and head for home.

It isn't until I'm at the top of Sepulveda heading down into the Valley that I realize I never asked him about my visitors earlier in the day. Not that Peanuts would know either of them, though he might. I find the whole thing bizarre. A slick young guy who used to be a hockey hero. A giant redwood with an oft broken nose wearing a pin stripe suit. A chubby little guy with a smutty vocabulary and a bad hairpiece and apparently they all want a piece of Ned Sharkey.

The big question is, why.

CHAPTER THREE

It's early Friday morning. Much too early for me to be up and about, especially considering how little sleep I got last night, but nonetheless I'm on my way to Wrigley Field. It's our final day of shooting at the ball park provided we don't get hit with more rain or some other unforeseen calamity. Movie making is full of them. They're not life threatening. All they do is cost money. But today the air is clear, the temperature brisk but comfortable and there are no calamities in sight. At least not yet.

My mission this morning is humanitarian. I am hoping to finally catch up with Ned Sharkey and/or Peanuts and warn them about the out-of-towners who seem to be much too curious about Ned's whereabouts. Of the two the big guy seems the most dangerous. I suspect the other one, while not a physical threat, may have the ethics of a Congressman. In either case, forewarned is forearmed.

I turn onto West Addison Street on the outskirts of Hollywood and there it is a few blocks ahead on the left. Strange, for this early hour there seems to be a lot of activity and I think I see flashing red and white lights from the roof of a police squad car. Sure enough when I pull up, there are cops all over the place.

A uniform stops me but when I show him my Warner

Brothers credentials, he indicates a place for me to park. When I ask what's going on, he shrugs. He's not sure. I park and exit my car and start for the main entrance. Just inside I spot Doris Day gabbing with a couple of girls from hair and makeup. I start toward her. When she sees me she hurries in my direction.

"Joe, what's going on?" she asks anxiously. "They're keeping everybody away from the field."

"I don't know, Doris," I say. "Just got here myself."

Doris is a real trouper and a good pal. We got to know each other last year when she and Reagan were filming "Storm Warning", a pretty grim film about the Ku Klux Klan. Filmed in black and white, Doris not only didn't sing, she got killed off in the middle of the picture. Her fans were less than pleased. I don't know whose idea it was to put Doris in a straight drama - I never could get an honest answer - but wherever it came from, Doris proved herself. She's a pretty face with a great set of pipes but she can also act with the best of them.

Gwen, the makeup girl, pipes up.

"I heard one of the cops say dead body," she says.

"Any idea who?" I ask.

She just shakes her head.

"I wish somebody would tell us what's going on," Doris says. "I think Ronnie's out there. Joe, could you ask the A.D. what the plans are?"

"Sure," I say. "Give me a couple of minutes."

I know what's going through her mind. Nobody works harder than Doris, but if the company's going to wrap for the day. she'd just as soon be home with her twin Irish Setters and her Pekinese and maybe her new husband, Marty Melcher, if he isn't off somewhere cooking up one of his big deals.

I walk through the passageway that leads out onto the field

and the first thing I see is a crowd gathered at the pitcher's mound. The forensic guys are checking out the crime scene as the police photographer snaps off a bunch of shots of the corpse from every direction. It's a body I can't see from where I'm standing so I walk over to Pat Gurney, one of our security guys.

"What happened, Pat?" I ask him.

"Location guys found him out there just after daybreak, spreadeagled across the mound. Phil Oxley says the guy has a little bullet hole right behind his left ear."

I frown. "Hmm, that sounds like---"

"It sure does," Pat overrides me. We're both thinking guys in shiny silk suits whose names end in a vowel.

"Who's the victim?" I ask.

"No idea. No wallet. No watch. No jewelry. Stripped clean. But he's not one of ours."

I stand on tiptoe and crane my neck trying for a better look. I don't get one but when I look over to the third base side of the mound, I spot a green plaid Irish cap. I look back at Pat.

"Short guy. 40ish. Lousy bleach blond hair job?"

Pat nods. "That's him."

It seems that somebody who was looking for Ned Sharkey might have caught up with him.

At that moment I look to my right and see Reagan standing on the steps to the visitor's dugout talking to a very familiar figure. I amble over. A wry grin crosses Aaron Kleinschmidt's face as he sees me approach. He shakes his head.

"I should have known," he mutters. "Bernardi," he says, "I'm going to issue you an official police card identifying you as a professional suspect."

Reagan looks from Kleinschmidt to me and then back to Kleinschmidt. He's totally at sea.

I grin. "It's okay, Ron. Sergeant Kleinschmidt and I go back a long way. It's a private joke."

"Then I won't bother to laugh," Reagan says. He turns to Kleinschmidt. "If we're through, Sergeant----"

"We are, Mr. Reagan. If I need you, I'll let you know. Thanks for your cooperation."

Reagan nods. "See you later, Joe," he says as he walks off toward the parking lot where the company vehicles are parked including Reagan's travel trailer which is provided for him at every location.

Aaron smiles at me. "So what do you know, Joe?" he asks.

"What do you mean? Know what?"

"Come on, amigo. You always know something."

"Let's take a walk," I say.

We wander out to left field where it is deserted. Aaron Kleinschmidt is a homicide detective working out of the Metro Division. When we first met he and his partner tried to frame me for murder. Since that time he has mended his ways and become a pretty damned good cop. We're not really buddies yet but we're working on it. I have his grudging respect and he has mine.

I look around to make sure no one can eavesdrop.

"You first," I say.

"What?"

"You talked to the medical examiner. I didn't."

"Okay," Aaron says. "He's been dead maybe eight hours. Not much blood at the scene so he died someplace else."

"Then why drag him to the ballpark?"

Aaron shrugs. "To make sure he got noticed. To send some kind of message, that's all I can come up with."

"Weird," I say.

"Also weird, he has no wheels. We searched the parking lot. Nothing. So he was brought here, Joe."

"You're sure? The other day he was driving one of those funny looking white 1950 Studebakers."

"No Studebaker. No nothing, Joe. Okay? Good. Your turn."

"The guy's name was Ned Sharkey," I say. "He owned a sports bar called The End Zone in Altadena."

"You sure?" Aaron asks. "Whoever snuffed him took his I.D."

"Positive," I say, "but I have a hunch Sharkey wasn't his real name."

"We've lifted his prints. We'll run him through the files."

"Fax a set to Chicago." I say. "That's where he's from."

I tell him about Peanuts Lowery and how I met Sharkey through Peanuts and how Sharkey was a good old boy around the ballpark back in Chicago.

"A star-fucker," Aaron says flatly. It's a term for hangers-on who like to get close to celebrities.

"No, I think he was more than that. I know that he and Lowery were good friends back then and Peanuts says most of the guys on the team genuinely liked him."

"I guess I oughta talk to Lowery," Aaron says.

"You could do that," I say, "but Peanuts didn't kill him."

"Probably not."

"I hear he got a small caliber pop to the back of the head right behind his ear. What does that tell you?"

"Al Capone."

"Capone's dead," I say.

Aaron shakes his head sadly. "Too bad. He'd have made a real good suspect."

"You want suspects, Aaron? I have personal knowledge of at least two," I say.

I tell him about the tree trunk with no neck wearing the pin stripe suit. Also the smooth article with the phony business card and how they were both really anxious to catch up with their old friend Ned.

"You get any names?"

"Nothing from the big guy. The sportswriter said his name was John Cody. John 'Hat Trick' Cody."

Aaron looks at me skeptically, "How old did you say this guy Cody was?"

"Early twenties," I say.

Aaron nods appreciatively. "Man must really take good care of himself," he says.

"What do you mean?"

"I mean for most of the 1930's Jack Cody played right wing for the Chicago Blackhawks hockey team. In '38 when they won the Stanley Cup, he scored the hat trick in two of the games. Oh, and did I mention he was 40 years old at the time?"

I frown. "That would mean---"

"Yeah, Joe, I can do the math. That would make him fifty four years old this year."

I nod.

"My guy's probably not him," I say.

"Probably not," Aaron agrees. "Hair dye can only do so much. Can you give me an hour or so to sit down with a sketch artist?"

"Sure."

"If these guys have any brains they've probably left town but you never know. The capacity of the criminal mind to do something really stupid is awe inspiring."

"No argument here," I say.

"Come by Metro right after lunch. I'll have it all set up."

"Right," I say.

"Meanwhile I'll send a black-and-white to Altadena to pick up the guy's wife and see if I can get an ID on the body."

We go our separate ways. I head back to the dugout looking for Peanuts but he's not around. When I ask the second assistant director Bud Aronson where he is, Bud says he gave all the ball-players a late call. The first setups today will be for fans in the stands and particularly Doris rooting for Reagan to strike the bum out or words to that effect. I ask Bud to have Peanuts call me at the office when he shows up. Will do, Bud says.

I'm back at the studio by ten and make a beeline for Charlie Berger's office. Charlie is my boss. He's been around since the days of the silents and he's seen it all. In truth he doesn't want to see any more of it and at 62 he really would like to retire but ever since his trophy wife walked out on him last year, leaving him to care for their seven year old twin girls, Charlie's options have been severely limited.

"Dead? What do you mean, dead?" he growls. "The only thing dead at Wrigley Field are the arms of those two-bit pitchers they keep bringing up from Pacoima."

"Dead, Charlie," I say, "and somebody helped him get that way. He has a bullet hole in the back of his head."

"Swell," he mutters, "and I thought the only problem I'd have today could be solved with Kaopectate. Who is this guy? Is he one of ours?"

I fill him in with what I know.

"How do you want me to handle it?" I ask.

He tents his hands on the desk and stares into space thoughtfully.

"Don't," he says. "No press release. If anybody asks, we don't know the guy, never heard of him, the police are investigating, it's a tragic situation, our hearts go out to the man's family, if he had one---"

"And he only put us a day behind schedule," I add, mostly kidding.

"You can skip that last part, Joe. Warner Brothers has a heart."

"Yeah?" I say. "When did that start?"

Charlie points to the door. "Out," he says.

I start out. "I'll keep you posted," I say.

"Do that," Charlie replies.

As I walk back into my office, I ask Glenda Mae to get me the Milwaukee Journal sports desk. I want to speak to a guy named Jack Cody. I sit down at my desk and skim the trades, then turn to Phineas's column in the Times. True to his word he has kept mum about the Reagan nuptials. Phineas knows a good deal when he sees one. Sunday he will have a major scoop which will permit him to thumb his prominent nose at his competitors. For a newspaper columnist, this is equivalent to multiple orgasms.

Glenda Mae buzzes me. Cody is out of the office but expected back momentarily. She left word. If he calls she'll put him through immediately.

I have nothing better to do so to kill time, I take out a sheet of paper and decide to give Doris a nationwide leg up. She is thrilled by this picture, I write. She is thrilled to be working again with her dear friend Ronald Reagan. She is thrilled at getting a chance to once more demonstrate her acting ability in a non-singing part. She is thrilled to be playing a real life American heroine like Aimee Alexander, the great pitcher's widow. By this time I am getting slightly overcome by nausea and I wonder if I can keep this up. Most of the foregoing is probably true but the last part has to be a lie. Doris' part is substantial but the script is weak in too many places to allow her to really shine. In the end she'll come off well but the picture isn't going to earn her any nominations.

Glenda Mae buzzes me.

"Cody," she says.

I pick up.

"Mr. Cody, thanks for getting back to me so quickly," I say.

"No trouble, Mr. Bernardi," he says. "What can I do for you?" I hear a lot of Canada in his speech.

"Well, maybe it's what I can do for you." I tell him about the film we're shooting, about Ned Sharkey and about the discovery of Ned's body early this morning at the ball field.

"Sharkey, you say? Don't know him," Cody says.

"I didn't think you would," I say. "But yesterday I was heading back to my office when I was stopped by this young man who was anxiously trying to find Sharkey, claimed to be a sports columnist for the Milwaukee Journal. Said his name was John 'Hat Trick' Cody and he handed me one of your business cards."

"The devil you say," he sputters.

"I do say, sir. He's about six feet tall, slicked back dark brown hair, brown eyes, swarthy complexion. Possibly Italian heritage. Maybe Greek."

"Could be anybody," Cody says.

"He stammers," I say.

There's a long silence and then Cody says, "Tom."

"Tom?" I say. "Tom who?"

"Tom Scalese. He's engaged to one of our copy editors, Madison Chase. Bright girl. Knows her business. What she sees in Scalese I'll never know."

"Any idea why he'd be passing himself off as you?"

"None. I think I'd better ask Madison. Since she obviously stole my business cards to give to him, she must know what he's up to."

"You would think so."

"She's not here right now but as soon as I talk to her, I'll get back to you."

"I'd appreciate it," I say and that's how we leave things.

I turn my attention back to Doris' press release and finish it up. I start on one for Frank Lovejoy who is playing the legendary Rogers Hornsby. It's not a big part but it's key. Frank has a lot more to do in another release set for this year, a Korean War drama called "Retreat, Hell!" We're all nervous about this one. They say a truce is imminent and the war is all but over but no one really knows if there is a public appetite for a war movie about Korea. After four years of letting the war genre lay fallow, suddenly WWII has had a resurgence with films like 'Sands of Iwo Jima' and "Halls of Montezuma." But they have to do with America's "good" war. Korea is something else and the public's acceptance level may be zero.

The phone call comes in around twelve-thirty and Glenda Mae buzzes me. I think it's Cody getting back to me from Milwaukee but it isn't.

"Some dame for you on line one." she says.

"Who?"

"She wouldn't give her name."

"Why not?"

"She says if she gave her name you wouldn't take her call."

"Odd," I say.

"What have you been up to, boss?"

"Nothing," I say.

"Too bad," Glenda Mae says. "I like her voice."

"Okay. Put her on."

"You sure?"

"Put her on and don't listen in."

"I never do," she says, insulted. "Well, hardly ever."

I punch the lit button.

"This is Joe Bernardi," I say.

"Hi, Joe. This is Jillian Marx."

Oh, oh, I think. Blind datus interruptus.

"Jillian," I say, faking it. "So nice to hear your voice. Sorry it didn't work out last night. I had other plans."

"You're a lousy liar, Joe," she says. "You just don't like ribs."

"How'd you guess?" I say.

"Probably don't care much for blind dates either. Neither do I."

"Really?" I say.

"Really," she replies, "but I told Lydia I just had to meet the man who wrote 'A Family of Strangers'."

"You read my book?"

"I did."

"I don't believe it. Nobody read my book and I can prove it."

"Why don't we talk about it over lunch?" she says.

"Well,-----"

"You have to eat, Joe. How about if I buy?"

"I'll buy," I say firmly.

"Excellent," she says. "I'll be standing by a yellow Volkswagen Beetle parked across the street from the main entrance. See you in five minutes. We have a one o'clock reservation at Tam O'Shanter."

"Well,---" I start to say again and I would have said more but she had hung up.

I lean back in my chair wondering how to deal with this. One thing occurs to me that seems to outweigh every other consideration.

I'm hungry.

As advertised she's across the street from the main gate,

leaning against a shiny new VW bug. A few feet away is a conveniently located telephone booth. Her arms are folded across her chest and she seems to be regarding me with amusement as she watches me dodge the traffic. She's tall and willowy, all angles and planes and her straight dusty brown hair falls to her shoulders and no further. For a prototype you'd say Lauren Bacall as opposed to Bunny who is all curves and pillowy like Liz Taylor.

"Hi, there," she says with a smile. It's a nice smile and she has nice teeth.

"Hi, yourself," I say, not knowing if I should go for the air kiss or a handshake so I do neither.

"Do you mind if I drive?" she asks.

"Why would I mind?"

"Some men do."

"Not me."

"I'll have to wear my glasses."

"Suit yourself," I say.

She opens her door and gets behind the wheel. I get in the passenger side. Either the Germans are very short or this is the cheap economy version of the car.

"My legs seem to be in trouble," I say.

"Scrunch down," she says. "You'll get used to it."

It's a short trip to the restaurant. Over the hill to Hollywood and there it is. All English Tudor and looking a little like Anne Hathaway's house in Stratford on Avon. We didn't talk about much on the way over. Weather. Traffic. No sense getting into a real conversation while she's dodging tractor-trailers and I'm trying to keep my legs from going numb.

She parks on the street and we go inside. The hostess greets her by name. She must bring all her ditched blind dates here. We get seated at a cozy table off in the corner near the huge fireplace that dominates the back wall. The main room, all done up in rich dark highly polished woods, boasts a vaulted ceiling and the flags of various clans jutting out from the walls. The waiters are all wearing Blackwatch vests and jaunty caps. The only thing missing is a piper band playing 'The Bluebells of Scotland'.

I order a Coors. She opts for a Bloody Mary. We start to peruse the menus.

"I'm thirty-seven years old," she says.

I look up from my menu. She's still perusing.

"Excuse me," I say.

"I'm thirty-seven, you're thirty two. I thought we should get that out of the way so you don't waste a lot of time wondering about it."

"Thanks."

"Don't mention it."

She flips the menu closed.

"I don't know why I'm looking at this. I always order the same thing."

"Which is?"

"Forfar Bridie," she says. Off my puzzled look she says, "It's a horseshoe shaped meat pie. Very tasty."

"I'll try it," I say.

She gives me a chiding smile. "No need to suck up to me, Joe."

I smile back. "I'm not. You're not fat and you're not dead so how bad can it be?"

She laughs. It's a nice laugh. Genuine.

She wants to know all about me but I asked first so while we eat she gives me the abridged version of her life. Named Jilliian after a friend of her mothers. Born Markowitz but shortened it to Marx for professional reasons at the urging of her agent.

Born in White Plains, New York, family well off, father a doctor, mother a professional shopper who never met a sale she didn't like. Educated at Bryn Mawr, post grad at Columbia in New York City. No siblings. Mother dead. Father remarried and living in Seattle. "I don't bother him and he doesn't bother me." She's single, never married, started in an ad agency in New York and got into kid's books by accident. It's her passion. She can't imagine doing anything else with her life.

Jillian tries to get me to talk about myself but I don't bite.

"You read my book. That's pretty much it," I say.

"Lydia wasn't in your book, Joe," she says.

"Lydia's none of your business," I reply.

She nods. "Fair enough. And Bunny Lesher?"

"Lydia talks to much."

"Is she coming back?"

"I don't know," I say.

She puts her fork down on her plate. There are scraps left but she's finished.

"I have a crush on the guy in your book," she says.

"He's not me. Not really,"

"Sure he is," Jillian says. "I have tickets to a performance of Miss Julie by an experimental theater group tomorrow night. Want to go?"

"I hate Strindberg," I say. "Too depressing."

She nods. "I have tickets for a performance of 'Lady Windemere's Fan' by the Glendale Community Theater Group tomorrow night. Want to go? And don't tell me Oscar Wilde depresses you."

I smile. "And how long have you had these tickets?" I ask.

"Since late this afternoon," she says with a straight face, "provided they haven't sold out."

I have to laugh. This lady is sharp and she's funny.

"Okay, Oscar Wilde but let me get the tickets through the studio. They'll be free. No sense paying if we don't have to."

She smiles. "My thoughts exactly," she says. "And shall we throw in dinner somewhere?"

"Let's," I say.

After lunch, Jillian drives me over to Metro Division for my appointment with Aaron Kleinschmidt and his sketch artist. She pulls up to the entrance and stops. I lean over and give her a noncommittal kiss on the cheek and then I extricate myself from the car. She drives off and I stand stock still while the circulation fights to find my feet and legs. I have to admit I'm curious about this Jillian Marx. I'm also a little concerned about what I may have let myself in for. On the other hand I've never had any great desire to live like a Capuchin monk. Interesting times may lie ahead.

CHAPTER FOUR

Things go well with Aaron's sketch artist. She's as good as they come and inside of thirty minutes, she's got pretty good likenesses of both these bozos. The sketches will be posted at all divisions and distributed to the squad cars. A couple of metros will go to the airport and check the counter attendants to find out if either or both boarded a flight back to Chicago. Ditto Greyhound and Union Station. I feel proud of myself having done my civic duty. As a key element in the investigation, I ask Aaron for a couple of copies of the sketches. He frowns, his eyes morphing into suspicious little slits.

"What for?" he asks.

I shrug nonchalantly. "No reason. Just to have."

Aaron recognizes this bald faced lie for what it is.

"I don't want you playing detective, Joe," he says.

"Never crossed my mind," I lie.

"Bullshit," he says.

Deceit isn't going to work. I decide to try honesty.

"Look, Aaron, when I put Sharkey's picture in the paper, I might as well have pulled the trigger myself. I feel like crap and I'm not going to feel any better unless I can do something to catch the son of a bitch who did this. I just want the pictures to show around, that's all."

I'm not sure he believes me but reluctantly he gives me one copy of each sketch. "If I catch you poking around where you shouldn't be, I'm going to toss your sorry ass into a cell and melt the key down into a paperweight. Do we understand each other?"

"Absolutely," I say. "And by the way, did they ever find Nick's missing Studebaker?"

Aaron glares. "Yeah, it was parked a block away from his bar in Altadena. So here's what I figure. He walked to the ballpark. No, he took a cab. No, wait, he took the bus. Which one do you like, Joe? Pick one. No idea? Then get out of here."

Chastened, I mention that I need a ride back to the studio. He smiles. No problem, he says magnanimously, and calls me a cab. Hey, what are friends for?

I return to my office to find a dozen telephone slips neatly arranged on my desk. Louella, Hedda, Jimmy Fidler, Sheila Graham, Phineas, it seems the entire western world has heard about the body at Wrigley Field and these champions of the free press want answers and they want them NOW. One by one I have Glenda Mae connect me. One by one I tell them I know nothing. The victim is a bar owner who has nothing to do with Warners or this production. I refer them to Aaron Kleinschmidt. One or two may believe me. The others are sure they have gotten wind of the story of the decade. I will hear from these people soon again and afterwards, soon again several more times.

The company has wrapped for the day. Shooting at Wrigley is impossible and there is no other set that's ready for filming. Burt Yarrow, the unit production manager, tells me that the Angels will let us have the stadium on Monday but that's it. We finish Monday. Period. Tuesday the ball players reclaim the field.

"Joe?"

I look up. Peanuts is standing in my open doorway.

"Is this a bad time?" he asks.

I shake my head and wave him in. He hesitates, then enters and sits in my visitor's chair. I can tell he's pretty shook up.

"What happened, Joe? Who coulda done something like this?"

"I don't know, Peanuts," I say.

"I mean, a nice guy like Ned. Never hurt anybody. It makes no sense," he says.

"I know." I hesitate as Peanuts clasps and unclasps his hands nervously. "Last night, I forgot to tell you this. A couple of guys came looking for Ned yesterday. I didn't like the looks of either of them."

He looks up sharply. "You get names?"

"No," I say, "but they were from Chicago. This one guy, the big guy, was pretty hard to miss. At least six foot four, maybe 280 pounds and just big all over. Big hands like hams, big chest, big head with cauliflower ears that stuck out like batwings and a big gnarly nose looked like it had been broken a couple of times. Maybe a one-time heavyweight in club fights. He said he'd flown in that morning."

I reach into my jacket pocket and takes out one of the sketches. I push it across the desk toward him. He looks at it for a moment.

"Gordo," Peanuts says quietly.

"What?"

"Gordo Gagliano. A friend of Ned's. They worked together, doing what I don't know. Once in a while he'd come around with Ned to the clubhouse. Mostly in '45, I think. The series year. Gordo seemed like a nice guy. Kinda slow and clumsy but what the hell, any friend of Ned's---"

I shrug. "He said he came because he saw Ned's picture in the newspaper."

Peanuts looks up at me. "You think that's what got him killed? The picture in the paper?"

I frown. "I don't know."

"Maybe Gordo wasn't the friend Ned thought he was," Peanuts says. "Why else would he suddenly jump on a plane and fly out here?"

I feel a little chill run up my backbone. I know it's possible. Somebody in Chicago sees Ned's picture in the paper, gets on a plane with murder in his heart. Maybe this Gordo guy. Maybe the phony Hat Trick Cody. Maybe somebody else. I don't want to think about it because if it's true, I had something to do with Ned getting killed. I remember how skittish Ned got when Brad Aronson asked if he'd like to fill as an extra. No, Ned wanted no part of getting his face on film. I know that now. I wish I'd known it earlier before I sent that photo to the Sun.

I lean back in my chair. "So let's say Gordo saw Ned's picture in the paper. Do you know of any reason he'd fly here overnight to see him?"

"No, like I said, we hardly knew the guy except that he was a friend of Ned's and they worked together."

Okay, I say, and take out the other sketch which I hand to him. He looks at it.

"Who's this?" he asks.

"That's what I'm asking you," I say.

Peanuts shakes his head. "No idea. Never saw him before."

I take back the sketch.

"How long are you going to be in town?" I ask.

"Me and Gene Mauch are leaving early tomorrow for Florida. Gotta report to training camp first thing Monday morning."

"Can you stay a couple of extra days? You might be able to help the cops if they find Gordo."

Peanuts shakes his head. "No can do, Joe. They fine you fifty bucks a day for being late. After three days they find somebody else to play your position."

"Wow. You guys are dealing with a tough crowd. Maybe what you need is a union."

Peanuts laughs. "Yeah, that'll be the day."

"Don't laugh. It could happen."

He shakes his head. "Joe, you just don't know baseball. Soon as you sign that first contract, they've got you for life. You want a raise, you beg for it. You've got no rights, no say-so, no nothing."

"There must be something you can do. Talk to Reagan. He's been president of the Screen Actor's Guild for the past seven years, a real die hard union man. Even if he can't help you personally, he can give you some good advice."

"You think so?"

"I know so. Give him a call. I know he'll help."

I get up from behind the desk and walk Peanuts to the door. We shake hands. "Whenever the picture's released, I'll make sure you and the entire Cardinal team get free tickets to a St Louis theater or whatever city you're playing in if you're on the road."

"Thanks, Joe. Darned nice of you."

We wish each other luck and he takes off. I'm glad I finally met him. He's everything I thought he'd be. Sometimes your idols don't turn out that way. I got lucky. Peanuts Lowery is one of the good guys.

My desk is clear, I have no appointments and nothing urgent on my plate, so I decide to take a walk around the studio. I do this often when I want to think without the clamor of the telephone demanding my attention and today I have a lot to think about. I tell Glenda Mae to take the rest of the day off and I start off at a brisk pace toward the back lot. In many ways a studio is like a little city. We have our numerous sound stages and office buildings, a restaurant we call the commissary, a lumber mill where wood is cut to build sets, a transportation department complete with gas pumps and service bays, beauty salons for the hair and makeup departments, prop storage for the set dressers, men's and women's clothing, run by Wardrobe, and a back lot where false fronts stand in for a Greenwich Village street in New York, a Mexican village south of the border, and a Parisian street complete with a patisserie and an outdoor cafe, just to name three. And there's more, much more, which is why I never tire of taking it all in. This is Magic Town, Emerald City and the Great White Way all rolled into one. It is the place where dreams come true, or at least pretend to.

I pass by Stage 12 where they are filming "The Jazz Singer". It's a remake of Jolson's historic film which introduced movie lovers to the miracle of sound. Jolson's gone now, a massive heart attack two years ago, so Danny Thomas, a Lebanese night club comic, is taking the role of the cantor's son who only wants to sing jazz and ballads. The red light is flashing over the stage door which means the camera is rolling. As I recall this is the synagogue scene where Thomas comes to services to sing in place of his ailing father. Jack Warner has high hopes for this picture. No rushing it into theaters to scoop up a fast buck. They're talking a December release amid all the other Oscar contenders.

It isn't until I find myself walking the cobblestone surface of the "Rue de la Fleurs" that I realize I have forgotten why I am out walking. I sent a photo of a very nice man, a man who could have become a good friend, to a Chicago newspaper and someone, upon seeing this man's photo, came West and killed him. I don't know this for sure but every sign points in that direction. In short, I am an unwitting accomplice to murder before the fact, despite anything someone might tell me to the contrary. I am sick. I would undo it if I could but I can't. I feel a deep rooted hate in the pit of my stomach for whoever has done this. Whatever Aaron needs of me, whatever help I can give him, I will give it gladly. I will not allow this murder to stand or its perpetrator to go unpunished. I congratulate myself. It's a helluva speech I have just made that no one has heard but I meant every word of it.

I hear a car approaching behind me and a quick beep-beep. I turn. It's a black late model Ford with black wall tires and COP written in invisible ink on the front door panel. Aaron Kleinschmidt is behind the wheel. He rolls down his window.

"I think we've got one of your boys down at the station," he says.

"Which one?" I ask.

"The phony sportswriter," he says. "Hop in."

I do so and on the way to Division headquarters, he explains that a couple of Metro uniforms caught sight of the phony Jack Cody at Union Station getting ready to board the train to Chicago. He ran for it. They chased him. Before they could run him to ground, he'd gotten rid of every piece of identification on his person. At the moment he's in a holding cell, lips sealed. They need me to make an I.D.

It's him. He's huddled on the barebones cot, a sullen expression on his face. It says, screw you, I'm not talklng and there's nothing you can do to make me talk.

"We're sending his prints back to Chicago," Aaron says, "but my gut says we get nothin'."

"Anything on Ned's prints?"

"Not yet."

I stare into the cell as he lifts his head and our eyes meet. He holds for a moment, then looks away.

"You got nothing out of him?" I ask.

"Nothing," Aaron says.

"Can you hold him?"

"For a while. He took a swing at one of the officers but if we don't get something solid in a day or two I'm going to have to kick him loose."

"Suppose I take a run at him," I say.

"Why would he talk to you?"

"He wanted to yesterday. Maybe he still does. Besides I'm not a cop."

Aaron nods. "I'll have him moved to an interrogation room," he says.

"No," I say. "He's not stupid. If he thinks you guys are listening in, he'll clam up. I'll talk to him in the cell."

Aaron frowns. "I don't know----", he mutters.

"Sure, you do," I say. "You've got zilch and maybe I'll get lucky."

A couple of minutes later I enter the cell carrying a couple of Pepsis. The jailer locks the door behind me and disappears. There are no cops in sight. I sit on the other end of the cot and hold out one of the sodas. He hesitates, then takes it.

"Th-thanks," he says.

"You're welcome, Tom," I say.

He looks at me, startled. He knows I'm way ahead of him. He just doesn't know how far.

"Madison sends her best," I say, increasing the pressure. "She's been worried about you. Do you want to call her? I think I can arrange it."

He hesitates, then shakes his head. "I'm fine," he says.

"What's with you and Ned Sharkey?" I ask.

"You seem to have all the answers," he says. "You t-tell me."

"Did you kill him?" I ask.

"No."

"Were you hired by someone to come to L.A. to kill him?"

"No."

"Scalese. That's Italian, isn't it?"

"So what?"

"Do you belong to an Italian-American social organization whose chief activities are breaking heads, extorting money and shooting people in the back of the head with small caliber pistols?"

"You're c-crazy," he says.

"Why did you get rid of all your identification?"

"None of your b-business."

I nod and take a long and leisurely sip of my soda. Tom Scalese is staring off into space. No doubt he wishes I were elsewhere.

"Tell me, Tom," I say, "do you think the police are so stupid that they would never find out your real identity? And moreover, were you aware that the police deeply resent suspects who do not cooperate with their investigations? And did you know that once this happens they zero in on this person and do everything in their power to hang an indictment for first degree murder around his or her neck? Do I approve of such tactics? Of course not. Do I understand them? Of course I do. Have I seen them up close? You bet I have. So I am going to leave you now in the tender care of Sergeant Kleinschmidt and I give you one and only one piece of advice. Start talking and don't stop."

I get up from the cot and walk to the cell door where I call out for the guard.

"Wait!" I hear.

I turn. Scalese is sitting up straight.

"I wasn't lying," he says. "I didn't kill him."

"And?"

He starts to speak, then thinks better of it and turns to face the wall. He has something to say but he can't get to it. Maybe someday he will but it won't happen today. When he does finally talk I want it to be because he trusts me enough to confide in me which is why I don't tell Aaron that I know his real name. I admit to total failure. Aaron pretends to be disappointed. He isn't. Not really. It never looks good when a civilian conducts a successful interrogation where police methods have failed.

I've had enough excitement for one day so after Aaron drops me back at the studio to pick up my car, I head for home. I'm looking forward to a leisurely evening. On the agenda, a steak grilled on my new hibachi, french fries and a slice of chocolate cream pie for desert. Then I will curl up on my chaise on the back porch with Herman Wouk's "The Caine Mutiny" and read until it gets dark. I'm not sure my heart will be able to stand this much excitement but I'll take my chances.

The moment I toss the steak onto the heated grill, the phone rings. It always happens like this. People have no respect for the supper hour. I pull the steak from the grill and set it aside. Annoyed I answer the phone.

"Joe, it's Cody. I hope I didn't catch you in the middle of supper," Hat Trick says.

"Not at all," I lie. "I'm a late eater."

"I talked to Madison Chase. She somewhat sheepishly admitted to taking a few of my business cards but she swears she has no idea what her boyfriend wanted them for."

"You believe her?"

"Sure. She's a good kid. Guile isn't part of her repertoire. She also says she's worried. She hasn't seen or heard from him in a couple of days and she's worried."

"I'm not surprised," I say.

"What's going on, Joe?"

"Quite a bit, some of which I can't talk about. Not yet. Jack, do me a favor and give the girl this number and have her call me."

"The boyfriend's in trouble," he guesses.

"You bet," I say.

"I'll give her the message without comment. Is there a story in here somewhere?"

"Might be."

"You'll let me know?"

"Absolutely."

"I'll wait to hear from you."

He hangs up. I put down the phone. Tom Scalese may or may not be a killer but he sure is hiding something, not just from me but from the rest of the world. At that moment my empty stomach gurgles. I look at the white hot coals in the hibachi and juicy red steak next to it. I take the receiver off the hook and start to broil.

CHAPTER FIVE

It's been a rough night. This is nothing new. I've been having rough nights for months now. I turn out the light. The room plunges into darkness. I snuggle up to the pillow, scrunching it under my head. I close my eyes. Within minutes they pop open again. No matter how tired I was, I am now tense and on edge. I can hear the clock ticking in the kitchen even though there are two closed doors in between us. The rose bushes outside my window are calling out to me. The grass is screaming for more water. The furnace goes on and off shattering the silence in my darkened bedroom. I sit bolt upright. The noise disappears. I lay down again and pull the covers close. The din resumes. I try to empty my mind but I can't. Bunny floats up from my subconscious. She smiles. I reach for her. We're in a music store buying a piano. She doesn't play. Neither do I. It costs more than I make in a year but I buy it anyway because Bunny thinks it will look good in the living room. I sit down at the keyboard. Suddenly I am playing a concerto by Chopin. I laugh. She laughs. I reach for her again. She runs away. I try to get up from the piano bench. I can't. My legs won't function. I start pounding on the keys. I wake up. I am sweating. I check the clock. Twenty one minutes have passed. I sit up. The room is deathly quiet. I lay down. It starts up again and continues for hours. Bunny laughing. Bunny just out of reach. Bunny playing with an infant. Bunny dressed in black standing by an open grave with dead flowers in her hand. I finally drop off around four-thirty. If I'm lucky I sleep until seven and wake up, bleary eyed and again soaked with sweat. The sun is now peering in the window. I stare at the ceiling, then close my eyes. One minute later it's eight o'clock and I am exhausted. I toss back the covers. Even though it's Saturday I have people to see and places to go. I get up and pad my way into the bathroom.

Thirty minutes later I'm in the kitchen, brewing a small pot of coffee, pouring myself an orange juice and looking for some milk to put on my Wheaties. Normally I'd be getting ready for our regular Saturday morning basketball game at the Y but three of the guys are out of town and two more are down with the flu including my lawyer Ray Giordano so the game's on ice until next weekend.

I open the morning Times and skim Lou Cioffi's story about the Wrigley Field murder. It isn't much of a story because when he wrote it I doubt he had much information. Aaron Kleinschmidt is liberally quoted saying almost nothing. A few of the ballplayers chimed in with little to say. There's a discreet photo, a guesstimate time of death and the rest is conjecture. But if I know Lou, who is the Times bulldog of a crime reporter, he's all over this story and by tomorrow he will have come up with a great deal more.

I scoop up a spoonful of Wheaties but before I can get it to my mouth, the phone rings. Not many people call me at home unless it's office business or bad news and being Saturday it's not likely to be work related. What then?

I lift the receiver. "Hello?"

"Mr. Bernardi?"

"Yes."

"My name is Madison Chase. Jack Cody said I should call you. About Tom Scalese."

"Oh, yes," I say.

"Is he all right?"

"Yes, he is."

"Is he there with you? Can I speak to him?"

"No, he's not here, Miss Chase, but I know right where he is and he is safe and unharmed."

She says nothing but I think I hear her crying.

"Please believe me, Miss Chase. I assure you, he is fine."

"Yes, I believe you," she snuffles. I hate it when women snuffle. They're not like a dog. You can't pet them and say 'There, there, everything's going to be all right.'

"I just don't understand. Suddenly he's like a different person. Unfeeling. He packs a bag. I ask where he's going. He won't tell me. He says it's none of my business. I've never seen him like this." She's trying to hold it together and doing a bad job of it.

"Tell me about him," I say.

"What?"

"Tell me about Tom. What kind of person is he? What does he do for a living? What's his family like?"

"Why are you asking me all this?" she says.

"Because I want to know."

"He's in trouble, isn't he?"

"He's in jail." I hear her gasp. "It's not serious. Resisting arrest. He might even be out in a day or two. I think I can help him."

"Why would you do that?" Madison asks me.

"Why don't you stop asking me questions and answer the ones I asked you?"

There's a lengthy silence coming from the other end before she finally speaks.

"He teaches General Science to freshmen at a local Catholic High School," she says.

"He seems young for that," I observe.

"It's his first year."

"Seems like an odd profession for someone with a stammer."

"It only comes out when he's under extreme pressure. The rest of the time he's fine. Anything else?"

"Who are his friends?"

"What do you mean?"

"Friends. Who does he hang out with?" I ask.

"Me," she say sharply. "He hangs out with me. He's been hanging out with me for over a year. Three months ago he moved in with me. As soon as the school year's over, we're getting married. Is that okay with you?"

"Absolutely. What about family?"

"None I know of. His mother died five years ago. He lived in the dorm his first year, then moved around a lot living with friends while he went to school. Carroll College. 4.1 GPA. Full scholarship. Four years varsity football. Wide receiver. Anything else you want to know, Mr. Bernardi?" She's getting really annoyed with me but I don't care. I have to find out what Tom Scalese is all about and if this really sweet but frightened girl on the other end of the line gets pissed at me, so be it. I'll apologize later.

"Congratulations, Miss Chase. He sounds almost too good to be true."

"Then lucky me," she says. "You know, Mr. Bernardi, I haven't the vaguest idea who you are and that being the case, I think this conversation is over."

"As you wish," I say, "but keep this in mind. Tom is facing a lot worse than resisting arrest. He may be involved in a murder. I don't say this to frighten you but to put you on notice. If he's innocent I'll do what I can to help set him free but if that means, I have to call you and ask you more questions, I'm going to do it and I'm going to expect straight answers. Do we understand each other?"

"Murder? You never said---"

"Do we understand one another?"

"Yes, but----"

"Good. I'll be in touch."

I hang up. I feel bad for her. She's young and in love and she can see no fault in the man of her dreams. But I need information unfiltered through rose colored glasses. Tom Scalese got on a plane to L.A. with the express purpose of finding Ned Sharkey. He refuses to say why and until I know why, I am going to assume the worst. In this game, personal politeness and sympathetic feelings are also rans. Until proven otherwise I will assume the worst.

I drain the rest of my coffee and put the now-soggy Wheaties into the garbage can. I had toyed with the idea of swinging by the little chapel to see how the wedding was going but now I decide against it. I think maybe I'll take a drive to Altadena. Were either Tom Scalese or Gagliano able to track Ned as far as the sports bar? I think it's something I need to know. I debate whether I should let Aaron Kleinschmidt know what I'm up to and decide against it. He'll only tell me to keep out of it which I don't intend to do. Monday morning is soon enough to touch base.

It's not really a long drive but Altadena is a mile or two short of entering an entirely different world. Just north of Pasadena, it sits in the foothills of the San Gabriel mountains, a hiker's paradise in summer and a land of snow and ice in winter. It's a very big town or a small city, depending on your point of view, but places like Altadena and Flintridge and Big Bear and Lake Arrowhead, farther west in the San Bernardino mountains, are home to people with a different mindset than the average Angeleno. They are rugged, self-reliant and clannish. Strangers are the enemy and not to be trusted. Conversely they take care of their own and close ranks to protect one another. Before I leave the house I go to my desk in my office and scoop up a handful of Warner Brothers passes. These are accepted in any theater, any time, and Warners picks up the tab for them. We consider them good-will builders. Today I may need lots of good will.

I drive in from the south and am passing the bus depot on my left when I spot Hovack's Bar and Grill a couple of doors down. Nick hadn't lied. It's a dump. Cramped and dingy, weatherbeaten and in need of a paint job. There's a kid out front with a squeegee washing the plate glass window. He looks to be about sixteen and even though this is not a school day I'm thinking high school dropout. I'm also thinking something doesn't quite fit. How does a guy who owns this kind of a dive come up with two million to make an offer on Nick's sports bar? Maybe he has a lot of pre-war gold stashed in coffee cans buried in his backyard.

The End Zone is located on Lake Avenue a few blocks from the center of town. It's a two story wood frame building, larger than I thought it would be. The windows are cluttered with promotional signs and lots of neon. Coors and Budweiser fight for the most space. I park about a block away which is about as close as I can get. When I open the front door to go in I am assaulted by noise. Hank Williams is belting out 'Hey, Good Lookin'', drowning out the click-click of billiard balls and the bell ringing pinging sounds of a dozen pinball machines lined up along the far wall opposite the bar. I estimate there are fifty to sixty people crowded into this main room, half of them at the bar or at tables tossing back pitchers of beer and munching on pretzels. If Altadena has anything resembling a social center, this seems to be it.

The walls are festooned with athletic uniform jerseys. Some may even be authentic. There's Cal McLish and Bob Muncrief and Clarence Maddern from the Triple-A Angels. L.A.'s a stopping off place either going up or coming back down. The Dons of the All American Football Conference are represented by Glenn Dobbs and Shorty McWilliams. Now that the Rams are in town as part of the National Football League, the Dons aren't doing all that well. In a well positioned place of honor are jerseys from Norm Van Brocklin and Bob Waterfield and Elroy 'Crazy Legs' Hirsch. I actually know two of these guys. Waterfield's been married to Jane Russell for the past eight years and Hirsch is trying to get in the movie business. In fact I hear Republic is planning to do a movie about his life and let him play himself. Will it work? God only knows.

I look around for some sign that the owner of the establishment has just been cruelly murdered. I see none. No black ribboned wreath on the door, no black draped framed portrait on the wall. Life goes on.

I take a seat at the far end of the bar next to the wall where I can get a panoramic view of the proceedings. I note that a lot of the natives are staring at me. None are smiling. This may be a little tougher than I thought.

The bartender comes by. I order a Coors draft. He leaves. In a minute he's back and plops the beer in front of me. "Half a buck," he says. Apparently The End Zone doesn't believe in running tabs, at least not for strangers in a fashionable suede sport jacket. I lay a buck on the bar. He scoops it up. It's 50-50 whether he will return with change. If he doesn't I won't make an issue of it.

I scan the room trying to avoid eye contact with anyone who doesn't seem to have shaved in the past week. I see this barrel chested guy enter followed by a younger, skinnier version. Father-son, brother-brother, I can't tell. The older guy spots someone and waves. The guy he was waving to gets up and comes to him. They embrace like reunited comrades and then when the guy hands over a small slip of paper, Barrel-Chest takes out a wad of greenbacks and starts to peel off a substantial number of them which he hands to his friend. I remember Ned telling me that there was someone in town who handled the betting action. I'd say this is the guy.

I'm only half finished my beer when the bartender returns. He has forgotten my change. He stares at me, gimlet eyed. "Something else I can get for you?" he asks. I take this as code for "Take a hike, stranger, you're taking up valuable space."

I smile. "Is Minerva around," I ask.

The bartender frowns. "You a friend?"

"I knew Ned," I say.

"She's busy," the bartender says.

I take out my card and hand it to him.

"She'll see me," I say.

He checks out the card. It's like magic. They see the words 'Warner Brothers' and suddenly I'm not an undercover cop or an immigration officer or some other kind of governmental pervert. He walks off and I see him disappear through a rear door. If he comes back with a guy six-six carrying a two-by-four I'll be leaving sooner than I'd expected.

But no, he emerges followed by a man and a woman. The man heads for the front door and waves goodbye.

"So long, Minerva", he says.

"You take care, Jesse," she says and when she does I give the guy a second look. Could this be Jesse Hovack of Hovack's Bar & Grill? He looks lean and mean with deep set eyes and a military haircut and even when he smiles in farewell, he exudes little warmth.

The woman watches him go and her gaze lingers just a moment or two too long. I get the feeling that whatever they were discussing in the back room, it wasn't business. She's not a bad looking woman. Past 40, she might have been a beauty some twenty years and forty pounds ago. Finally she turns her attention to me and approaches.

"Minerva?" I smile as she reaches me.

"Who are you?" she demands to know.

"Joe Bernardi," I say. "I was a friend of your husband."

"He didn't have any friends," she says. "He only thought he did. And he wasn't my husband. He was mostly my partner. What do you want?"

I try smiling again, a sweet smile tinged with poignant regret.

"First I want to express my sincere condolences on your loss----"

"Mister, I got no time for this. I was getting ready to fry up a batch of chitlins when Ralph interrupted me so excuse me. I'm busy."

She turns to leave.

"I need your help finding the man who killed your hus ---person. I mean, partner," I say quickly.

She stops and looks at me with a very puzzled expression. "And why in hell would you want to do that?" she asks. "Is there some kind of reward?"

"No----"

"Didn't think so." She points. "There's the door, mister. Don't come back." Again she turns.

"Take a look at a couple of pictures and I'll leave."

She comes back and leans across the bar, eyes boring into me. "You'll leave anyway. Now git."

"I don't think so," I say. "If you won't help me, I'm going to walk all around this room and ask everyone here to help out. Maybe someone won't want to. Maybe one of these folks will take a poke at me. Fine. Then I press charges for assault and sue for damages, including you as the owner of the premises, who failed to provide me with a safe environment. Now this'll drag on for months, maybe a year and you'll have to pay a lawyer which I won't because I have a movie studio backing me up. So now I ask you, Miss Boggs. Which is it? Are you going to look at the pictures or are you going to spend the next twelve months giving depositions?"

She glares at me and then suddenly breaks into laughter.

"Jesus, man," she says, "that is one high falutin' line of crap you've got there. I am so terrified I am quaking in my gym shoes." She juts out her hand. "Lemee see 'em," she says.

I take out the sketches of Tom Scalese and Gordo Gagliano. She holds them up, side by side, and scans them, first one, then the other. Finally she hands them back. "No and no." she says. "Never saw 'em before."

"You're sure?" I say.

"Mister, you're the first stranger we've had in here for the past two weeks. Believe me, I'd remember."

"Okay. Sorry to have troubled you." I slip the sketches back into my jacket pocket.

She regards me with curiosity. "You really work for that movie studio?" she asks.

"Absolutely," I say. "You got a movie theater in this town?" I ask reaching in my pocket for the studio passes.

"Hell, mister, we ain't a ghost town. Got five of 'em."

I hand her the passes. "Here. Use these anyway you want, any theater, any film. They're good as gold."

She looks at them and nods appreciatively. "Obliged," she says.

"You're welcome, Miss Boggs. You've got my card and if either of these guys show up, which I doubt, give me a call."

She nods. I head toward the door. She calls after me. "Come back any time, hear?" she says and she's actually smiling.

"I will," I say and smile back.

As I get to the door I spot the barrel chested guy in deep conversation with a young kid with long greasy swept back hair wearing a black leather jacket. Barrel Chest is writing something in a little notebook. The kid hands him a couple of bills and Barrel Chest rips off a receipt from the notebook and hands it to him. If there's a plainclothes cop in the room, which I doubt, he's not paying attention and I suspect if he were, he wouldn't care much.

Barrel Chest walks over to the bar, signalling to Minerva who walks over to greet him. He takes her hand and says something. She laughs. He reaches over and pinches her cheek and she laughs some more. The merry widow, I think to myself. I have a sudden vision of Nick being stuffed into a plain pine box and shuffled off to Potters Field. Grief is in short supply around this place.

Just then I look to my left and Barrel Chest Jr., the younger version who came in with him, is staring at me hard. I look away and open the door and go out onto the street. I manage to get halfway to my car when the young guy catches up with me.

"Hey!"

I turn as he reaches me.

"What are you doing around here?" he asks.

"Sightseeing," I say. "I'm Joe. Who are you?"

"You a cop?"

"No."

"You seem awful interested in what my old man is doing," he says.

"Not really. What did you say your name was?"

For the second time he avoids my question.

"You're a nosy guy. We don't like nosy guys around here, especially strangers."

"I'm no stranger," I say. "I was a friend of Ned Sharkey's."

He looks at me with contempt.

"That won't get you much around here, mister. Sharkey was a dead beat loser. Nobody had much use for him."

"Really?" I shake my head. "Looks to me like he ran a pretty popular place."

"Minerva runs it. Sharkey just ran off at the mouth most of the time. Talked big, acted big. Nobody'll miss him much."

"I'm sorry," I say innocently. "I don't think I caught your name."

"Drive out of here, mister," he says. "Don't come back."

He turns and heads back to the bar. I watch him go. The bookie and the bookie's son. Interesting combination. Junior let slip one thing he probably shouldn't have. Or maybe he didn't care. When a bookie calls someone a dead beat loser, it usually means three things. One, the bookie was getting the guy's action. Two, the guy was a lousy gambler and didn't win. And three, and worst of all, he wasn't conscientious about paying his debts. Depending on the book this sort of behavior can get you a sharp slap on the wrist or something worse. A lot worse.

Altadena doesn't have it's own police force and relies on the L.A. County Sheriff's Department to keep the peace. As I'm heading out of town I spot the Sheriff's station off the main road and pull into the parking lot. I go inside and ask for the commander. Within a few minutes I find myself talking to Captain Floyd Willard. Willard is potbellied, grey haired, soft spoken and pleasant. Not so pleasant is the noxious little cheroot he's smoking. The clouds of smoke make his office smell like a stable but he doesn't seem to mind. Matter of fact, I don't think he minds much. The word 'mellow' comes to mind. If I were a betting man I'd say he was coasting toward a 30-year retirement and he's not about to let anything get in the way of that.

I tell him why I've driven to Altadena this morning, the murder of Ned Sharkey whose body was dumped at Wrigley Field early Friday morning. Obviously he already knows all about it. I show him the two sketches. Like Minerva Boggs, he's never seen either of them in town. I ask his opinion of Sharkey. Willard is circumspect in his answer but I read between the throat clearings and the pauses. Ned was an irresponsible blowhard with few friends and who had earned little respect from the townspeople. Finally I mention the father and son bookie tandem. He tells me the older man is Eddie Braverman. He handles all the action in town. He's divorced and lives with his son Andy, a high school dropout who is learning the business. People in Altadena genuinely like Eddie. They think Andy is an arrogant pain in the ass.

"I don't suppose you've ever considered arresting the man," I say.

Willard laughs. "Hells bells, young fella. Eddie'd be out on the street inside of three hours. A good lawyer'd get the arrest knocked down to a misdemeanor, Even if he didn't, Eddie'd never go to jail. They're too damned crowded. Besides if I put Eddie away, the town'd lynch me."

"I was in The End Zone," I say. "I guess maybe they would."

Willard laughs again. "Damned straight, young fella," he says, "Damned straight."

I head for the door but before I get there, I stop. I turn back to Willard.

"Jesse Hovack," I say.

Willard's expression darkens and he gets squinty eyed. The smile has disappeared.

"What about him?" Willard asks.

"You tell me," I say.

"One of our leading citizens."

"Yeah. I saw his bar and grill."

"You got a question for me, son, spit it out."

"Ned Sharkey told me Hovack had offered him a couple of million for the sports bar. Doesn't seem to fit the little I know of him."

"That's make two of us, Mr. Bernardi, but Jesse's been here in town two years now, obeys the law and minds his own business. He doesn't bother me and I don't bother him."

"Ever run a check on him?"

"Son, I think you've just about exhausted your quota of questions for the day." He takes me by the arm and leads me to the door. "Drive safe now," he says.

"And don't come back?" I say.

"Don't believe I said that," Willard says.

"No, you didn't, Captain. Not in so many words."

I head for my car. I can feel his eyes boring into my back. I am definitely not a stranger in paradise.

CHAPTER SIX

It's pushing two o'clock when I pull into my driveway. There's a Metro squad car parked at curbside and I don't need tea leaves to tell me that the uniform behind the wheel is here to see me. His name is Sanchez, he's soft spoken and all apologies but Sergeant Kleinschmidt has sent him to bring me in and to not come back without me. Am I under arrest, I ask. No, sir, Sanchez tells me unless I refuse to come in which case he is authorized to slap the cuffs on me and toss me in the back seat of the cruiser. Sanchez hopes it will not come to that.

I tell him I am going to drive myself and he can follow. The last time I was caught car-less at police headquarters it cost me a five buck cab ride home. That won't happen again.

Even though it's a Saturday, I know what that means. Aaron's a divorced Dad who gets his kid Josh every other weekend. The weekends he doesn't, he works which helps him forget what a really crappy life he has.

I find him hunched over his typewriter hunting and pecking as he fills out a report. When he sees me, he straightens up and leans back in his chair.

"What are you doing?" he growls.

I shrug. "Visiting?" I suggest.

"I mean, what are you doing in Altadena? A half hour ago I get a call from my friend, Floyd Willard, at the Altadena substation wanting to know who the Nosy Nellie is poking around in the Sharkey murder. I thought I told you----"

"Wait a minute. I told you that I was going to try to find out what this is all about. I'm the one who got Sharkey killed-----"

"Oh, bullshit. He got himself killed and you know it. Stop whining and keep out of this. I don't want to find you in the morgue someday with a tag on your toe."

"I can take care of myself."

"No, you can't, Joe. These people play rough and they play for keeps and they're not going to be scared by the likes of you."

I frown, puzzled.

"What do you mean, 'these people'?"

"We just got a reply from Chicago about the fingerprints we faxed them."

"And?"

"Your friend Sharkey's name wasn't Sharkey, it was Scalese. Nicholas Scalese."

Ping. Another piece of the jigsaw puzzle just fell into place. I don't know what it means yet, but it answers a couple of questions.

"Okay, his name was Scalese. And?"

"He was a low level hustler for what was left of the old Capone gang. Mostly he was a bag man who dealt with the cops. He had a juvie record, nothing big. Did six months on a bad check charge. A couple of bunco arrests that were dropped. Aside from that, nothing."

I nod. "Not a violent guy," I say.

"Not so you could notice," Aaron says.

"So what's he doing in Southern California calling himself Ned Sharkey?"

Aaron smiles. "I thought you might ask that being the inquisitive fellow that you are. In 1946 the Feds scooped him up on a major charge, no one knows exactly what it was. Apparently he was looking at serious prison time so he flips and agrees to rat out the higher ups in the mob. This goes on for about six weeks and suddenly one day, he's gone. Completely disappeared. No trace. His wife and his kid haven't a clue. The cops think the wiseguys got wise and Scalese is at the bottom of Lake Michigan wearing cement shoes but nobody knows for sure. After a couple of months, nobody cares."

"You said wife and kid?"

"Yeah. She died of a stroke just before the kid was supposed to go off to college. Cops lost track of him, too, but by that time, nobody was looking."

I nod. Ping. Ping. More pieces of the puzzle.

"So you think, what? "

"I think that maybe the mob knew they hadn't gotten him and maybe they put a contract out on him with a nice price tag and maybe somebody with a good memory recognized him from the newspaper photo and came west to collect the jackpot."

"Makes sense," I say.

"Although I find it hard to believe that the kid we've now got stashed in county jail is a mob hitman."

"Maybe he's not," I say. "What are you holding him on?"

"Resisting arrest. Assaulting a police officer."

"Pretty low level beefs," I note. "No bail?"

"He doesn't want it. Or a lawyer either. Not even a Public Defender. He just sits in his cell. eats a little, sleeps a lot and says nothing. We had Chicago run his prints through their files. They came up empty. Any ideas?"

"None at the moment," I say, deciding that Aaron doesn't

have to know that the kid's name is Tom Scalese and in all likelihood he is Nick Scalese's son. I know how the D.A.'s office works. Tom is a made to order patsy for the murder and if there is a way to make the few facts that they have point to Tom, they'll do it, even if they have to use moves that no circus contortionist ever heard of. No, for the moment, I'll keep Tom's identity to myself.

"By the way," Aaron says, "we got a lead on the big ugly guy. Showed his picture at the Hertz counter at LAX. Last Thursday morning he rented a car."

"A big black Cadillac sedan?" I ask.

"That's right. But how did you----?

"He's been following me around. Why, I don't know. You get a name?"

"Sure. Robert Smith."

"Clever. How about the passenger list in the incoming flight from Chicago?"

"Not on it. His brother apparently was. James Smith."

I nod. "James or Robert, whichever, is certainly working hard to keep a low profile."

"Seems so."

"And did you find out who the guy was that jumped Ned-- I mean, Nick--- in the pool parlor?"

"Not yet," Aaron says. "The manager wasn't there when it happened. The bartender and the cocktail waitress say they never saw the guy before but it's my guess they're lying. The other patrons aren't coming forward and your ballplayers have all left town. We can't even get a decent sketch."

"Let me know when you find out who it was," I say.

"What for?" Aaron glares at me.

"I just thought----"

"Joe, go home. Better yet, get a life. Go downtown and get laid. You need it. If you want a phone number, I've got a few. Nice girls and not too pricey."

"Thanks," I say, "but I can handle my own love life."

"Yeah?" Aaron says, "and when did that start?"

I smile. He has reminded me that I have a date tonight. Maybe tonight will be an evening to remember. I sure hope so. I could use one.

The tickets for "Lady Windemere's Fan" will be waiting at the box office and paid for, courtesy of Warner Brothers. Before I leave the house, I check everything else. Wallet, fly zipped, car keys, breath mints. At twenty to six I leave to pick up Jillian Marx at her apartment stopping first at the florists to buy a dozen white carnations. Her address is written on a piece of paper in my shirt pocket. I also have her phone number just in case. We have a six-thirty dinner reservation at Musso & Frank's. An hour to eat and we're on our way to Glendale for an eight o'clock curtain. It's a good schedule. If the gremlins are not watching it might actually work out.

Her apartment's on Franklin Avenue just north of Hollywood Boulevard a couple of blocks west of Highland Avenue. Except that when I get there the apartment has transformed itself into a house built into the hillside with a panoramic view of the Los Angeles basin. And when I say house, I mean house. Where did I get the idea she lived in an apartment? Maybe because she's single and never married and what the hell does she need a house for anyway? It's then I realize that I made a stupid assumption based on stereotypes and I tell myself not to make that kind of mistake again.

I park at curbside and bound up the dozen steps that lead to her front door. I bound because, in case she's looking, I want her to know that even at age thirty two, I'm a remarkable physical specimen. If I've learned one thing at Warners. it's that it pays to advertise.

Before I can reach the massive lion's head knocker, the front door swings open and she is standing there in greeting. I can't tell you exactly what she's wearing because high fashion and I are not on speaking terms and never have been but I do know it's steel grey satin and it clings to her like grease on grits and if she's wearing undies I see no sign of them. Around her neck is a collar of pearls and on her wrist is a diamond studded gold watch that charges by the hour to tell you the time.

"Hi," she smiles.

"Hi," I smile back, handing her the flowers and giving her a little non-binding kiss on the cheek.

I walk in and when I say this house is a house, I do it no justice. The foyer is warm and welcoming and just beyond to the right is the living room which boasts a sixteen foot ceiling and walls that are covered with contemporary art in all shapes and sizes. I recognize a Jackson Pollack, a Grandma Moses and two Georgia O'Keefe's. As opposed to the "new" paintings on the wall, the furniture is old. That is to say, they are antiques. Nothing heavy. Mostly delicate. A sofa, three padded chairs, a couple of tables, a secretary off in one corner, a baby grand in the one opposite.

I turn and look at Jillian who has been regarding me with amusement.

"The kids' book business must be good," I say.

"No," she says. "My grandfather's hosiery business was good. When he died he made sure I'd never want for anything."

"Nice man," I say.

A little glint of sadness shows in her eyes. "Yes, he was," she says. She recovers quickly. "How about a drink?" she suggests.

"We don't have a lot of time," I say. "I made a six-thirty at Musso & Franks."

"Cancel it," she says. "We're eating in."

"We are?"

"In addition to writing books about singing snails and turtles that fly, I also cook. Quite well, in fact. We're having broiled lamb cutlets with mint jelly, asparagus hollandaise, scalloped potatoes and a caesar salad. Any problem with that?"

"None I can think of," I say.

"Good. I'll have an Old-Fashioned. The bar's hiding in the breakfront in the dining room. The Coors are chilling in the refrigerator. I'll be in the kitchen."

I find the bar and fix her drink, then join her in the kitchen. I uncap a long necked Coors while she washes the romaine lettuce for the salad.

"I'm wasted on myself, you know, Joe," she says. "I rarely have someone in that I can cook for. This is a real treat."

"Happy to oblige," I say. "Do you also do needlepoint?"

She smiles. "Only when I haven't enough time to put together an entire ensemble for a white tie ball."

"Ouch. I think I deserved that."

"You certainly did," she says. "We have a few minutes before I have to start things. Come on, I'll show you around."

We carry our drinks and take the tour. Downstairs she also has a formal dining room, a guest bathroom out near the front door for company and a second at the rear of the house for her household help and any workers like the landscaper who comes twice a week or the occasional plumber or electrician.

There are three bedrooms on the second floor. Her bedroom, the master suite, has its own bathroom complete with bathtub and walk-in shower. The other two bedrooms share a bathroom situated between them.

I am impressed but not envious. It's a magnificent edifice but

Jillian is a woman of taste and she has done a great deal with it. It seems almost criminal that she lives here alone but apparently that's the way she wants it. But it's when we hit the third floor, the converted attic if you will, that envy starts to creep in.

For the first time I realize that she not only writes her books, she illustrates them as well. Two skylights have been added to the roof and one can see that in daytime the room will be exceptionally bright and airy. Off to the right are a couple of easels and a workbench that holds a huge assortment of paints and brushes, colored chalks, canvas, poster boards, pens and pencils, and anything else a professional artist would need to get her hands on. Off to the left is her desk and a side table that holds her typewriter. Papering the walls are all sorts of sketches, some finished, and some only half started. Gophers in red velvet suits, frogs wearing top hats and tails, kittens wearing tutus and puppies sporting bib overalls. Each drawing is more charming than the last. I'm beginning to think I've missed something by not reading a few of her books which, I suspect, are written for Mom and Dad as much as they are or the kids. When I suggest this to her, she laughs. Spot on, she says. The parents buy the books and often read them out loud. If they aren't happy you become a former author very quickly.

Dinner is everything she said it would be. If the book business goes belly up, I'll recommend her to Musso & Franks. We chat easily, first about kids and their collective imaginations, then about the movie business and how it could use a lot of improvement. Admitting her bias, she says Disney has the right idea. Kid's movies the family can attend. Ten years ago she bawled like a baby at "Bambi". She thinks "Song of the South" about Brer Rabbit and his crowd is a national treasure and should be re-issued every year. She has well thought out opinions on a wide range of topics but she's not didactic and has the capacity to listen. She can also be very funny in a dry ironic way but I can also see that she has steel in her spine and a need for control. It makes me a little nervous but it's not so overt that I can't enjoy her company.

When I have the temerity to remind her that we have an eight o'clock curtain for "Lady Windemere's Fan", she just smiles.

"I've seen it," she says.

"So have I," I say and now I know what kind of evening this is going to be. She brings out the coffee and brandy and we move into the living room. She puts the latest Montovani on her LP player and before I know it we are slow dancing to "Stardust". Some allusion to a spider and a fly keeps caroming around in my brain but I am able to ignore it. She melts into my arms and I can smell the Chanel No. 5 dabbed behind her ears. Our faces move toward one another and then my lips and hers are conjoined and before long we are entwined together in her bed and exploring places in one another heretofore unseen. She makes tiny little noises of passion but her eyes remain open, the better to see and be seen. She's good. She's very good but I suppose at her age she's had plenty of time to refine her skills. I don't complain. I go with it. I remember hoping for a night to remember. I got what I wished for. Sometimes Murphy and the gremlins will just have to go bother somebody else.

CHAPTER SEVEN

t's ten after nine on Sunday morning and I wake up in my own bed and how I got there I am not quite sure. I vaguely remember kissing Jillian goodbye at her front door after several hours of bump and tickle and her saying that she preferred sleeping alone in her bed as she had been doing it all her life and I saying I could understand that since I had been doing it for the past couple of years. So as I perform my morning ablutions I remember the previous evening with fondness and look forward to a second evening of delight with the sexually enthusiastic and athletically accomplished lady who has jolted me out of my doldrums and reignited my moribund libido. I think we have another date on tap. In fact I'm sure we do. I just can't remember where or when.

Unlike most Sunday mornings I do not slip into a worn pair of blue jeans and a floppy sweatshirt. I take out my best dark suit, find a relatively clean white shirt, a silk tie sans gravy stains and a pair of highly polished patent leather shoes. After rummaging around in my bedroom closet, I find a well worn briefcase and then head off to the kitchen.

I fix a hurried breakfast settling for toast and jam, juice and coffee and a quick look at the Times. I search for Phineas' account of Reagan's wedding and I find it featured on the first page of the entertainment section. There's a two column photo of Ronnie and Nancy waving and smiling for Buddy Raskin's camera and in the text I find both Ronnie and Nancy liberally quoted. Phineas, that sly walrus, managed to get them to sit still for an interview. I read it through. It's well put together. The Reagans will be pleased. Charlie Berger will be pleased. Who will NOT be pleased will be Hedda and Louella and the dozens of their ilk who will be after my hide for not giving them a piece of the action. My response to this will be simple. Phineas got the tip, Phineas followed through and Phineas got the exclusive. If the others had gotten off their dead duffs and done the same they'd have gotten the same deal but they didn't so shut up about it. I won't couch it in exactly those terms but the message will have been given and received.

Satisfied I put the paper aside and call my flu-stricken lawyer Ray Giordano. His wife Trudy answers the phone.

"How is he?" I ask.

"A lot better," Trudy says, "but he's still acting like a baby so that I'll keep waiting on him."

"I need to see him. What do you think?"

"Oh, he'll see you, Joe, if only to play martyred tough guy. This sort of thing happens about once a year. I've learned to live with it."

"See you in thirty minutes," I say and hang up.

Ray lives on a quiet residential street in Santa Monica. His house is a forty year old English Tudor once owned by Lionel Barrymore. The law business is good and he's good at it. Why he keeps me for a client I'll never know. Maybe it's my high free throw percentage.

Trudy answers the door.

"He's in the living room watching 'Meet the Press'," she says. "When he starts reaching for the Kleenex, make a fuss."

"Will do."

He's on the sofa, wearing his robe, swathed in a wool blanket, with a box of tissues at his side. When he sees me, he grunts a feeble hello. If I didn't know better I'd be calling the county coroner.

"How are you doing, Ray?" I ask.

"I'll be okay," he whines pitiably. Snuffle. Sneeze. Tissue.

"You sound awful."

"All you can do is tough it out," he says. Snuffle. Sneeze. Tissue.

I glance over at the television screen. Martha Rountree and her parade of newspaper reporters are grilling Illinois governor Adlai Stevenson about his Presidential aspirations. Since it's highly likely that Eisenhower will run on the Republican ticket, I'm pretty sure Adlai's wasting his time. On the other hand if Taft gets the GOP nomination, maybe not.

"I need about a half dozen of your business cards," I tell him.

"What for?" he asks.

"If I don't tell you, you can't be indicted," I say.

"Oh. Like that," he says.

"Nothing serious. Just a mild impersonation."

"Tell me."

"You sure you want to know?"

"Tell me," he says again, a bit more forcefully. "If I'm going to be disbarred I'd like to know why."

He listens carefully to what I have in mind and when I finish, he nods. "Okay. They're in the top left drawer of my desk. Ask Trudy. She'll get them for you."

"Thanks."

"Kleinschmidt's not going to like this," he warns me.

"I'll deal with Aaron when the time comes. Don't forget he once tried to railroad me for first degree murder and I never let him forget it."

"Keep bugging him and he may try again," Ray smiles. "Good hunting, Sherlock," he says as he turns his attention back to the talking heads on the TV screen.

A short time later I pull into the parking lot at the County Jail and stride in as authoritatively as I can manage. I tell the sergeant at the main desk that I am here to represent the John Doe they've been holding for the past day. The sergeant just smiles and tells me the John Doe doesn't have a lawyer and doesn't want one. I hand him one of Ray's cards. On the back I have written 'Madison Chase'.

"Tell him I've been retained by Madison Chase," I say. "I think he'll see me."

The sergeant looks dubious but he signals one of his nearby assistants and hands him the card. The assistant goes off while I take a seat. Ten minutes later the assistant returns and speaks quietly to the sergeant who waves me over.

"He'll see you." he says. "Go with Officer Jacoby."

I follow Jacoby through security and soon he has me parked in a small room reserved for prisoners and their attorneys. There's a table with two facing chairs. On the prisoner's side of the table is a huge U-bolt to accommodate handcuffs. It is an overgrown cubicle without windows, without air and with only a single fluorescent bulb overhead to provide light. I look to the floor for any signs of vermin. There are none. Even the rats won't come near this place.

Just then the door opens and Tom Scalese enters, his hands cuffed in front of him. Instantly he recognizes me and stops short. Just as quickly I'm on my feet.

"My name is Ray Giordano. I've been hired by Madison Chase to represent you. Please sit down."

I can see he's confused but Madison Chase has the same effect as presto, abracadabra and alacazam. He's too curious to walk away. Jacoby sits him down, then uncuffs his left wrist and attaches the cuff to the U-bolt.

"You've got twenty minutes," Jacoby says.

"No, Officer, I'm this man's attorney and I've got as long as I want and if you don't want your sergeant to step on you like a cockroach, you'll come back when I summon you and not a second before."

Jacoby gives me a hard look and then goes out without comment. I learned this kind of chutzpah from Ray who is very good at it.

Tom Scalese stares at me hard.

"You're not Giordano," he says.

I make an imaginary check mark in the air.

"One for you. And you're not John Doe. So, Tom, where were we when last we met? Oh, that's right. you were stonewalling me."

"Why did you bring M-Madison into this?" he asks.

"She's in because she wants to be in and stop that damned stammering. You're in no danger from me. I'm here to help, if I can."

"And why would you d-do that?" he asks.

"Because I'm a damned fool," I say.

"Tell Madison to stop wasting her time on me."

"What do I look like, a Western Union boy? Tell her yourself."

He glares at me.

"Spare me the look, Tom. I know exactly who you are. Ned Sharkey, the stiff on the pitcher's mound at Wrigley, his real name was Nick Scalese. Sound familiar?"

He continues to stare at me and says nothing.

"Six years ago he walked out on you and your mother. That means I put you at twenty-two, maybe twenty-three. Want to tell me about it?"

Again, silence.

"You know I'm just a dumb press agent but if I can put it together how long do you think it will take the cops to come up with your identity? And when they do, how long do you think it'll take them to charge you with first degree murder?"

"I didn't k-kill him."

"I'll have it carved on your tombstone."

I stare him down. I see him calculating. Up side. Down side. What'll it be?

"You have it right," he says finally. "One day he's there, drinking a beer, telling a joke, helping me put together a m-model airplane. The next day he was gone. No note. No warning. No nothing. He left all the m-money in the bank but the rest of it, his suitcase, clothes, a lot of personal stuff. Just gone. M-Mom near went out of her mind thinking he was hurt somewhere or maybe even d-dead. I knew better. I knew he'd run but I didn't know why. Even today I'm not really p-positive."

"So you didn't know what he did for a living," I say.

"I knew what he told us, that he sold advertising in the yellow pages which was why a lot of nights he was never home, talking to advertisers at their houses. Like I said, that's what he told us. But I never saw a paycheck from the yellow pages and neither did Mom. It was always cash and some days he'd have a roll on him big as a baseball, all tens and twenties and fifties."

"And what did you think about that?" I ask.

"I thought he probably wasn't selling ads in the yellow pages."

"So what did you think he was really doing for a living?"

"Isn't it kind of obvious?" he says.

I nod. "Okay, so he disappears. Then what?"

"Mom's sick. Then she gets even sicker. The summer before I'm supposed to start classes at Carroll College she died. She just gave up and died."

"You loved your mother," I say.

"Damned right."

"And you hated your father for what he'd done to her."

He hesitates for a long while. "No," he says. "I was angry and disappointed but I didn't hate him. I knew his instinct was to back away, to run and hide when things got tough. It's just how he was. He couldn't do anything else or be anyone else."

"So you didn't come out here to kill him."

"God, no," he says. "I just wanted to see him, to talk to him, to tell him what Mom and I had gone through. It was a door left open that needed to be closed."

"And to this day, you don't know why your father ran away and left you," I say.

"No, I don't," he says. I realize that for the past several minutes he has not stammered. In letting his pain and anger out into the open, he seems to be finding some kind of peace.

"Shall I tell you?" I ask.

He frowns, then says, "Sure. Why not?"

I tell him.

When I finish, he looks at me sadly. "Poor bastard," he says.

"Yes," I say. "He ran to the end of the world to hide and it wasn't far enough."

"So that's what you think? Someone from Chicago came and killed him?"

"I don't know," I say. "It's possible. Maybe even probable. What do you know about a man named Gordo Gagliano?"

"Nothing," Tom says. "Who is he?"

"Someone your father worked with back in Chicago."

"I told you, I didn't know anything about that part of his life."

"So you did, Tom. So you did."

Our eyes meet. I like this young man and I believe him. Even more than his dead father, he is a victim in all this.

"You need to get out of here. You need to go home," I say.

He nods.

"The cop in charge of the case needs to know who you are. He's a pretty fair guy. I can talk to him."

"Thanks," Tom says.

"I can have a lawyer in to see you tomorrow morning. Not today because he's home pretending to be sick but he's a good guy and I'm sure he can work something out for you. Can you hang on here until morning?"

"Sure."

I get up. "Okay, then. He's the real Ray Giordano. I'll have him here before nine."

"Thanks," he says.

"Don't thank me, thank Madison," I say as I rap on the door for the guard. "Nice girl, Tom. A keeper."

From the County Jail I drive over to the offices of the L.A. Times and head for the morgue in the basement. I search through six year old files on microfiche for any mentions of Nicholas Scalese or Gordo Gagliano. I find none. This confirms my feeling that they were very low level on the mob's operational chart. I check out news items on the Capone gang activities just after WWII. There isn't much. Eyes red and bleary, I go home.

I call Jillian to say hi and what a wonderful time I had and to discover whether we actually have an upcoming date. It turns out we do. A six o-clock cocktail party Tuesday evening at her publisher's to celebrate some kind of anniversary. After that, dinner somewhere nice and then on to Jillian's for act two of 'getting to know you'. I can hardly wait.

I settle down on my porch chaise with a book and a beer and promptly fall asleep. I'm awakened at five by Lydia who wants to crow about her friend Jillian and wasn't she right about her and didn't I have a wonderful time and really, isn't it obvious you two are made for each other? It seems to me that these two dames have spent at least an hour today jabbering about my good points and fretting about my shortcomings but on balance deciding I am a quarry worth pursuing. At least that's the way I read it. I could be wrong but I can't shake the feeling that I'm like a turkey on the last Wednesday in November.

Monday morning. I walk into the office feeling like a million bucks. Within minutes Glenda Mae has me reduced to a buck and a half in loose change. As I feared the gossip brigade with the exception of Phineas Ogilvy is after my scalp. The Reagan wedding was a major story and all these also-rans never had a whiff of it. No fewer than thirteen phone slips are on my desk and oh, yes, Mr. Berger wants to see me as soon as I walk through the door.

"We don't play favorites around here, Joe," Charlie says to me as I stand uncomfortably in front of his cluttered desk.

"I know that, Charlie----"

"Jack is very unhappy about the phone calls he's had to take. Calls to his home, Joe. To his home," he repeats for emphasis.

Jack Warner doesn't like to be annoyed by minutiae and in his eyes, the marriage of a B-level actor to a C-level actress comes across as a non-event. And yet the gossipmongers are screaming for blood and my fear is that when he looks around for a donor, his gaze will fall on me.

"Now look, Charlie," I say, mustering wounded indignation, "the fact is that I saved this studio from a major headache and a really disgruntled star who also happens to be the president of a major labor union in this industry." I tell him about Phineas, his tip, his threat to print the rumor and the deal I made. When I finish, Charlie nods thoughtfully.

"Good work, Joe. Well handled. I should have known you were on top of things but goddammit, when Jack starts screaming, I lose all sense of reality."

"Which is why I really don't want your job," I say.

He wags a finger at me.

"Oh, no, you don't," he says. "As soon as I get my life straightened out and can ditch this place. you've got the job, like it or not. Now, what do we do about the Reagans and the malcontents in the press corps?"

"Press conference," I say.

Charlie laughs in my face. "Oh, sure, that'll do it," he says sarcastically.

"Press conference at Scandia's," I continue. "We book their best private room, set up an open bar, tons of food, the newly married Reagans attend and exude charm, and pose for pictures. Ford Frick, the baseball commissioner shows up and gushes over Reagan's new movie, "The Winning Team", the heroic saga of Grover Cleveland Alexander, an iconic American hero and his lifelong romance with his beloved wife Aimee."

"Stop!" Charlie says, raising his hands in surrender. "In a minute you'll have me bawling like a baby."

"Okay?" I ask.

"Okay," he growls.

"You'll handle Jack?"

"Leave him to me," Charlie says.

I leave his office jauntily feeling pretty good about my quick witted ingenuity. Now all I have to do is talk Ronnie and Nancy into participating and roping Ford Frick into an appearance.

CHAPTER EIGHT

No time like the present, I think, so I head down to Stage 17 where the company is shooting a scene with Ronnie and Doris and her on-screen parents before their marriage and before he embarks on his historic baseball career. Doris, who is 28, has no trouble passing for Aimee who is barely 20. Ronnie, who is 41, is unconvincing age-wise as a 20 year old Grover. But this is Hollywood and movies are built on fantasy so who cares?

The red light is unlit so I walk through the stage door and immediately run into Doris who is headed for her dressing room. The crew is setting the lights for the next set-up.

She smiles at me. "Joe, just who I wanted to see," she says.

"At your service," I grin.

"Did you know? About Ronnie and Nancy, I mean. Getting married and all."

"I did, just at the last minute but Ronnie swore me to secrecy."

Her eyes flare a little in annoyance.

"You would think," she says, "that he might have dropped a hint to his closest friends." She includes herself in this group.

"Now, Doris, you know better. One hint to the wrong person and half of Hollywood's press corps would have been standing outside the chapel Saturday morning."

She frowns.

"Yes, I suppose," she says. "It's only that----" She stops in mid-sentence.

"Only that what?"

"Walk with me," she says.

"Sure."

We go back outside and start toward her dressing room.

"Joe, is he okay?" she asks.

"Ronnie?"

"Yes. He just, well, I don't know. He's acting so strangely. It's not just the secrecy about the wedding. I just think maybe there's something wrong. Maybe not. Maybe it's just me but----."

Again she hesitates.

"But?"

"Well, last year when we were doing 'Storm Warning', I know he thought I was politically naive and so he kept talking to me about government and how it should work and how it had a responsibility to the working class and also to the poor and how the big corporations were getting fat at the expense of the little people."

I shrug. "Well, he is a Roosevelt Democrat, you know."

"How could I not know?" Doris says. "the way he goes on and on. I remember what Jane Wyman said when they got divorced. She just couldn't stand him talking her to death."

"Doris," I say, "he is a man of firm beliefs."

By now we're at her dressing room. She turns toward me with a quizzical look.

"You think so? Friday we were talking and he told me that if Eisenhower got the Republican nomination, that he was going to vote for him."

"What?" I say in disbelief. "No, Doris, you have that wrong."

"I do not," she says indignantly. "Ask him yourself."

"I can't believe it."

"Neither could I," she says. "That's why I thought something might be wrong with him. Like major depression or a brain tumor or something, God forbid."

I shake my head. "This is the first I've heard of it," I say. "I'll ask him about it."

"Do that, Joe," Doris says. "I love him so much. We all do. I'd hate to think there was something seriously wrong with him."

She starts to open the door to he dressing room then she turns back with twinkle in her eye.

"And Joe," she says, "in case you hadn't heard, they're turning the film into a musical."

I look at her dubiously.

"They're letting me sing 'Take Me Out to the Ball Game'," she grins and goes inside.

I love Doris. Great gal and a great kidder and I wonder if she's on the level or just pulling my leg. It sure didn't sound like kidding. I scratch my head. Reagan voting Republican. This is like Lorelei Lee giving up diamonds or Marcel Marceau talking.

I head for Reagan's dressing room which is nearby. I knock. He bids me enter. I find him sitting in an easy chair reading the latest issue of 'Human Events', a conservative newspaper. He quickly folds it up, covering the masthead and slips it under the chair's cushion. He gets up with a smile and extends his hand.

"Good to see you, Joe. Tell your friend Ogilvy Nancy and I both liked his story very much. Just the right touch."

"He'll be pleased to hear that, Ron, but I have a problem and only you and Nancy can solve it for me." I tell him about my thirteen phone messages and the bind I'm in, not only with the press but with Jack Warner as well. Ronnie's sympathetic.

What can he do? I lay out my plan for the press conference and he's immediately on board. He is sure Nancy will be delighted to participate now that the wedding's behind them and besides, he's looking forward to meeting Commissioner Frick. I don't tell him this piece of the arrangements has not yet been secured.

Finally I ask, "How are you feeling these days, Ron?"

"Wonderful," he replies with a grin. "Joe, I'm a newlywed. How else could I feel?"

"Absolutely," I say as I segue clumsily into, "Looks like an interesting political year, wouldn't you say?"

"I would," he says as he slips out of his silk lounging robe and back into the baseball warmup jacket he wears in the scene. He doesn't elaborate, strange for a man as loquacious as he is.

"Seems to me Eisenhower's a cinch to get the Republican nomination," I say, still fishing.

"I wouldn't bet against it," he says, looking in the mirror and carefully combing his hair. I wait for more. There is no more.

"Too bad Truman doesn't want to run again," I say. "I think he'd be formidable, don't you think?"

He heads for the door, taking me with him.

"Well," he says, cocking his head to one side, "no, I don't, Joe. I think twenty years of Democrats is more than enough. See you later." And he walks off toward the sound stage leaving me staring after him. Twenty years is more than enough? Doris is right. Something strange is going on with Ronald Reagan. I just hope it isn't fatal.

The rest of my day is wall to wall aggravation. It takes three phone calls but I finally get Scandia to give us a good sized private room this coming Thursday evening from five until seven. I contact my thirteen also-rans whose reactions run from total delight and anticipation to 'This had better be good, buster.'

This last from Hedda who has her own unique way of expressing dissatisfaction. Two of my calls were unavailable but I expect to hear from them by the end of the day. Now all I have to do is wheedle an acceptance out of Ford Frick.

I am about to ask Glenda Mae to run the commissioner to ground when she buzzes in and tells me Aaron is on the phone. I pick up.

"Good news?" I ask.

"I'm not sure," Aaron says. "The sergeant on the desk at County Jail says Ray Giordano got in to see the John Doe this morning."

"Good," I say. "The kid needs a decent lawyer."

"The sergeant said that Giordano was about six-one, maybe one ninety, clean shaven with sandy brown hair and moderately good looking which I find odd since the Ray Giordano I know is about five-ten, two hundred pounds, sports a thin pencil mustache and has his jet black hair slicked back with goose grease. What do you say to that, Joe?"

"Moderately good looking? Is that what he said? Moderately?"

I hear Aaron sigh. "Jesus, Joe, what are you trying to do?"

"Get some answers which you apparently don't have, Aaron."

"Tell me."

"Maybe tomorrow, after Ray talks to your John Doe. What have you got? Anything?"

"We got the car."

"What car?"

"The black Cadillac. The one that's been following you around. We found it parked on Century Boulevard in a really sleazy section of Inglewood that features a so-called adult book shop, a peep show palace, a porn movie theater and a couple of stripper night clubs."

"Lovely."

"A squad car spotted it from an APB we sent out. We staked it out right away but the guy never came back. I think our plain-clothes guys were spotted."

I laugh. "You think so? A couple of guys sitting in a black unmarked Ford sedan with black wall tires and a big radio antenna. How could that have happened?" I say.

"Fine. Laugh," Aaron says.

"It's not that far a walk to the airport," I suggest.

"No, it isn't, but we have all the airlines covered, especially the flights to Chicago. He's still around but on foot. We're distributing the sketch to all the cab companies, the car rental places and the bus lines. He can walk but he can't ride."

"I have a question," I say.

"Shoot."

"Let's say he comes here to kill Sharkey. He finds him and kills him. Why doesn't he leave? Why does he follow me all over Los Angeles?"

"Maybe when we catch up with him he'll tell us."

"But until then you have no idea."

"Not a clue," Aaron admits.

Hey, Aaron, I think to myself, guess what? I don't either.

After Aaron hangs up, I go after Ford Frick. His secretary says he is not in his office, that he is in Boston in talks with Lou Perini, the owner of the Boston Braves. I ask what hotel he is staying at. I'm told that information is not available but she will leave a message that I called. He's on a tight schedule and might not be able to get back to me today. This is odd. Frick's not known for avoiding the press but I get the feeling that I'm being shined on. But why? Something tells me I'd better start thinking of a suitable substitute for this coming Thursday evening.

I wait around for another hour for my call backs. They finally get back to me, I fill them in and add their names to the Thursday guest list. It's now well past seven and Glenda's long gone. So is Charlie. By the time I get out to my car, it's getting dark. Storm clouds hover overhead, Rain seems imminent. I head for home. I stop at the grocers just as the rain lets loose. I hurry into the store. A pound of hamburger, a pint of cole slaw, a six pack of Coors, and a bag of chips later and I race back to my car pelted by the rain. Thunder roars and lightning flashes and by the time I park and then scurry through my kitchen door into my darkened house, I am soaking wet and my disposition is surly. I may need to increase my nightly quota from one beer to two. My crankiness is not helped when I flip the light switch next to the door and nothing happens. Great, I think, a burned out bulb and I am positive I don't have a replacement. I plop the soggy bag onto the kitchen table and start for the pantry when a massive hit of sheet lightning illuminates the room. That's when I see him standing quietly in the corner, staring at me. The big man in the pin-striped suit. Gordo Gagliano. In his hand is a huge chrome finish .45 automatic aimed squarely at my gut.

The lightning has passed. He's in shadows again. I force myself to stand very still.

"What are you doing here?" I ask.

"Waiting for you," he says. "Sit down."

I'm standing next to the kitchen table. I grope around for one of the chairs and when I find it, I slowly lower myself onto it.

"How did you find out where I live?"

"You got a license plate on your car, don't you?"

"That's confidential information," I say.

He just laughs. I love it when I amuse people.

"How did you get here?" I ask.

"I walked."

"Are you going to shoot me?"

"I don't know yet," he says.

Lightning flash. Then boom, thunder! The storm is directly overhead. He is on the move edging toward my food pantry. The gun continues to be pointed at my midriff.

"What do you want?"

He ignores my question.

"You should have told me where I could find Nick. If you had told me he might be alive today."

That's an odd thing to say.

"I was trying to protect him," I say.

"That's what I was going to do," Gagliano says. He opens the pantry door and reaches in. On the wall is the electrical box. I hear him open it. In a moment the lights come on in the kitchen.

"The cops think you killed him," I say.

"The cops are wrong," he says. He pulls out one of the other chairs, swings it around and straddles it, facing me. "Why would I kill him? He was my friend."

"Money."

"I know about the money. That's why I came. I knew others would be looking for him. I came to warn him."

"I don't believe you," I say.

"He was like my brother."

"I still don't believe you. How much?" He looks blank. "What was the price on his head?"

"A hundred thousand dollars," Gagliano says. I react visibly.

"Jesus," I mutter quietly. "Who'd he kill?"

"Good question," Gagliano says. "At first it was only ten

thousand because they said he was just a rat. Then the cops picked up Mr. Tony Accardo's nephew, Pietro, who was really just a kid but they convicted him of a couple of lousy charges based on what Nickie told the cops."

"Nickie Scalese, your friend."

Gagliano nods.

"They sent Pietro to Joliet. It was supposed to be two years. A couple of guys got interested in the kid. He got caught in the middle of a fight and somebody knifed him. Nobody knows who. He died. When Mr. Accardo found out what happened he changed the contract on Nickie to a hundred G's. But nobody knew where he was. He was just gone. That was six years ago. And then Wednesday. I saw his picture in the newspaper. I don't think I was the only one."

By now I'm beginning to feel how Judas might have felt except his betrayal was deliberate and mine was inadvertent. I wonder if I am going to feel lousy about cashing my next paycheck.

"So you didn't come here to Los Angeles for the money," I say.

"I have money," he says.

"Do you have a hundred thousand dollars?"

"I don't need a hundred thousand dollars."

Mr. Moneybags in a cheap suit.

"And so did you find anybody else from Chicago who might have come out here to kill your friend?"

"Only the fat man," he says.

I sit up straighter. Ping. Another piece of the puzzle suddenly pops up.

"Fat man? What fat man?" I ask.

"Fats McCoy. That's what he called himself in Chicago. He's a comic, you know, baggy pants, pie in the face, dirty jokes. Not really a funny guy."

"What's a burlesque comedian have to do with your friend Nick?"

"About ten years ago, Nick's banging McCoy's wife but real soon he feels bad about it, him being married and with a kid and all, so he breaks it off. Then four years later, Fats and Sylvia are on the outs, you know what I mean, and she's leaving him and taking her kid who is three years old and Fats says nobody takes his kid away from him which is when Sylvia---that's his wife's name--- when Sylvia tells him he's not the father, that Nick is. By this time Nick is gone. Fats goes nuts, beats her up, does sixty days for it, comes out and now she's gone, the kid's gone and his life is total crap. He goes back to work but now he's really not so funny and there's a lot of hate in the guy and he keeps talking about Nick like if he ever finds him he's gonna kill him."

"And then he sees the picture in the paper," I say.

"No," he says.

"No?"

"No. Soon as I see the picture I check up on Fats and I find out he quit the club he was working at last November and went to Los Angeles and this stripper I know at the club tells me he was crazy out of his mind and going to find the son of a bitch who ruined his life and kill him."

"How did he know Nick was in L.A.?"

"I don't know. Somebody must have tipped him."

I nod. "Okay, so where is this Fats guy now?"

"He's working at a club in Inglewood. Calls himself Dickie Divine. From what I hear, same routines, same bad jokes. I was looking for him when the cops spotted my car. I was lucky. I spotted the cops first."

"Maybe you should tell the police what you know?"

Gagliano smiles. "Where I come from the only thing you tell the police is where to shove it."

"Okay, you say no cops. What do you want from me?"

"Wheels," he says. He looks at his watch. "Fats goes on at ten o'clock. We can just make it."

"What do you mean, we?" I ask.

"You're driving," Gagliano says. That gun is still pointed at my belly button.

CHAPTER NINE

We head over the hill toward Inglewood. It's quite a ways and if Gagliano walked it earlier his feet must be killing him. If so he gives no sign of it as he stares stoically straight ahead through the rain swept windshield. The rain has slowed only slightly. The traffic hasn't. Southern Californians consider wet highways an inconvenience to be ignored. Also a good chance to use their horns.

He has stowed his gun in a shoulder holster. I guess he figures I can't assault him and drive at the same time. Either that or I'm a hapless wimp not worth worrying about. I try to make conversation but it's obvious he doesn't want to talk. I'd like to find out more about what makes him tick because I have this gut feeling he's exactly who and what he says he is.

"So you and Nick worked together?" I say trying to get a dialogue going for the third time.

"Yes," he says.

"What did you do?"

Out of the corner of my eye I can see him turn his head toward me and for a moment he is silent.

"Why do you want to know?" he asks.

"Just curious," I say. "In case you decide to kill me, I'd like to know a little bit more about the man who's doing it."

"I'm not going to kill you. I only kill bad people," he says.

"I'm relieved," I say. "What about Fats McCoy? Are you going to kill him?"

"You don't have to know that," Gagliano says.

"I just thought---"

"You talk too much," Gagliano says.

"Right," I say, shutting up.

For several minutes we ride in silence. Then he says, "Nick paid money to the police. I went with him, to make sure he didn't get robbed or somebody tried to hurt him."

"And did they?" I ask. "Try to hurt him, I mean."

"No. People don't like me. They stay away from me. When they stay away from me, they stay away from Nick. Even when we were just having a beer in a bar, people stayed away."

I wonder why.

Vermont Avenue looms straight ahead. I take a left turn. From here to Century Boulevard in Inglewood it's a straight shot. We drive in silence the rest of the way. When we reach Century Boulevard I turn right because I think I know the section of Inglewood Aaron was talking about. Sure, enough it's coming up on my right hand side.

"That's it," Gagliano says, pointing.

The Pink Lady isn't anything to look at it. It's small, one story, stucco, with a couple of shuttered windows on each side of the recessed entrance. We park on the street and walk toward the doorway which is flanked by a couple of imitation potted palm trees. On the right side of the doorway is a billboard featuring three gals who probably no longer look as good as these photos and a large head shot of a rotund comic. Below his picture it says, 'America's Favorite Comic, Dickie Divine'. I wonder if America is in on the joke.

"Stay close to me," Gagliano says as we go in. "Don't do anything stupid." I hadn't planned to.

From the darkened foyer I can hear the band. Piano, trumpet, sax and drums. They're playing tinny stripper music and the drummer is punctuating everything with a kick to the bass drum, a rim shot and the cymbals. I catch a glimpse of her through the curtains as the greeter appears. The bleached blonde babe is down to her pasties and her g-string and if anybody in there cares, I hear no sign of it. The greeter, bald with a hawk nose and rheumy eyes, gives us a toothy smile as he bids us enter and shows us through the flimsy curtain.

"Right this way, gentlemen. I have an excellent table right up front."

The room is small with a tiny stage illuminated by two badly positioned spots. There are maybe twenty small tables throughout the room but only a dozen or so breathing bodies.

Gagliano points. "We'll sit back there in the corner," he says.

"Up front's better boys. Gives the ladies someone to play to, if you know what I mean."

But Gagliano's already on his way to a little table by the wall in a semi-darkened section of the room. I tag along. So does the greeter. Gagliano sits and holds up two fingers. "Two Jack Daniels neat," he says, "Doubles." He looks at me. "Bottle of Coors," I say. I take no chances with this place's plumbing apparatus.

The guy scurries away to fill our order. I suspect he is everything. Greeter, manager, waiter and bouncer. If he thinks he's going to bounce Gagliano anywhere, he has another think coming.

It turns out I am wrong about Hawknose going to get our

drinks. He is also the master of ceremonies. As the faux blonde struts off stage with her pasties and g-string still intact, Hawknose strides onto the tiny stage, exhorting the bored patrons for a round of applause for Darlin' Lily, or whatever the babe's name was, and then he goes into an overwrought introduction for the star of the evening, you guessed it, America's favorite funnyman. When Fats McCoy aka Dickie Divine walks out on stage, I can sense Gagliano stiffen. I look over at him. He's leaning forward grimly, his eyes riveted on the chubby comic with the bad rug.

Without turning his head, he says, "You can go now."

"No," I say.

He looks at me sharply.

"I say you go."

"No, I'm staying."

"What I have to do is none of your business."

"I think it is. I want to talk to this guy before you kill him."

"There is nothing to talk about," Gagliano says.

I vaguely hear Fats yakking, then a rim shot and I look to the stage where he's strutting around, shaking his belly like a bowlful of jelly while the drummer helps him out with a bass accompaniment. Thump-a-thump-a-thump. Nobody's laughing.

Hawknose brings our drinks and the tab. Five bucks for a beer, seven fifty each for the two Jack Daniels, and a ten dollar cover charge. I wonder what their weekend prices are like. Gagliano tosses two twenties onto the tray and tells the guy to get lost. The guy smiles and gets lost.

I lean over to Gagliano. "You don't know that he killed your friend, not for sure."

"I know," he says.

More rim shots. More thump-a-thumps. Fats is babbling one bad joke after another. Nobody cares, least of all me.

I lean closer. "You kill this guy and you get it wrong, it means Nick's real killer gets away with it. Is that what you want?"

Gagliano looks at me. "He ain't gonna tell you nothin'," he says.

"You don't know that."

"I know," Gagliano says and looks back at the stage just as Fats winds up his act. He gets up. "Come on," he says.

We go back into the foyer. Off to the side is a door that's marked NO ADMITTANCE. Gordo tries the handle. It turns. He opens the door and starts down a cramped hallway that leads to the rear of the building. I follow. Sure enough we find ourselves backstage. By now another stripper is out front prancing and swaying, almost in step to the music. Off to the right is a door with a cardboard star tacked to it. The star is covered with gold sparkles. I suspect this is Fats McCoy's dressing room. So does Gagliano who heads straight for it, opens it without knocking and charges in with me right behind him.

Fats is sitting at his dressing table, scanning a girlie magazine and smoking a roll-your-own cigarette that doesn't even come close to smelling like a Lucky Strike. He looks in the mirror and sees Gagliano charging at him. He tries to get up but it's too late. Gagliano grabs him by his shirt collar and yanks him to his feet and then shoves him hard against the wall.

"Jesus Christ---" Fats wails.

"I'm gonna kill you, you son of a bitch," Gagliano says, taking out the chrome .45 and laying it alongside Fats's sweaty head.

"Gordo, I swear to God, you got it wrong," Fats screams.

I barge in very close, getting in his face.

"Bullshit," I say. "You jumped Nick at the pool parlor. He ran out the door. You chased after him, caught up with him----"

Fats stares at me, confused. "Who the fuck are you?" he wants to know.

"I'm the guy who's going to save your life if you come up with the right answers," I say.

"Screw you," Fats says.

Gagliano pulls his head back and then slams it against the wall.

"Be polite to my friend, Fats," he says.

Just then Hawknose dashes into the room.

"What's going on in here?" he demands to know.

Gagliano swings the automatic around and points it at the guy's head. "Get the fuck out of here," he says.

Hawknose stops short, then turns and runs from the room.

"You chased Nick from the pool parlor, you caught up with him," I say. "Then what?"

"Then nothin'. I lost him. He was gone. The next day I hear he's found dead at the ball field but it wasn't me who done it."

"I don't believe you," I say.

"Me neither," Gagliano echoes, jamming the barrel of the gun against the base of Fats's skull.

Suddenly Fats throws an elbow backwards and catches Gagliano right in the pit of his stomach. He wriggles loose as Gagliano staggers backwards. He throws a well placed kick right into Gagliano's crotch and the big man doubles over in pain. The pistol falls from his grasp and clatters to the cement floor. Fats makes a move toward it but I'm faster and scoop it up. I point it at Fat's chest.

"Four months ago you came out here to find Nick Scalese to kill him. Now cut the crap. What happened?"

In the distance I can hear the wail of police sirens approaching. I lean down and tug at Gagliano's arm.

"Cops on the way," I say. "Go out the back."

He's on his feet now, still in pain and gasping for air.

"Gimmee my gun," he says.

"No," I say.

He glares at me, takes a step in my direction but when he hears the police sirens stop right outside the club he staggers from the dressing room. I swing the gun toward Fats.

"I just saved your life," I say.

"Thanks, Boy Scout," he says, "but I could handle that lug."

"And could you handle this?"

I click back the hammer and aim it between his eyes. He starts to grin. "You ain't gonna shoot. You ain't the type," he says dismissively.

At that moment two Metro officers enter the room, guns drawn. The first guy through the door takes dead aim at my head.

"Drop the weapon! Now!" he orders.

I spread my arms in obeyance, kneel down and lay the .45 gently on the floor.

"Aaron Kleinschmidt. Sergeant. Homicide. Call him. He knows me," I say, remaining on my knees as I raise my hands above my head.

CHAPTER TEN

espite my name dropping, the two Metro cops hauled me down to headquarters where they finally placed a call to Kleinschmidt. It was fast approaching midnight and Aaron had no intention of dragging himself out of bed to rescue me from overnight incarceration. He talked to one of the cops for a couple of minutes and then the cop whose name was Ortiz handed me the phone.

"What the hell are you up to now, Joe?" he asks grumpily.

"The fat guy that jumped Nick Scalese in the pool hall. I found him."

"Thanks for sharing that with me," Aaron says.

"I couldn't do it earlier," I say. I tell him about coming home and finding Gordo Gagliano in my kitchen and my forced participation in confronting Fats McCoy at the Pink Lady.

"Wait a second," Aaron says. "I'm writing this down." Long silence. Then, "Gagliano? That's the big guy we've been looking for?"

"Gordo Gagliano. He and Scalese were business associates back in Chicago."

"The mob."

"What else? They were also very good friends. He said the

only reason he flew to L.A. was to warn Scalese and try to protect him."

"I'll bet," Aaron says. "And this other guy? Fats McCoy, is that what you said?"

"Here in L.A. he calls himself Dickie Divine. He's a baggy pants comic, at a dive called The Pink Lady, not so funny. Fats McCoy is his real name. He's from Chicago."

"Chicago? Oh, in that case, I'd better talk to him," Aaron says, "or did you already beat me to it?"

"I tried," I say. "I didn't get very far."

"Pity," Aaron says, his voice dripping sarcasm. "Now listen to me, Joe. Officer Ortiz is going to release you on my say-so so I want you to drive home, climb into bed and get a good night's sleep. Then tomorrow morning you go to the studio and you do whatever it is you do and you keep your nose out of police business. Do you understand?"

He's suddenly gotten very loud and I can tell he's a bit peeved. I tell him I hear him loud and clear. How could I not? I do not assure him I am going to stay out of this because I'm not. More and more it becomes clear none of this would be happening and Nicky Scalese would still be alive if I hadn't arranged to have his picture sent to the Chicago Sun. Aaron can huff and puff all he wants but I am in this until the end.

I drive home on rain soaked streets. Traffic is light. My mind wanders as I try to fit Fats McCoy into the puzzle. It's certainly possible, perhaps even likely, that he killed Nick. He's a strong man with a propensity for violence, he certainly had motive and chasing Nick outside the pool hall he had opportunity. His denial sounded sincere but then so did all those Nazis in Nuremberg who kept saying they were only following orders. The cops had wanted to arrest Fats as well as me but I talked them out of it.

Fats in a jail cell does me no good at all and I have plans for the fat man the first chance I get.

I pull into my driveway. The house is dark. I go inside cautiously just in case Gagliano is back for another visit. I softly call his name. No answer. I lock all the doors and windows and go into the bedroom. I take my .25 Beretta from the night stand drawer and check to see if it's loaded. It is. When I finally get into bed, I slip it under my pillow. For the next seven hours I sleep fitfully if, in fact, I sleep at all.

Shortly past nine I follow Aaron's advice and show up at my office to do whatever it is that I do, Glenda Mae says I have not received a call back from Commissioner Ford Frick. I ask her to try again and after a few minutes she buzzes me. He's still in Boston and incommunicado. Frustrated, I ask her to get me John Galbreath in Pittsburgh. Galbreath is the new owner of the Pirates and I met him through Bing Crosby who had been one of the team's previous owners. Glenda Mae buzzes back after ten minutes. Galbreath's out of town. He's in Boston and not available. Boston? What the hell is going on in Boston?

I place a call to Chick Fullmer, the knowledgeable baseball writer with the Times. If anybody has the answers, he does, and I know him well enough to get the straight story. I get through and we exchange pleasantries and then I tell him what I've been going through trying to reach Ford Frick. He listens in silence and when I finish he says, "Perini? Your sure his office said he was seeing Lou Perini?"

"That's what they said."

"Holy Toledo," Chick says. "It may actually happen."

"What may happen?"

"The move. They've been talking about it for months. The Braves may be moving."

"You're kidding. Where?"

"Nobody knows for sure. They keep mentioning Milwaukee and Kansas City but nobody's talking. Anyway, thanks for the tip, Joe. I owe you one."

"Wait a minute. What about Frick?"

"Forget about him. He's got bigger things to worry about than your press conference. If I were you I'd try to get Hornsby." And he hangs up.

Swell. I advertise a Commissioner and I haven't got one. There have only been three. Judge Landis is dead. That leaves Happy Chandler, the second Commissioner, but then I remember reading that he is back in Kentucky, running from town to town, laying the groundwork for another run for the governor's office. I am a man with a very big problem. And then I think, Chick had a pretty good idea. Rogers Hornsby is a major character in the movie, played by Frank Lovejoy. We could do a lot worse.

I ask Glenda Mae to get him on the phone. He's at the St. Louis Browns training camp where he's managing. I expect to have to get a call back later in the day so I wander into the anteroom to get myself a Nehi and then wonder of wonders, Glenda Mae tells me she has him on the phone.

I hurry back into my office and pick up.

"Mr. Hornsby?" I say.

"Yeah. Who's this?" comes the gruff voice in the other end of the line.

"My name is Joe Bernardi, I work for Warner Brothers pictures and it is a privilege to talk to you."

"Save the soft soap, son. What do you want?"

I'd heard that Hornsby could be prickly. This guy is a full grown cactus plant.

"Well, sir, you may not be aware but we are filming the life story of a good friend of yours, Grover Cleveland Alexander."

"He wasn't a friend, he was a teammate and I've got three Triple A pitchers waiting for me outside on the mound none of whom can reach home plate with a cannon and if you don't get to the point I'm hanging up."

"Yes, sir. I'm calling to invite you to a party and a press conference here in L.A. to celebrate the movie and give you a chance to meet Ronald Reagan and Doris Day and Frank Lovejoy who plays you in the picture."

"Who'd you say?"

"Frank Lovejoy. He's a well known movie star."

"Never heard of him. Maybe that's because I don't go to the movies. What's he look like?"

"Tall, athletic, good looking."

"Well, that'll be alright then."

"Then you'll come?"

"No, I won't come," he says.

"All expenses paid. Air fare, first class hotel---"

"Listen, whatever your name is," Hornsby says, "I don't smoke, I don't drink, I don't go to the movies and I hate parties. Thanks for the call." And he hangs up.

I sit there staring at the phone, not really disappointed when I think of what a cheerful addition he would have been to the festivities. Back to the drawing board, I think, but before I do, Glenda Mae reminds me that I have a date this evening. With all that's been going on, I'd almost forgotten and I call Jillian at home.

"Hi," she says. "Ready for tonight?"

"Ready as I'll ever be," I say, "but be forewarned. I'll do my best but I'm really not comfortable around an artsy-fartsy crowd. To much manure being spread around."

She laughs. "Spread some of your own. Most of these people don't know what they're talking about. Use a lot of four syllable words and they'll be eating out of your hand."

"Is this black tie," I ask, "or can I wear my pajamas?"

"Absolutely not," she says. "Tweed sports jacket with leather elbow patches, faded blue jeans, white button down shirt with no tie, uncombed hair, briar pipe with or without tobacco in it and horn-rimmed glasses, the latter being optional."

"Sounds comfortable," I say.

"Actually, it's a uniform. Everybody wears one."

"So I'll blend right in."

"Absolutely," she says. "Remember, wardrobe and manure, You'll do just fine. Pick me up at six o'clock. We'll arrive fashionably late."

I laugh and hang up. Tonight might be fun. Jillian has a devilish antisocial streak in her that I like. And I sure need respite from this damned murder case which is giving me a permanent headache.

The other night it was the sleek sultry look. Tonight it's Bohemian casual. Her dress is blue cotton from v-neck to ankles, six strings of colorful beads around her neck, a white suede vest over the dress and sandals on her feet. She wears a coronet of tea roses on her head and jangly copper and silver bracelets on both wrists. The look is both interesting and bizarre. She tells me it's the coming thing. I hope it doesn't come too quickly. Being a red blooded male I still lean toward form fitting sweaters and silk that clings, not shapeless body bags. Still for all that, she looks pretty damned good.

We get to the publishers around six-thirty and the place is half filled with all sorts of artistic types, some already half loaded on champagne. Nubile young things in short skirts are passing through the throng with plates of cocktail wieners and crabs legs and cold shrimp. For some of the less successful in the crowd these will be dinner. Jillian introduces me around to a bunch of people I do not know and would just as soon forget. I meet her publisher who is a suave Scotsman with a wry sense of humor and her editor, a frumpy 40-year-old with her hair in a snood. She talks through her nose and when she mentions for the third time that she graduated from Sarah Lawrence, I whisper to Jillian that it's time for us to go.

I let her pick the dinner spot and she chooses perfectly, a dimly lit family-owned Italian restaurant in West Hollywood, We sit side by side in a tiny booth near the back of the room, surrounded by a mural that depicts either Rome or Florence, I'm not sure which, because the Pitti Palace is sitting right next to the Coliseum. We order calamari to start and a bottle of house chianti and allow ourselves to relax.

She asks about my day and I tell her. First about the movie I'm working on and then my bind with the press over the Reagan wedding and then my futile attempt to lure the baseball commissioner to the press conference which will actually be a party in disguise.

"What about inviting Mr. Alexander himself?" she suggests.

"Dead. Two years ago."

She thinks about that for a moment.

"How about the catcher?" she asks.

I look at her puzzled.

"What about him?" I ask.

"You said Alexander won three games in the 1926 World Series. That means his catcher caught three games. Aren't they like a team? I don't know, maybe it's just me, but I think I'd be really interested in talking to the man who caught those three games."

I stare at her for a few moments, speechless. I'm supposed to be the professional and this amateur who writes books about singing butterflies has just made me feel like a dunce. I lean over and give her a kiss. "You are fast winning my heart, lady," I say. Tomorrow I will find out who Alexander's catcher was. I pray he is still alive and lucid.

We chat aimlessly throughout dinner. Nothing special. Nothing really worth remembering but the talk comes easily as do the laughs. Even as we talk, I measure her. There's little to not like about Jillian Marx. She's attractive. sexy without working at it, intelligent, well read, a good conversationalist with a sassy sense of humor and I enjoy her company. Her shortcomings are minor. She's a tad too sophisticated for a country boy like me. She's sure of herself which is good but now and then it comes off as superiority which is bad. It's not deliberate, it's just there. She has only one major drawback. She isn't Bunny. It's unfair and not her fault but there it is. We may very well have a future in front of us but I sense already that it will never be complete. I think if I can come to terms with that, we might do well together. Anything is possible.

We're finishing our coffee when I glance at my watch and tell her that this will be a short night together. She arches an eyebrow.

"Oh, two dates in one evening and I'm just the opening act?"

I laugh.

"Nothing like that," I say. "I need to chat with a fat man and it won't keep." I haven't told her about the night before or my involvement in the Wrigley Field murder. It's too difficult to explain and my participation is too hard to justify. If it ends well, some day I'll tell her about it.

"I'm disappointed but not possessive," she says. "Shall I call you or will you call me?"

"How do you feel about Martin and Lewis?" I ask.

"Hilarious."

I smile. "They're doing a benefit for the March of Dimes Saturday evening at the Shrine Auditorium. Also Gene Kelly and Cyd Charisse, Nat King Cole, Les Brown's band and where Les goes, Doris Day follows for old times sake. I have two tickets, compliments of the studio."

"Shall we say Saturday evening then?" Jillian says.

"Why don't we?" I say, "I'll be at your door at six o'clock on the dot and we'll grab dinner before the show."

"Can't wait," she says.

I reach over and squeeze her hand. She squeezes back.

I drop Jillian back at her house and then head for Inglewood. At nine fifteen, I walk in the front door. Hawknose is standing next to a small podium making notes on a seating chart. When he looks up, he recognizes me and his automatic smile dissolves into a grimace.

"Hey, I don't want you in here, Jack. Take a walk or I call the cops."

I reach for my wallet and take out a business card.

"I come in peace, friend. Tell Dickie I'm alone and here on business. It'll be worth his while and if it works out, there may be something in it for you as well."

He scans the card suspiciously, looks up at me, looks back at the card. Then he says, "Wait here."

He goes through the NO ADMITTANCE door and I step to the curtain and push it aside. Things have changed little since last night. The band is wheezing out some provocative music, the drummer is underscoring every bump and grind and the stripper looks bored enough to fall into a deep trance if she hasn't already done so. The crowd is about the same. Small and silent.

"Hey!" Hawknose calls to me in a half-whisper from the open doorway and when I turn he waves me forward. "He'll talk to you," he says.

I find him sitting at his makeup table scanning a copy of weekly Variety. His hair is sitting on a nearby table. His eyes flick up toward me in the mirror as I enter with Hawknose right behind.

"You want me to stick around, Dickie?" he asks.

"Blow," Fats says. "I can handle this guy."

Hawknose leaves, closing the door. I stare into the mirror. Fats stares back.

"Where's your friend?" he asks.

"Don't know," I say.

"The big ape. Not a brain in his head. What are you doin', hangin' around with a guy like that?"

"It wasn't by choice."

"That I can believe," Fats says. "So what do you want?"

I look around, see a rickety chair against the wall, bring it over and straddling it, face the fat man.

"You ever do any acting?" I ask him.

"Yeah. Some. Why?"

"There's a script floating around the studio called 'Man on a Clock'. It's all about Harold Lloyd and the silent movie days. It's got a producer assigned and they're working up a budget so I'm pretty sure it'll get made."

"So?"

"So there's a decent part in the film for somebody to play Fatty Arbuckle."

I can see his eyes light up.

"I could do that," he says.

"I thought you could. That's why I'm here. I can make it happen."

His eyes narrow.

"What's the catch?"

"You have to talk to me."

"About what?"

"Nick Scalese."

"What do you want to know?"

"Everything," I say.

"That's a lot to talk about," he says.

"I know what happened back in Chicago. I know about your wife and the boy and the deep hate you had for him. Start with November when you quit the club in Chicago and came to L.A."

There's a sharp knock on the door and a man's voice. "Twenty minutes, Mr. Divine."

"Yeah, I hear ya!" Fats yells. "Like I can't hear the music," he mutters. "Like I don't know that chubby Verna is putting the place to sleep." He reaches for a box of Regents on the table and lights up. "Where were we?"

"November." I say.

"Yeah." I can see him collecting his thoughts. "Right before Thanksgiving, I get a call from a pal, one of the guys from the old days, four a days, lousy theaters, crappy pay. He knows about Scalese and what he did so when he spots Scalese at Santa Anita one afternoon, that night he calls me."

"Scalese told me he never went near the place."

"Well, this one day he did. My pal says his hair was dyed like a blonde and he was wearing dark glasses but there wasn't any question, it was Nick."

"So you quit your job to come here and find him."

"That's right. Find him."

"And kill him," I say.

"That's right," he smiles. "What's the sense of finding him if I don't kill him?" He takes a long drag on his cigarette. "I spent all of December and most of January lookng for the guy. Every racetrack, every poker parlor, every sports bar, every lousy dive in the city. I checked out the bookies. Now I figure if anybody can tell me where I can find a deadbeat like Nick Scalese, it'll be a bookie."

"What do you mean, deadbeat?" I say.

"Just what it sounds like. The guy couldn't pick a winner in a one horse race. He gets in deep to a book, then suddenly he gets hard to find. Back in Chicago, because he was connected the books didn't lean on him too hard but they kept after him. Sometimes he paid up, sometimes he didn't."

I shake my head. "Doesn't sound like the Nick I knew," I say.

"Look, he could be a really nice guy. He was my friend for years before he went after my wife, but the man had a sickness and he couldn't handle it. My pal in Chicago, the one I told you about, he says when Nick disappeared he was into this one book for over 20 G's."

"This bookie have a name?" I ask.

"He was a Jew guy. Bernstein. Birnbaum. Yeah, that's it. Birnbaum. Solly Birnbaum."

"You think maybe Birnbaum came here to Los Angeles when he saw the picture in the paper?"

Fats shakes his head. "Naw. Solly had trouble with his legs, walked around with these metal braces. If he needed something done he paid for it."

"Maybe he hired Gordo Gagliano," I suggest.

He shakes his head again. "Anybody but Gordo. Gordo and Nick were tight. The way I heard it a few years back Nick was into this other book for maybe 10 G's and he was threatening to break Nick's legs, mob or no mob. Gordo paid him a visit. That was the end of that."

"And so you're telling me the local books never saw or heard of Nick. None of them."

"That's it," Fats says. "I had this picture with me. Me and Nick and our wives sitting in some nightclub. Happier days. Nobody recognized him. Nobody. After ten weeks I sort of gave up. My buddy from the old days must have got it wrong. Whoever he saw at the track that day, it wasn't Nick."

"What about Altadena?' I ask.

"What about it?"

"Did you check it out? The End Zone sports bar?"

He nods. "Sure. The End Zone. Pretty big place. Everybody knows about it. I was there. The owner was home sick that day with the flu or something but I caught up with this guy named Eddie Braverman. He's the biggest bookie in town. He'd know Nick if anybody would so I showed him the picture. He told me he never saw him before but he'd keep a lookout." Fats frowns and I can see him recalling something. "Yeah, that's when it was," he says.

"When what was?"

"A couple of nights after that, I was coming out of one of the poker parlors in Gardena when these three guys jumped me. Young guys, like teenagers only maybe a little older. One of them hits me from behind. I swear to God it was a sap, and I fall to my knees and then they start kicking the shit out of me. Now I'm a pretty handy guy but against three of them with my head busted open, I didn't have a chance. So I'm laying on the ground and this one kid leans in and he says to me, 'Go back where you came from, fat man', or something like that and then they walk away. I got cash in my pocket, an expensive watch, gold cuff links and they walk away. So I get it. Nick knows what I'm doing and his pals rough me up to make me quit."

"And did you?"

"Not right away. I keep at it another three or four weeks and then I say to myself, screw it. If I fall over him some day, fine. If not, I'm not going to waste any more time."

Another sharp rap on the door. "Five minutes, Mr. Divine!"

"I hear ya!" he yells and gets up and goes to a nearby table where his toupee sits atop a mannequin head. He sticks it on his bald pate with spirit gum and adjusts it in the mirror.

"And then you fall over him."

"Yeah. This same pal from Chicago calls me, tells me about the picture in the paper and how they're filming this movie at the ballpark. Ha, I say to myself. Gotcha, you son of a bitch, but even then it isn't easy. I only get lucky when somebody on the crew says he heard that a bunch of the guys were shooting pool at this place downtown."

"So you jump him, a fight breaks out, he runs for it and you chase after him----"

"And I lose him. I go home so's I can get after him again in the morning. Around seven o'clock I drive to Wrigley Field. The cops are already there. I find out what's going on. Somebody describes the dead body to me. Not being stupid I get the hell out of there. Somebody did my job for me. Not as satisfying as doing it myself but pretty damned close."

He slips into his oversized purple jacket with the wide lapels and heads for the door.

"That's it, buster. There ain't no more. I'll be waiting to hear from you about that movie." And he's gone.

CHAPTER ELEVEN

I'm tired. I mean tired. I'm thirty three years old and feeling every month of it. Ten years ago I was a twenty-two year old stud based at Fort Ord in Monterey, California, getting famiiiar with the Information and Education arm of the United States Army. For whatever reason they decided I needn't carry a rifle and a pad and pencil would do just fine. I wasn't about to argue. Weekends were spent down at the wharf scoping out the female wildlife. Beer, booze and babes. I nailed everything I could find in a skirt and 99% of them turned out to be women. Life was sweet.

This morning I am thinking about those days as I climb unsteadily out of bed. This is my third straight night without decent sleep and I am feeling it from hairline to toe nails. I wonder if I have gone crazy. I know that I am obsessed with Nick Scalese's death. What I don't know is if it will kill me. I think I may have to seriously consider shoving my guilty conscience aside and let Aaron Kleinschmidt solve this murder all by himself.

And even while I am thinking this, even while I am ready to abandon the chase, I am irritated like an oyster is irritated by a grain of sand. Except I am not going to produce a pearl. If I am lucky I also will not produce a huge kidney stone which is often caused by stress of which I have plenty. A piece of this puzzle doesn't fit and it won't fit no matter how hard I try to jam it into place.

Fats McCoy, in search of Nick Scalese, goes to the End Zone sports bar in Altadena. The owner is not there. He is home sick with the flu but Fats shows a photo of Nick to Eddie Braverman, the town's bookie. Eddie doesn't recognize the man who has owned the sports bar for the past four years. I ask myself, why not? Myself answers me. I have no idea, myself says. Like I said, my energy level is zero. I do not feel like driving to Altadena. I have obligations at the studio. Yes, I am determined to lay this one off on Aaron and see what he comes up with.

It's shortly past eight. Cops start work early and Aaron's at his desk. I tell him I'm coming over. I have information better relayed in person as it is lengthy and complicated. I can tell by the sigh in Aaron's voice that he can't wait to see me.

I find him at his desk doing the morning crossword puzzle. Crime must be on hold this morning. He bids me sit and tells me not to take too long as he has a 9:30 in City Hall with an Assistant District Attorney named Harlow Quinn. I cringe. Quinn I know. He is bad news.

I am two sentences into my narrative regarding Fats McCoy when Aaron raises his hand to still me.

"Before you get too wound up, Joe, there's a couple of things you ought to know. Your pal Ray Giordano was in to see the kid early this morning."

"John Doe," I say.

Aaron smiles. "You say John Doe. I say Thomas Scalese. I say the victim's son."

I hesitate, then nod. "Yeah, I was going to tell you about that."

"And were you saving it for a Christmas present? The kid doesn't have a record but when he was eighteen he got a summer job with a delivery service. He had to be bonded. That's how we matched his prints."

"Look, Aaron, I screwed up. I'm sorry. But the boy didn't do it. I just didn't want him caught up in the system. Not yet."

"Well, he's in it now, friend. And stop calling him boy. Twenty two is not a boy. Scalese goes into court this morning and the D.A.'s office has amended the complaint from resisting arrest to first degree murder."

I'm stunned. "You people are crazy."

"For years he's been saying lousy things about his father, how he and his mother were abandoned, how his mother died of a broken heart. Over and over he told people he was going to kill his old man if he ever got the chance."

"That was just talk----"

"Right before he got on the plane for L.A., he borrowed a .38 snub-nosed revolver from a friend. That sound like just talk to you?"

"He must have had a reason," I say.

"He did and I can tell you what it was."

I shake my head. "You didn't find a gun on him."

"Joe, we didn't find anything on him. He'd ditched it all. Wallet, identification, chewing gum, loose change and a .38 short barreled police special."

"Does Ray Giordano know about the new charge?"

"He will when he shows up in court this morning."

"You guys are making a mistake," I say.

Aaron shakes his head. "Not me, Joe. It's the D.A.'s call and as far as he's concerned he has the right guy. My Captain agrees. Now what do you suggest I do?"

I have no answer to that question. Aaron's in a tough spot

with both the District Attorney's office and his superior officer arrayed against him. Even if I voiced my misgivings about Eddie Braverman's inability to identify Nick Scalese, Aaron can't act on it. He needs the equivalent of a smoking gun to get this investigation re-energized.

"By the way, I don't suppose you got a return visit from Gagliano."

"Thankfully, no," I say.

"Well, just so you know, as far as we can tell he hasn't left the city so be careful."

"Will do," I say as I rise to leave. "I know you're in a tough spot, Aaron, but this time you've got it wrong. Just keep an open mind."

He looks at me hard. "Sure, Joe," he says. "You do the same."

When I arrive back at the studio Glenda Mae's busy sorting my mail. A lot of it will be forwarded to the mail room. A few are actually intended for me personally. I have no phone calls but Reagan wants to see me as soon as possible. Glenda Mae says they are still shooting on stage 17. I ask her to call Chick Fullmer at the Times and ask him who Alexander's catcher was in the '26 series. If he's got a name, find out how I can track the guy down so I can invite him to the press conference tomorrow night in lieu of Frick.

"On it," she smiles as she reaches for the phone.

I hurry down to stage 17 to see Reagan. Something's amiss because Ronnie normally doesn't leave phone messages, especially ones that end in "as soon as possible".

He's sitting on his folding camp chair with his name printed on the back reading the morning paper. He sees me and waves me over. There's a nearby chair marked "Cast". I grab it and pull it over to him.

"What's up?" I say, probably looking a little concerned.

He smiles putting me at ease. "Nothing earth shattering, Joe, but I think we need to get a couple of things ironed out. I got a call last night from Peanuts Lowery. On your suggestion, he said."

"Right. It was just a casual thing. He needed some advice. I thought you could help him."

"Well," Reagan says, "he was looking for a little more than advice. He and some of his teammates are thinking about forming some kind of player's association. I think they mean union. They want to challenge the reserve system and they want me to head the effort."

"Oh, my gosh, Ron, I am so sorry. I thought they were just looking for some guidance. I had no idea they had this in mind."

"Well, I straightened him out on that score. I'm coming to the end of my tenure with the Screen Actor's Guild and frankly, Joe, I have no intention of getting involved in union activity of any kind from here on in."

"I understand completely, Ron. I'll make sure Peanuts understands as well."

"Thanks," Reagan says.

"Though it is kind of sad, I mean, the way they have to live with that reserve clause. It's pretty darned close to indentured servitude."

Reagan nods thoughtfully. "Well, yes, I guess you could think of it that way. On the other hand, you might say the owners are entitled to some stability in building and maintaining their ball clubs." I look at him oddly. Did I hear right? He smiles. "Think about it, Joe. If every ballplayer could put himself up for sale to the highest bidder, in a short time you'd have chaos in both leagues and a clear division between the haves and the have nots.

Floundering clubs like the Phillies or the Boston Braves would be out of business within a year. No, I think the club owners are entitled to better than that."

I sit there in disbelief. Who the hell has he been talking to? J. Paul Getty? This notion of a brain tumor may require extensive exploration. I am saved from continuing the conversation when he is called to the set. He gets up and smiles. "See you tomorrow evening at Scandia, Joe. Nancy and I are both happy to help out."

Clearly worried about our star's mental state, I head back to the office. When I arrive Glenda Mae tells me Ray Giordano needs to talk. He's at his office. I ask about the catcher situation.

"Done." she says with a smile.

"Done?"

"His name's Bob O'Farrell, he lives in Waukeegan, Illinois. 'Knute Rockne' is one of his favorite pictures and The Gipper is right up there on his A-list of actors with Bogart and Gable. He arrives tomorrow a little past noon on United and I've already booked him into the Beverly Hills Hotel for two nights."

I stare at her in unabashed admiration. "You know, gorgeous, if you weren't already married----"

"Yeah, yeah. I've heard it before, boss. Save it for your new lady friend."

Again, I'm taken aback.,

"What new lady friend?" I ask.

She shakes her head. "Do you really regard me as a piece of furniture around here, boss?"

"My mistake," I say contritely.

"You bet," she says. "I'll get Ray for you."

I'm seated at my desk when Ray comes on the phone.

"Where do you find these guys, Joe?" he asks.

"They find me, Ray. What's going on?"

"What's going on is assistant D.A. Harlow Quinn who has his eye on the big man's office when he retires this November and he's trying hard to build a tough-on-crime resume."

"I know the guy," I say. "He's a total jerk."

"No," Ray says, "he's not that smart. He's got a couple of bits and pieces and he's trying to build them into a dead bang case against our client."

"So he's got nothing."

"Not nothing but not enough. All he can do is spread trouble and misery while he's preening for the cameras."

"And meanwhile the police stop looking for the actual killer."

"Precisely," Ray says.

"Bail?"

"Not a prayer."

"So now what?" I ask.

"You tell me," Ray says.

"I'd better not. You're an officer of the court."

"Oh, like that."

"I have one lead I need to run down. Let's see where that takes us."

"What's this 'us' business, pal?" he asks.

And this is why, shortly before one o'clock on a Wednesday, I find myself driving to Altadena to have a casual chat with Eddie Braverman.

I walk in the front door of The End Zone at 1:40 and it's deader than Jersey Joe Walcott's chances of keeping the title against Rocky Marciano this fall. There are a couple of solitary bar flies sitting at the far end nursing beers and three more sitting at a table watching some dumb TV show about fly fishing. One-forty's an odd time. Too late for lunch, too early for Happy Hour. My chances of running into Eddie Braverman are slim.

I take a stool at the bar and signal to Minerva who is busy washing glasses. She comes over, wiping her hands on her apron, and tosses me an amused smile.

"Ah, the jailhouse lawyer from Warner Brothers."

"Good memory," I say.

"Them free passes helped," she says. "Coors draft, right?"

"Right," I say.

She takes a glass and starts to pour.

"On the house. Man who drives all the way up here gotta have a thirst."

"Right again," I say as she slides the glass in front of me. I take a deep swallow. "Thanks."

"Those two fellas you was asking about. Still haven't seen 'em."

"Actually I drove up here to talk to Eddie Braverman."

"Eddie. Naw, not at this time of day. If you want to make a bet, his son Andy's over at Hovack's bar. Every day from 9:00 to 10:30 and afternoons from 1:30 to 2:30."

I smile. "Horses and me don't get along that well," I tell her, taking a deep swallow of the Coors. "No, I just had a couple of questions."

"Well, Eddie's got this little place up the block where he lives with his kid, but like I said, this time of day, Eddie most likely will be down at Santa Anita, hanging around the clubhouse and laying off bets." I look puzzled. "You really don't play the ponies, do you?" she says.

"Not really," I say.

"A bookie like Eddie gets a good sized bet on a longshot, he goes to the track and bets it. He doesn't make any money on it but he doesn't lose his drawers either. Say Eddie books a c-note on a 50-1 shot. He gets hit for five thousand. That's too big a risk."

"He could always refuse the bet."

She shakes her head. "It don't work that way. A customer wants to place the bet, Eddie accommodates him. It's part of doing business."

"And I guess Eddie accommodated Ned a few times," I say.

She laughs out loud. "That's real funny, mister. Eddie hadn't booked a bet from Ned in almost two years. Even when Ned had cash, Eddie wouldn't do it. You gotta understand, Eddie and Ned were friends. Eddie knew Ned had a sickness about the horses. A few years back Ned dug himself in real deep and barely got out in one piece. Eddie wasn't going to let that happen again. No bets. Period."

"Funny, I was sure Ned told me last week he'd made a bet on a horse."

She shrugs. "Maybe at the track. Maybe some other book, but not with Eddie. That's for sure."

"They were close."

"Very close," Minerva says.

It's beginning to come into focus.

"So if a stranger came in here, say with a photograph of Ned, and asked Eddie if he knew him or where he could find him----"

"You're talking about the fat guy."

"You remember him," I say.

"Hard to forget him, the obnoxious son of a bitch. You never know about strangers, who they really are and what they really want."

I nod. "I know how Ned left Chicago and the loose ends he left behind."

She stares at me thoughtfully. "Then I guess you know his name wasn't Ned."

"Yes, I know that, too, and I know he had every right to be

scared to death of some of the people who someday might come looking for him."

"Yeah, well, he was scared all right. That's why he stuck pretty close to home. Couldn't resist the movie shoot, though. Damned shame. Pops his head up one time and gets killed for it."

"You think it was one of the Chicago boys?"

She shrugs. "Who else? A hundred G's is a lot of money."

"Sure is," I say. I'm silent for a moment, then I say, "Did you ever consider that maybe we're missing the obvious here, that maybe it was just a simple case of robbery?"

She snorts derisively. "Robbery of what? Those rings on his fingers were glass, the watch was a copy somebody bought in New York City and brought him as a present and as for cash, he'd carry maybe seventy or eighty dollars around. No more than that."

"Even on the day he died? You know, Minerva, despite what you've told me, Nick gave me the impression he was going to make a sizeable bet on a horse. Could have been a lot of b.s. Maybe not."

Minerva's been wiping the bar down with a damp rag. Now she stops and looks at me curiously. She's remembering something.

"What?" I say.

"The day Nick was killed he wrote out a check for a thousand dollars. I noticed it around noon because I had to pay the beer guy. It was strange because Nick never did anything like that. I called Pansy down at the bank, she said Nick cashed the check first thing in the morning, right after they opened." She shakes her head. "Damn. Putting good money on a horse. Man never learned."

"Maybe he never placed the bet," I say. "He was at the ball

park with me and the others until well past noon, before the track opened its windows. Maybe he went to the track in the afternoon. Maybe he didn't. If he didn't he was carrying around a lot of cash. If he opens his wallet in front of the wrong person----" I shrug. "It could be as simple as that."

Automatically she starts to wipe the bar again but her thoughts are elsewhere. Then she looks at me and shakes her head. "No, it wasn't no robbery. Dragging him to the ball field. putting a bullet in the back of his head, that's how the mob does it. Kill a double crosser and make sure everybody knows about it and who did it." I can see her eyes getting a little moist. "I told him we oughta get out of this town. Sell the bar. Move away. A long way away. I said, you stay too long in one place like this, sooner or later they find you. He just laughed."

I nod. "He told me you'd gotten tired of the place."

"Hell, yes. Over five years, working seven days a week, turning a dinky little bar into something special. We had offers, mister. Big offers. But I couldn't get him to sell. I got papers say I'm a partner but I'm a junior partner which means what I had to say didn't mean squat. I finally figured he wasn't gonna move from here. Not ever."

"Depressing," I say.

"Damned straight," she says. There's sadness in her eyes. "Damned straight."

A few minutes later I exit the place. I had questions for Eddie. Maybe I'll ask them of his punk son. Maybe I'll even get a chance to chat with Jesse Hovack himself. It might be enlightening.

I find a parking spot across the street from Hovack's bar and jog across to the entrance. Going through the main door is like entering a mausoleum. It's dark and it's dank and it may even have dead bodies hanging around since I don't see or hear anyone moving. As my eyes adjust I see the bar off to my left. The bartender's a squat and porky Hispanic. There are two guys sitting at the other end nursing beers. Toward the back of the room I see the kid who days ago was outside washing the front window. Now he's mopping the floor and my guess is he hasn't ever had much success with either chore. At the near end of the bar is Andy Braverman sitting alone scanning the racing form. I walk over and take the stool next to him. He looks up at me curiously.

"It's me. The nosy guy," I say.

"Get lost."

"I take it you're not a member of the Chamber of Commerce," I say.

"What?" He screws up his face, totally bewildered.

"Why are you so anxious to run me out of town when all I want to do is ask a few questions."

"I'm busy," Andy says.

"Yeah, I can see that," I say, looking around.

"You want to make a bet, okay. Otherwise, shove off."

"Okay," I say, grabbing the form from him.

"Hey!" he yelps.

"You want a bet, don't you?" I scan the paper, check the so-called expert handicappers picks and pull ten bucks out of my wallet.

"Soda Fountain Baby in the seventh. Ten on the nose."

He takes my ten, shaking his head and starts to fill out a betting slip. "You must need a half a buck pretty bad," he says.

"What's that supposed to mean?"

"It means the nag is chalk. I mean REAL chalk. If you're lucky she'll pay two-ten for two."

He hands me the betting slip which I fold over and put in my wallet. "It's risky," I say, "but I'll take my chances. Now how about answers to a couple of questions?"

"Such as?"

"What do you know about the fat man that came into The End Zone a couple of months ago and started asking questions about Ned Sharkey?"

"Nothin'. Next question."

"Okay, what do you know about three punks who beat the crap out of the guy two nights later and nearly sent him to the hospital?"

"Nothin'."

"How about---"

"How about you said a couple of questions and that was them." the kid says. "Scuse me while I get back to work, sport."

He turns away from me but at that moment, the main door opens and a man strides in. I recognize him from The End Zone the last time I was there. I get up from my stool and intercept him.

"Mr. Hovack?"

He regards me with suspicion.

"Yeah?"

"I was a friend of Ned Sharkey's. You got a minute?"

"What for?" he asks coldly. Another member of the Chamber of Commerce. The town is loaded with them.

"I'm working with the LAPD on Ned's murder. I was told you were a good friend who would help out any way you could."

He hesitates for a moment, then shrugs.

"Sure. Why not?" he says. He leads me over to a small table. "What are you drinking?"

"Coors in a long neck," I say.

Hovack signals to the bartender.

"Chico. Two Coors." he says as we sit. He turns his attention to Andy who is still sitting at the bar. He checks his watch.

"Hey, kid! Aren't you supposed to be in Glendale?"

Andy looks at the time and slides off the stool. "On my way, Mr. H," he says, heading through the bar to a door that leads to the back of the building.

Hovack turns his attention back to me.

"So, Mr.-----?

I hand him my card. "Joe Bernardi," I say.

He looks over the card and nods.

"You guys make good pictures," he says. "So, Mr. Bernardi, what can I do for you?"

"I understand you made Ned an offer for The End Zone." I say.

"Where'd you hear that?"

"From Ned before he died. He said you offered him two million dollars."

For the first time a smile crosses Hovack's face. "Two million, he said? Interesting," he says.

"Not two million," I say.

"Not even close. Maybe a million-two. I think that was my last offer. The first was a million-three."

"You offered him less the second time around?"

"Damned right. You say no to me, you pay a price. The next time it would have been a million-one."

"I would say it's worth a lot more than a million-two," I say.

"It's worth what somebody's willing to pay for it," Hovack says. "He was wavering."

"No doubt because you had Minerva on your side," I say.

He sort of smiles again. "Why are you asking me all these questions when you seem to have all the answers?"

"Just a guess."

"And what has my business proposition have to do with Ned's murder?"

"Maybe nothing. No offense but a million dollars is a lot of money." I look around pointedly and then back at him. He cocks his head with amusement. He knows where I'm coming from.

"I had a loan guarantee from the bank. I was going to sell this place for the down and if I needed more, I have other assets I can lay my hands on."

"Such as?"

"Mr. Bernardi, I think you really don't want to know."

At the moment the front door opens. Hovack looks past me. I turn to look. A woman is standing in the entrance. Bright daylight is at her back so I don't immediately see her features but she is fashionably dressed in grey and as she steps inside she looks around with difficulty trying to adjust her eyes to the gloom of the interior. Hovack gets to his feet and approaches her solicitously. They speak quietly and I cannot hear the conversation but she seems upset about something. As he leads her to a table the phone rings and in a moment, Chico, the bartender, calls to Hovack.

"Phone, Mr. Hovack," he says.

"Tell 'em I'll call 'em back", he says.

"It's Chula Vista," Chico tells him.

Hovack hesitates, then leans close to the woman, whispers something and heads for the bar to take the call. At this moment, I realize that I know her. Her name is Vivian Phelps and the last time I saw her was last summer when she was co-chairman of a charity event at Pasadena's Civic Auditorium featuring the city's symphony orchestra. They were presenting an evening of themes from Warner Brothers films composed by Erich Korngold and

Max Steiner and Franz Waxman. I remember her as quite an elegant woman, very composed with a warm sense of humor. I consider walking over to say hello but as I look at her, I realize she is extremely nervous and on edge. She reaches into her purse for her cigarette case and as she does so, she drops the purse on the floor. I get up and move quickly to her side and retrieve it for her.

"Thank you so much, young man," she says.

"You're quite welcome, Mrs. Phelps," I say.

She is surprised and looks at me more closely.

"I'm sorry. Have we met?"

I refresh her memory about the charity performance. She smiles and seems to brighten somewhat but her hands are shaking as she puts the cigarette between her lips and fumbles with her lighter. I take it from her and light her cigarette.

"Thank you again," she says, inhaling deeply and blowing the smoke out to the side. She looks off anxiously toward Hovack who is deep in a phone conversation at the bar.

"And how is your husband Howard?" I ask. "I remember he was a delightful man but not well."

"He died," she says matter of factly. "Last October. I've been alone ever since."

"I'm so sorry to hear it," I say.

"Yes," she replies, again looking nervously toward Hovack. She is all of sixty but her makeup is excellent and she looks terrific but now I notice that she is beginning to perspire and the make up is starting to blotch.

"Are you feeling all right, Mrs. Phelps? Can I get you something? A glass of water?"

"No, no, I'm fine," she says when she clearly isn't. Her cigarette is only half-smoked but she stubs it out in the ashtray just as Hovack gets off the phone and returns to the table.

She reaches up and tugs at his sleeve. "You do have it, don't you, Jesse? I don't want to have to make another trip."

He smiles. "I have it, Mrs. Phelps. You needn't worry." He looks over at me. "I think we were just about through, Mr. Bernardi."

"We were, Mr. Hovack, and thanks for your time."

I get up and smile down at Vivian Phelps.

"So nice to see you again," I say and I leave.

I squint as I step into the sunlight. When my eyes finally adjust I find myself staring at a beautifully maintained four-door pre-war Bentley parked at curbside directly in front of the bar. Old money speaks for itself so I don't need to see the registration to know that this is Vivian Phelps' transportation. The guy in the chauffeur's uniform rubbing the hood with a soft cloth is also a giveaway.

"Nice wheels," I say.

"You bet," he says.

"How's she handle?"

"Like a baby carriage."

"Really?"

"Yeah, with square tires."

I nod in understanding and look in the window.

"Real leather," I say.

"Real leather, real burlwood on the dash"

"1939, 1940?"

"'37" he says. "425 litre saloon."

"Gas?"

"Six miles to the gallon. Downhill."

"Big on economy," I say.

"One of kind," he says. "Wanna buy it? Then maybe she'll buy a Caddy or a Lincoln, something I can actually drive without getting a hernia."

"Sorry," I smile. "Already have one. It's home in the garage."
He laughs.

At this moment Vivian Phelps emerges from the bar. Her step is lively and her eyes are clear and I see none of the fumbling and bumbling I witnessed a short time before.

"You seem much better, Mrs. Phelps," I say as she approaches.

"Better? I'm fine, young man. Feel wonderful."

The chauffeur has raced around to the back door and holds it open. "Thank you, Hamilton," Vivian says. She steps in, throwing me a last smile. "So nice to see you again," she says just before the door closes. A minute later the Bentley is headed south out of town in the direction of Pasadena. I stand there, watching it go and then I look over to the bar. I see Hovack standing in the open doorway. He is watching me watching the Bentley. Our eyes meet, then he turns and goes back inside.

I cross the street and get in my car. I sit quietly for a few moments mulling over what I've learned. Most importantly, I know that Nick had a thousand dollars on him the day he was killed. That in itself could be a reason to kill him. He may or may not have bet it on a horse. If Minerva's right Eddie Braverman would never have taken his action but he still might have made the bet at the track. I remember he said the horse was running in the seventh race. I make a mental note to check it out.

I start the car and head out of town. My mind is still trying to sort things out and I realize that something else is bothering me. Vivian Phelps. This is a woman of impeccable credentials, a leading lady of Pasadena society whose money is so old it was first counted in pounds sterling. Yet she walks into a moth-eaten little bar and greets the equally moth-eaten proprietor like he was an old friend of the family. In Vivian Phelps' world Jesse Hovack should have been a footman at the rear of the carriage and nothing more. I'm also bothered by the sudden metamorphosis in personality. Bumbling, unsteady, in the grip of the shakes one minute, then perfectly fine five minutes later. If she was a boozer I could understand it. Got the shakes, needs a drink, gets a couple of belts down the hatch and feels immensely better. And where better to get a couple of belts than a bar? But why this puddle of a watering hole? There are plenty of upscale cocktail joints in Pasadena even if the cupboard is bare at home. No, booze isn't it and there's only one other explanation that makes sense but it's so absurd I dismiss it as soon as I think of it.

I am so deep in thought that I'm not aware that I am being followed and when I glance up into my rear view mirror, I see the red and white flashing light array atop the squad car on my tail. I pull over. He does likewise. I look in my side mirror as Floyd Willard exits his his cruiser, hefts his gun belt, and approaches. I wind down my window.

"Hello, again, young fella," he says.

"Hi."

"Saw your car parked outside Hovack's."

"You have a good memory," I say.

"About some things," he says. "I promised my good friend Aaron Kleinschmidt I'd keep an eye out, just in case you showed up here again, nosing around."

"I call it inquiring."

"Well, whatever you call it, it's going to stop."

"Look, Captain, you can't---"

He interrupts me sharply. "I can and I will," he says. "You're nothing but trouble, Mr. Bernardi, and I don't like trouble. I don't like dealing with it and I don't like cleaning up after it."

"You're going to an awful lot of trouble to keep me from talking to Eddie Braverman," I say.

"You weren't talking to Eddie. First Minerva, then Jesse."

"You have a problem with that?"

"I have a problem with you in general, Mr. Bernardi."

"Yeah, I kind of thought you did, considering."

"Considering?"

"Well, you take Eddie Braverman, for instance. The man's a lawbreaker yet he's not in jail. I wonder why."

"I told you why once, Mr. Bernardi. I won't tell you again."

"Yeah, I know. Eddie's just a good old boy providing a public service to the people of Altadena."

"That's right."

"And except for his son Andy, he doesn't have any partners, silent or otherwise."

"That's also right."

"Including you?"

"Including me. Be on your way, Mr. Bernardi, and don't break any speed laws leaving town. I'd hate to see you spend a night in jail on a lovely day like this."

Message received. I drive away at a sedate thirty miles an hour. I check the mirror. He's still there, arms folded across his chest, leaning against his grill watching me go. I don't speed up until I reach Pasadena.

Altadena's an odd little town, I think to myself. There's an invisible sign posted at the city limits and if you could read it, it would say 'Strangers Need Not Apply'. The law is administered by a man who openly permits illegal bookmaking, raising the question, what else does he permit? Since he seems pretty cozy with Jesse Hovack, I suspect the answer may be very revealing.

CHAPTER TWELVE

I decide to skip the office for the rest of the day. I'll call Glenda Mae from home to see if anything crucial needs my attention. As I turn into my street I spot a new yellow Volkswagen Beetle parked in front of my house. I have company. I try to remember. Do we have a date tonight? I don't think so but my synapses have been so overloaded of late that we could be flying off to Vegas tonight to get married and I wouldn't remember. Well, whatever the reason she's here but I sure wish I knew why. I'm not crazy about people dropping in no matter who they are.

I pull up into the driveway by my kitchen door and even before I walk inside, I can smell the coffee.

"Hello!" I call out. "Anybody?"

"In the living room!" Jillian responds.

I find her lounging on the living room sofa, shoes off, reading the latest issue of 'Photoplay' which is the least grating of the fan magazines.

"This is a welcome surprise," I say as I lean down and give her a quick kiss in the lips.

"Welcome? I doubt it. I've violated your space and you probably are annoyed as hell," she says.

"No,---" I start to protest.

"Save it, Joe. You forget I talk to your ex-wife at least three times a week. You are anal compulsive about your privacy."

I shrug. "Well, I wouldn't say----"

"SHE would," Jillian says, cutting me off. She eyes me suspiciously. "So what's going on, Joe?"

"About what?"

"Lydia says Mick told her that you're hip deep in a murder investigation."

"Not really, I say."

"Not the way she tells it. I need coffee."

She gets up and brushes past me on her way to the kitchen. I get a whiff of her Chanel. No. 5. I'm a sucker for Chanel No. 5. I follow her into the kitchen.

"Lydia exaggerates," I say.

"Did you or did you not get into a shoot out at a burlesque house Monday night with some gangster from Chicago?" she asks.

"Not exactly," I say.

She shakes her head in disgust. "Not really. Lydia exaggerates. Not exactly. Joe, what the hell are you involved with and could I please get a straight answer."

She's locked on with a very defiant look and though I wanted to keep her out of this, I see that I can't. I ask her to sit down at the kitchen table. I grab a coffee and sit across from her. I tell her everything. She listens intently.

"So the way it plays out, Jillian, is this. If I hadn't put Nick's photograph in the Chicago papers, he'd still be alive today."

"You don't know that, Joe," she says.

"I do know it," I say.

"And you're not a cop."

"I know that, too. but I can't pretend I'm not at fault."

"Most people would just walk away."

"I suppose they would."

"But you won't."

I manage a shrug. "I can't."

She looks at me with a faint smile.

"I guess I shouldn't be surprised," she says.

She stands and straightens out her dress, then walks past me back into the living room. "I need my shoes," she says.

I follow her back in.

She sits on the sofa and slips her shoes on,.

"How about dinner?" I ask.

"Can't," she says, glancing at her watch. "My editor's coming by with proofs from my next book.:"

"Then how about a quick romp in the sack?"

"Next time," she says. "Look, maybe I had no right to come here this afternoon and butt into your private business. But I like you an awful lot, Joe, and Lydia scared the crap out of me."

"I can handle myself," I tell her.

She nods. "Yeah, I think you can."

She gets up and takes my face in her hands and kisses me like next time is already here. As she pulls away she smiles and says, "Remember where you got that from."

I walk her out to the front door and stand on the stoop as I watch her get in her funny little car. I wave as she backs out and starts down the street. I'm about to go back inside when an LAPD squad car pulls up in front of the house. This is like the third time this week. These guys are giving the neighborhood a bad name. When he gets out of the car, I see that it's Officer Sanchez again.

"Nice to see you again," I say. "What have I done now?"

"I wouldn't know, sir, but Sergeant Kleinschmidt needs to see you as soon as possible."

"And why is that?" I ask.

"I'm not sure, sir, but he said to tell you the big guy beat the snot out of the fat guy and that the big guy is still at large."

I nod. "I'll follow you. Where are we going?"

"County General Hospital and you're to come with me, sir. The sergeant doesn't want you left alone. I'll drive you back when you're done."

"Okay," I say and we hurry across the street to the squad car.

Aaron's on the second floor deep in conversation with a Metro officer and someone from hospital security. Another Metro officer is seated on a chair outside one of the hospital rooms. Aaron waves when he sees me.

"We've been looking all over for you. Where were you?"

"Here and there," I say. "What happened?"

"McCoy showed up at the club a little after one o'clock. Gagliano was waiting for him in the parking lot in the back. He started beating the crap out of him. I think he intended to kill him but a couple of maintenance guys came out the back door and when they saw what was going on, they jumped in. They were both pretty big guys so Gagliano ran for it. "

I look to the hospital room door.

"How's he doing?" I ask.

"Not good," Aaron says. "Fractured skull, broken jaw, dislocated shoulder, internal injuries. He's pretty much doped up right now. When he's lucid I'll talk to him."

"And Gagliano's still on the loose."

"Which is why I wanted to see you. I don't like the idea of you being alone in that house with only your little pop gun for protection."

I ignore the slur on my handy little .25 caliber Beretta which twice has saved my life.

"I can stay at the studio overnight if you really think it's necessary," I say.

"I do. I think this ape has a screw loose, attacking the fat guy in broad daylight and if he's nuts he's doubly dangerous. We have an APB out on him, armed and dangerous, but he's found someplace to hole up so until we get him, I want you totally protected."

"Tell me what to do, I do it," I say.

"Sleeping overnight at the studio is a good start," Aaron says.

"Done," I say. "although I find this curious since neither McCoy or Gagliano seem to have any connection to young Tom Scalese whom the D.A. has already tried, convicted and sentenced to a life stretch in Folsom."

"Let's say I'm keeping an open mind."

"Better yet," I say, "let's say you are not convinced that you've locked up the right guy."

"That, too," Aaron says, "but don't spread it around."

"I won't. Now let me ask you something. How well do you know this Floyd Willard?"

He glowers at me. "Is that where you were? Altadena?"

"Shoot me at sunrise," I say, "but first answer my question."

"We worked a case together a couple of years ago. I see him at law enforcement seminars. Why?"

"There's a bookmaking operation going on up there under his watchful eye," I say.

"I wouldn't be surprised." Aaron says.

"Last time I checked the penal code, bookmaking was illegal."

"Still is. It's also illegal in Pasadena, Glendale, West Hollywood, Brentwood and various other enclaves of Greater Los Angeles."

"So it's all over the place."

"And as long as violence doesn't get involved it'll probably stay that way."

"So you don't think Willard is looking the other way in return for a piece of the action."

"I didn't say that," Aaron replies. "I have no idea and I really don't care as long as he keeps the peace. Joe, you're a big boy. Think like one. The state can pass all the anti-bookmaking and anti-prostitution laws it wants to but it's so much hot air and always will be. As long as no one is getting hurt, as long as the mob isn't involved, then guys like Eddie Braverman will continue to operate. And yes, I know who Eddie is and have for a long time."

"Enough said," I respond. "I guess I was wandering up a blind alley. Thanks for setting me straight,"

"No problem."

"Any chance I can talk to Fats after he wakes up?"

"None," Aaron says. "I don't know how many ways I can phrase this, Joe, but stay out of it. This is dangerous business and I don't want you getting in the way."

"And have I? Gotten in the way?"

"Not yet. Let's keep it that way. Sanchez!" He signals to my chauffeur that I'm ready to go. "I'll let you know when we catch up with Gagliano. Meantime, as they say in your business, Joe, don't call us, we'll call you."

Sanchez drives me home where I pack a small overnight bag. I slip my Beretta into my pants pocket, turn down the heat and lock up. I drive myself to the studio with Sanchez right behind me. He sees me through the main gate and then peels off.

I walk into my office anteroom just as Glenda Mae is closing up for the day. She spots my bag and smiles.

"Forgot to pay the rent, did we?" she asks.

"No. I'm fed up with that boring fifteen minute commute every morning. Anything interesting going on?"

"Nada," she says.

"No crises to attend to?"

"None."

"Phone calls to return?"

"Zero."

"Mail to open?"

"Sorry."

"In that case, go home," I say.

"Goin', boss," she says scooping up her purse.

"See you in the morning."

She eyes my overnight bag.

"How can I not?" she says. "Sweet dreams."

Out she goes and I amble into my private office and set down my bag. I look at the sofa which converts to a bed. In four years I have never once opened it. I'm not sure I know how. I open the door to my private bathroom. Towel, toilet paper, soap in the dish. Looks okay. I go around my desk and sit down. I lean back. I check my watch. Quarter to six. I twiddle my fingers. I am a man with nothing to do and no place to go. I wonder what the special is at the commissary tonight.

I walk over there and find out. I wish I hadn't. I return to my office and resume reading "The Caine Mutiny". This lasts about an hour and then I give up. It only takes me fifteen minutes to get the bed open and then two hours to finally drop off to sleep. The bed measures six feet, three inches. I am six feet one inch. I do a lot of scrunching. I toss and turn like a jib in a wind storm. The skimpy blanket is guaze-like. I'm mostly cold. When I awaken in the morning I check my watch. It's six-thirty-nine. I try to go back to sleep. I can't. Finally I stir myself and pad into the bathroom. I am so miserable, if Gordo Gagliano were to walk through my office door at that moment I would shoot him on sight.

Once dressed I go into Glenda Mae's office and start to make coffee. This is always an adventure because, even though I know how to make the coffee, I don't know how much chickory to add. I am saved from having to deal with this ordeal when I see that we are out of chickory. Uh-oh, I think. It's going to be one of those days.

At this moment, the phone rings. I look at my watch. Seven-oh-nine. Who the hell is calling me at seven-oh-nine? I lift the receiver.

"Mr Bernardi?"

"Yeah."

"This is Leo down at the main gate. I've got this young lady here. She's not on the list but she says she needs to see you. She says if I give you her name, you'll see her."

"And what's her name?"

"Madison Chase."

I was sleepy and groggy. Suddenly I'm alert and bushy-tailed.

"You want me to send her up?" Leo asks.

"Hold her there. I'm coming down."

I'm still about thirty yards away but I can already tell that she's a looker. Petite, dark haired, blue eyed, heart shaped face, no more than twenty years old, reminds me of Kathryn Grayson.

"Thanks, Leo," I say to the gate guard. "Good morning, Miss Chase. You are a long way from home."

"I'm sorry to bother you, Mr. Bernardi, but I didn't know who else to contact."

"No bother," I say, taking her arm and leading her onto the lot. "Have you had breakfast?"

"No, I came here directly from my motel."

"We'll chat while we eat," I say.

It's a few minutes past seven and the commissary is beginning to thin out. Working crew members come in around six and finish up by six-thirty. Secretaries and others not due at their desks until nine start drifting in around eight.

Madison and I are in the lull and we have our choice of tables. Mamie, the little gal from Oakland who'd rather be doing Crawford's hair than hustling eggs over easy, takes our order. Whetena for Madison, a waffle with bacon on the side for me, and coffee all around.

Madison tells me she was so worried about Tom that she couldn't stay in Chicago, she had to come. She got in last evening and is staying at a motel near the airport.

"How is he, Mr. Bernardi?" she asks. "What's happening?"

Telling her isn't my business, I should leave that to Ray, but she's so distraught it would be cruel to stay silent. I tell her what I know. It isn't what she'd hoped to hear and I can see she's afraid but I can't force myself to soft pedal the reality of Tom's situation.

"Will I be able to see him?" she asks.

"I don't know. Maybe Ray can arrange it. You'll like Ray. He's a good lawyer and a good person."

We remain quiet as Mamie brings our breakfasts. Then I say, "I was told Tom brought a gun with him. Is that true?"

"My brother forced him to take it. For protection."

"Why?" I ask.

"Why what?"

"Why would your brother assume Tom would need protection? When we talked on the phone, you gave me the impression you had no idea why Tom was flying to Los Angeles."

"I didn't."

"Sorry. I don't believe you. I think you knew he was going to seek out his father. I think you and your brother knew there was a price on his father's head and I think you knew why."

She pales and I sense an onslaught of tears.

"Tom didn't kill him. He loved his father."

"He never said he hated him? He never said he was praying for the day when he'd find him and kill him?"

She shakes her head. "That was in the beginning when he'd first been abandoned and later when his mother died. He was just a boy then, full of resentment. When he got older, he became more understanding. He learned about his father's work with the police and then about the contract that was put out on Nick's head. He felt sorry for his father. He prayed for him."

Her eyes are still moist but the tears don't come. She's fighting them back. "You don't know him the way I do, Mr. Bernardi. He's a good, decent man. That gun my brother gave him? He handed it back to me at the airport. He wouldn't hurt a soul. He couldn't. These people are wrong. He's innocent."

I reach over and take her hand and squeeze it. She looks up at me with a smile.

When we get back to my office, I call Ray. From now on, Madison Chase is his problem. Me? I've got a press conference to attend to.

CHAPTER THIRTEEN

t's four-thirty. I have been at Scandia's for an hour already, checking to make sure that everything is in order. I have gone over the menu with the manager. In the center of the room is a huge table. The centerpiece is a champagne fountain consisting of dozens of champagne glasses stacked atop one another in a pyramid shape. At some point we will start pouring champagne into the upper glasses and the wine will cascade downward from glass to glass filling each one to the brim. It doesn't make the wine taste any better but it does get a lot of oohs and aahs which is the whole idea. Beating the drum, selling the sizzle, filling the air with flash and dash. Make it big. Make it memorable. Welcome to the world of promotion and publicity, Hollywood style.

Arrayed around the champagne are iced platters of cherrystone clams, oysters, cold shrimp and cocktail sauce, steaming trays of mini-weiners wrapped in bacon, stuffed mushrooms, chicken satay and peanut sauce, swedish meatballs and toothpicks, and for ambience, crystal bowls filled with peanuts and popcorn and crackerjack.

At the end of the room, next to the open bar, is a raised platform with a piano, a set of drums, and a bass fiddle. A talented trio of studio musicians will be playing unobtrusively for most of the two hours. A standing mike has been placed at the front of the platform. I'll emcee the proceedings. I think Ronnie intends to say a few words and maybe Doris will favor us with her latest hit single. Along the walls are hastily prepared posters with stills of scenes already shot and eight foot cutouts of Ronnie and Doris and Frank in character. Souvenir baseballs and bats marked "The Winning Team" will be handed out at the door. And finally a velvet curtain has been hung against one wall, flanked by six baskets of flowers and it's here that the various photographers will shoot their pictures of the beaming newlyweds.

In addition to the thirteen gossip columnists and entertainment editors, we've invited the press from all over including several television stations. Bill Holden said he'd drop by as did Nancy Olson. We may also get a quick visit from Randolph Scott who's filming 'Carson City' and even better, we may get Ray Bolger who's shooting 'Where's Charley?' If we're lucky Ray might even do a little dance turn for us. I can only hope.

They start to appear shortly after five. Our newest staffer, Donna Brown, has picked up Bob O'Farrell at the Beverly Hills Hotel and he turns out to be a pleasant outgoing guy, totally awed by the proceedings. He can't wait to meet The Gipper. He's even brought his old catcher's mitt which he plans to give to Reagan as a gift. My boss Charlie Berger shows up early and makes a bee line for the shrimp followed by the open bar. Doris and Frank Lovejoy wander in around five fifteen and the Reagans arrive a few minutes later to the popping of flashbulbs and a lousy version of 'O Promise Me' from the bandstand trio.

By six-fifteen, I have sweet-talked every member of the press in attendance. Half of them are now well lubricated and the laughter level has risen by several decibels while the quality of conversation has dropped by an equal amount. Doris has declined our request for a song but Ronnie takes the microphone willingly and does thirteen minutes on the grand and glorious game of baseball and how it is an integral part of the American way of life and how men like Grover Cleveland Alexander and Bob O'Farrell have served as heroes to a generation of young people who were brought up to love and respect the freedoms that their country had given them and---. There was more but by that time I had tuned out. In small doses, Reagan can be a spellbinder but he is unfamiliar with the notion of small doses. Still you can't help but admire him. He talks a lot but you know that he means what he says and he is unapologetic about his deep love of country. I guess that is why most people, me included, can't help but like the guy.

As the polite applause for Reagan's speech subsides, I spot Phineas Ogilvy slipping in the door. He heads straight for the food table and fills a plate to overflowing, then walks over and tugs at my sleeve, pulling me to one side.

"What are you doing here?" I ask. "You got your scoop last Sunday."

"I'm here for the food," he says unashamedly, "and where is the cheese fondue?"

"A free meal and you're bitching?" I say.

"It's in my genes. In any case, old top. I am actually here on behalf of others. Chick Fullmer wants to know if you've learned anything more about the clandestine activities in Boston."

"I have not," I say.

"I thought as much and told him so. I will tell him so again. Now, as for Lou Cioffi---"

"Nothing."

His eyes flare. "I have not yet asked the question," he says indignantly.

"You don't have to. I know absolutely nothing that Kleinschmidt hasn't given to the press."

"According to Lou, your friend the policeman has given the press absolutely nothing."

"He's been busy."

"Who's the John Doe he's got stashed in County Jail?"

"Next question."

"That sort of answer will not earn you a gold star in Lou's little black book."

"Probably not."

"Is he guilty?"

"How should I know?"

"Is he from Chicago?"

"He could be from anywhere."

"Is he a hitman out to collect on a hundred thousand dollar contract?"

"No."

"Really?"

"He's not a mob killer and that it is the only information you get from me tonight."

Phineas smiles. "Lou will be pleased, He can write an entire column on that one fact alone."

"I know," I say. "I've read his stuff. Phineas, your plate's empty. Go get a refill while there's still something left to get."

"An excellent suggestion," he says and waddles off in the direction of the food table. I've made a good move. I've given Lou, who is the Times' premier crime reporter, a tidbit of truth. He'll fashion a decent story out of it and be grateful to me. At some time in the future I might be able to make it pay off.

At six-thirty, the Man himself walks through the door. Jack Warner seldom attends these outings unless a major celebrity has been invited, i.e. the President or the Governor or a visiting head of state. But here he is and the press crowds in on him. He smiles warmly and handles them deftly, even as his eyes search the room. Finally they settle on what they've been looking for. Me. He throws a little head nod toward a deserted corner of the room and I nod in understanding and amble over there to wait for him. Charlie Berger has caught the exchange and he, too, moves toward the corner as Warner breaks away from the crowd and heads towards me.

"Keep the jackals away, Charlie," Jack says. "Joe and I need privacy."

"Right, J.L.," Charlie says, heading off Louella who is striding toward us, martini in hand.

Warner takes me by the elbow and we move even farther away from the crowd. I can hear Louella whining and Charlie quietly trying to steer her back to the open bar.

"First of all, Joe," he says. I hate it when he says 'first of all' because it is a sure thing that I am not going to like 'second of all'.

"You have done a bang up job here, as usual. Love the champagne thing. Between that and the open bar most of these hacks are totally sloshed. They may not remember what went on but they'll remember they had a good time and that Warners provided it. Four gold stars."

"Thank you, Jack," I say.

"However, about an hour ago I got a call from an Assistant District Attorney named Quinn complaining loudly about your unasked for interference in the investigation of the unfortunate murder that took place last Friday at Wrigley Field where we were filming."

"Sir, if I may say----"

"No, you may not say and don't call me sir. I don't care if

they've got your fairy godmother behind bars, the coverage of the so-called Warner Brothers murder at Wrigley Field has fallen to a trickle and I want it totally gone, dead and buried. Do we understand each other?"

"Yes, but---"

"And I do not want to read in the paper a day or two from now that you have continued to poke around in this affair---"

"I hear you----"

"Because if I do, as much as I love you, Joe, and respect and admire the wonderful work you do for us, I will kick your ass into the gutter without a second thought. Do you understand THAT?"

"I do."

"Good." He smiles and claps me on the shoulder. "Now lead me to the microphone and introduce me so I can say something that sounds plausibly sincere about Reagan's marriage."

It is quarter past seven when we finally clear the room. Scandia's people are carting away what's left of the food and drink and starting to clear away the debris. I am sitting on a folding chair, a cold Coors in my hand, contemplating my future. Jack Warner has erected a brick wall which I may not skirt around or surmount if I want to keep my job. To stay employed I have to keep silent and I'm not sure I can do that. Having spoken to Madison Chase I am more and more convinced that Tom Scalese is innocent. Worse, I am also convinced that Harlow Quinn, that poor excuse for an assistant D.A., is going to use Tom's conviction as his first major move to win the election for District Attorney.

It would be nice to think that other studios besides Warners might be interested in my services but I've seen no sign of it. Every studio in town is hurting as audiences dwindle. Profits are hard to come by. They are experimenting with everything from 3D to stereophonic sound to a new wide screen process called Cinemascope. With money tight, if I leave Warners, and especially if I am fired, it might be months or even a year before I could find work elsewhere. No, common sense says to mind my own business. I drain my beer and head for the door.

Outside, Stan Sinkowitz is waiting for me. He's a Warner's security guard who followed me here earlier and is supposed to tail me back to the studio at party's end. This on orders from the studio's security chief who got his instructions from Aaron Kleinschmidt. Everybody's worried about me. I should be flattered. Mostly I'm just aggravated.

"Ready, sir?" Sinkowitz asks.

"You can take off now, Stan. I'll be okay."

He shakes his head. "Sorry, sir, I'm under orders to stay with you all the way back to the studio."

"I'm not going back to the studio," I tell him.

Sinkowitz is perplexed. "But, sir---"

"I'm going to County General to visit a sick friend."

"Sir, are you sure---?"

"I'm sure."

"All right, I'll follow you," Sinkowitz says.

"I'll be fine," I say.

"I'll follow you," Sinkowitz says again, this time more firmly and he doesn't blink.

"Suit yourself," I say as I slip behind the wheel of my car. I take off and look behind me. Sinkwitz is in his studio cruiser and he is following me closely.

I pull into the hospital's underground parking area and stop in a space near the staircase. Sinkowitz pulls in beside me. I get out. He gets out.

"Do you want me to come in with you, sir?"

I start to say no, then hesitate.

"All right, but I want you to do something for me. I'm going to the second floor. I want you to follow me but then I want you to go into the men's room. It's at the end of the corridor." I look at my watch. "At precisely eight-fifteen, I want you to fire two shots into the water in one of the commodes."

"What? But---"

"I have my reasons, Stan, and they're important. If you can't help me, then get out of my sight."

He stares at me long and hard and then he says, "Well, I know you're not crazy, Mr. Bernardi, so what the hell. Go ahead. I'll be right behind you."

I climb the steps, open the second floor door and step out into the corridor. At the far end I can see the room where Fats McCoy is convalescing.

Seated on a folding chair by his door is a Metro officer reading a newspaper. I start down the hallway toward him.

As I get near I see he's not famliar. He's heavy set like a wrestler, jowly and losing his hair. His name tag reads "Hoffman". He looks up at me curiously.

"Hi," I say. "I need to speak to Mr. Divine for a couple of minutes. It won't take long." I start toward the door. He throws a meaty leg in front of me, blocking my way.

"Sorry, sir, no visitors," he says.

"Oh, this isn't a visit. I've been working with Sergeant Kleinschmidt on the case. Check with him if you like."

I try to move past the leg but it's not budging. Hoffman smiles up at me.

"Is your name Bernardi?" he asks.

"That's right. Thanks, Officer."

I try to press forward. The leg is cemented in place.

"The sergeant said to keep a special eye out for you," Hoffman says with a knowing smile.

"Excellent," I say. I'm going to get past that leg if I have to leap over it.

Hoffman is still smiling.

"Sir, I think you misunderstand the situation," he says.

Just then two loud pistol shots echo through the corridor coming from the other side of the building. Hoffman is on his feet instantly, reaching for his service revolver.

"What the hell----" he says starting down the hallway, gun in hand. For a beefy man he's amazingly quick and agile. I watch him go and then duck into the hospital room.

Fats McCoy, bandaged just about everywhere, is sitting up doing a crossword puzzle. He looks up in a panic and then relaxes when he sees it's me.

"What the hell's the racket?" he says.

I go to his bedside and try my best to look threatening.

"I need answers, Fats, and I need them quick. I haven't much time."

"Got no answers. Get lost," he says, turning back to his puzzle. I snatch it out of his hands and toss it across the room.

"Hey!" he yells.

"Tell me what I want to know or I tell the cops that you confessed to me that you killed Nick Scalese."

"That's a damned lie," he screams.

"It sure is, but I can screw up your life for months if I stick to it."

"Okay, okay. What do you want to know?"

"You checked out The End Zone in Altadena."

"That's right."

"And you talked to this bookie named Eddie Braverman who said he didn't know Nick Scalese."

"So?"

"And then the next night or the night after you get jumped in a parking lot by three young punks who beat the hell out of you but don't rob you."

"Get to the point, man," he says.

"And this young kid leans over you and says 'Go back where you came from' or something like that."

"Yeah. Something."

"So I guess you must have told somebody you were from out of town."

"No, I never did."

"You never said you were from Chicago?"

"You got a hearing problem, bud. I said no."

"But they were sure you were from out of town."

"Yeah, I suppose."

"Now, think about this, Fats. You ask about Nick. You show a photograph. Everybody plays dumb but the next night three punks jump you and tell you to go back where you came from. Not go home. Not mind your own business. Not keep out of this. No, they say 'go back where you came from'."

"You're grabbing at straws, Mister."

"Did you know that the owner of The End Zone was Nick Scalese and that Braverman had known him for over four years."

That piece of information brings Fats up short. For a moment he's silent. "Is that right?"

"That's right and I think maybe you scared the piss out of him asking about his friend because Eddie knew who Nick was and about the contract out on him and he figured you were there to collect and needed to be scared off."

"It wasn't the bookie who beat me up. He's an old guy. Like I said, it was three punks."

"Eddie's got a twenty year old son. The son has friends. They wanted you out of Southern California real bad."

I think I hear the door open and the curtain sweep back. I turn, expecting to see Officer Hoffman. I have my apology all ready. But it isn't Hoffman. It's Gordo Gagliano and he's holding his chrome plated .45 automatic and the look in his eye tells me he's there to use it.

CHAPTER FOURTEEN

et out of the way!" Gagliano says to me reaching out with his huge paw to shove me aside.

"No!" I say, backing up but still keeping myself between Gagliano and Fats who is screaming at the top of his lungs.

"Gordo, he didn't do it!" I yell.

"Don't make me hurt you, Joe," Gagliano says, his hand on my shoulder now and shoving me violently. From outside I can hear fast approaching police sirens. Gagliano can hear them, too. He looks toward the window.

At that moment Hoffman comes charging through the door. "What the hell is going on----?" He stops short as Gagliano whirls toward him, brandishing the .45. Insanely, Hofffman claws at his holster for his revolver.

Without thinking, I leap at Gagliano who now has his back to me and I grab him around the neck. The sirens are loud now, the squad cars pulling up outside the hospital. I try to get a good grip on Gagliano but effortlessly he shrugs me off his back and onto the floor. In the same motion he swipes his gun hand at Hoffman and catches him aside the head, slamming the burly Metro officer back against the wall. At that moment the hospital alarm system starts to wail. Gagliano is startled. He turns back toward the bed, leveling his pistol but Fats is no longer there.

By now Hoffman has gotten himself into a kneeling position and his revolver is just clearing the holster when Gagliano hits him again, slamming the .45 into Hoffman's head. Hoffman doubles over and sprawls to the floor as Gagliano steps to the door and goes out. I hear him race down the corridor and then I hear a shot.

"Is he gone?"

I turn as a terrified Fats rises up from the floor alongside the bed where he'd thrown himself when Hoffman dashed into the room. I give Fats one look and then I hurry out into the hallway. A grey uniformed figure is crumpled on the floor near the far end of the corridor. Stan Sinkowitz. A nurse is bending over him as a doctor races to help. I look around. Gordo Gagliano is nowhere in sight. I hurry to Stan's side.

"How is he?" I ask the doctor.

"Flesh wound to the arm," he says. "Through and through. I don't think it's serious."

Sinkowitz looks up at me and forces a smile through the pain. "What the hell's going on, sir, if you don't mind my asking."

"Well, Stan, for one thing, we just prevented a murder," I say.

"Good for us," he grimaces.

I can hear more sirens approaching outside. I run to the window at the end of the hallway and look down. Three more squad cars are pulling in and I suspect more are on the way. In a few minutes this place will be crawling with cops. If Gordo is still in the building he won't have a prayer of escaping.

I turn away from the window just as the elevator doors open and two helmeted officers wearing body armor step into the corridor. They are cradling riot guns and they take in the scene in a matter of seconds. Directly behind them, Aaron Kleinschmidt appears. His bulk says he's wearing a vest. He carries a pistol in one hand and a walkie-talkie in the other. He looks around and spots me. His expression goes from grim to unpleasant as he strides toward me.

"What the hell are you doing here?" he asks, "And where's Hoffman?"

"In the room. I think he's okay. So is McCoy," I tell him.

He starts quickly for McCoy's room. I follow behind.

"Where did Gagliano go?" Aaron demands to know.

"I don't know. When he heard the squad cars arriving, he ran for it."

"How long ago?"

"Two minutes," I say. "No longer."

As we get to the room, Hoffman emerges. He's unsteady on his feet but otherwise looks all right.

"You okay?" Aaron asks him.

"A bang on the head, Sarge. I'll live."

"Get it looked at."

"I'm okay---"

"Now," Aaron barks gruffly. "That's an order."

"Yes, sir," Hoffman says and starts off in search of a doctor,.

Aaron's radio squawks. He talks to the police downstairs covering the lobby and the other exits. The alarm that had sounded automatically locked all the emergency doors. No sign of Gagliano. Gordo's in the building somewhere. Now it's just a matter of time before they flush him out. I feel a chill. He won't surrender, I'm sure of it. People are going to get hurt. Some may even die. It's a lousy situation.

I hear a new sound, the whirling of rotor blades. I glance out the window again. An LAPD helicopter is circling overhead. Its spotlight is poking into the dark hiding places around the building and on the roof.

"How'd you get here so fast?" I ask.

"A nurse was leaving, spotted him going in a service entrance. She phoned it in. Now get out of here," he says.

I shake my head. "I can help."

"No, you can't. Move."

"No," I say.

"I'll have you dragged out of here."

"No, you won't. He won't surrender, Aaron. We both know it. You may kill him but he could take one or two of your men with him. You really want that?"

"And what's your great idea?"

"Let me talk to him."

Aaron's radio squawks again. The helicopter has spotted Gordo on the roof. Aaron relays instructions to the other units working the building and hurries toward the elevator. I follow and when the door opens I step in alongside him.

"Get out!" he says angrily.

"He might talk to me. He sure as hell isn't going to talk to you."

"He'll shoot you the minute you get close to him."

"No, he won't."

"If you're wrong, you're dead," Aaron says.

"I know that," I say.

Aaron hesitates, then pushes a button. The doors close. The elevator cab starts to rise toward the top floor. We ride in silence. When the elevator doors open, we find ourselves on the very top floor. Across from us is a door marked STAIRS. Aaron crosses the hall and opens it. We both enter the stairwell and start to climb the few steps that lead to the door that opens onto the roof.

Cautiously Aaron opens the door and steps out with me right behind. The air is chilly and there is a mild breeze. The chopper is hovering several hundred feet above the roof, it's searchlight stabbing through the night air at a cluster of heating and air conditioning units. Over to the right we see a trio of cops in body armor approaching from a different direction. I grab Aaron by the arm and tell him to have the men hold up for a few minutes. He shakes his head and shrugs me off, then starts barking tactical orders into the walkie-talkie. At any moment this is going to turn into a firefight. Without really thinking, I shrug out of my suit jacket and raising my hands, I start walking quickly toward the spot marked out by the helicopter search light.

I hear Aaron behind me screaming my name. I ignore him. I am betting my life that Gordo will not shoot me. I am not so sure about the police but I am committed. I am determined that Gordo will not be slaughtered in a hail of bullets if there is the slightest chance I can talk some sense into him.

I am about ten yards away, the wind wash from the chopper whipping at my shirt and trousers, when I hear him call out to me.

"Stop! Go back!" Gordo yells.

I can barely hear him. The noise from the helicopter is drowning out everything. I pretend I haven't heard him and move closer, my hands still high above my head. I see Gordo now, crouching in the shadows, gun in hand. With his other hand he is waving me back. When I am ten feet away I stop.

"Don't do this," I shout.

"Get out of here or I'll kill you!"

"No, you won't! You only kill bad guys!"

I am aware that the chopper is moving, climbing higher. The searchlight is still focused on me but it's a little quieter now. The turbulence of the rotors is not as severe.

"Gordo, be smart," I say. "You came to kill Fats. You didn't. If you die up here, Fats will still be alive and you'll be dead. Is that what you want?"

He doesn't answer because he has no answer, not one that makes sense.

"Did you know they're holding someone for Nick's murder?" He looks at me curiously. He didn't know. I didn't think he did. "Do you know who they have?" I ask him. He doesn't answer. "They're holding Tom, Gordo. Nick's son Tom. They've charged him with murder."

He looks at me in disbelief and he starts to slowly shake his head. "No," he says.

"Yes, Gordo. He's in a cell in County Jail and they say they can prove he killed his father. And if they can't, maybe they can prove that he told you to do it for him. Maybe they can prove that. Can they, Gordo? Did Tom tell you to kill his father?"

"No, it's a lie."

"Then maybe you should tell them everything you know but you won't be able to tell anybody anything if you're lying dead on this roof." I move forward. I'm close now. I could reach out and touch him.

He looks up at me from his kneeling position. There is real pain in his expression. I think I even see tears forming in his eyes.

"What do I do?" he says.

"First, lay the gun down. Then stand up and get behind me. Very close so we're touching. Then we walk out to the middle of the roof with our hands raised so everyone can see us. And then very slowly we are going to lower ourselves onto the roof and lay flat on our stomachs with our arms and legs spread and wait for them to come to us."

"They won't shoot us?" he asks.

"No, they won't shoot us," I say.

And they don't.

Thirty minutes later I'm sitting in a waiting room, suit jacket back on, huddled with my arms wrapped around my torso, shivering. My teeth are chattering and I don't know if it's the cold or my nerves. Aaron sits opposite me, filling out some paperwork. Gordo is on his way to Metro Division headquarters where he'll be booked and then stashed in the lockup until Aaron can get to him for questioning. It won't be fun but it's better than bleeding to death on a tar paper roof with a half dozen slugs in you.

A uniform enters carrying two containers of hot coffee. I get one, Aaron gets the other. I thank the cop for his kindness. Aaron just grunts. He finishes the paperwork and sets it aside, then takes a sip of the coffee.

"I ought to arrest you," Aaron says.

"Don't," I say. "It'll cost me my job."

"Can't have that," he says. "You might apply to the Police Academy."

"Very funny," I say without humor.

"What's it going to take to keep you out of my hair?" he asks.

"Keep the investigation alive. Tom Scalese isn't your killer. Neither is Gordo Gagliano."

"Then who is?"

"Person or persons unknown. Some guy who flew in from Chicago we don't even know about. Why not? A hundred grand's a lot of money."

"I don't believe that and neither do you," Aaron says.

"You're right. I don't. But it's still possible."

"Maybe it is," he says. "You need a ride?"

I shake my head. "I've got my car." I finish the coffee and get to my feet. "Where's Sinkowitz?"

"Third floor. They're keeping him overnight for observation."

I nod.

"Don't forget, Aaron, no matter what, I wasn't here tonight."

"I'll do my best to remember that," he says.

I go in search of Stan Sinkowitz. I find him in a third floor hospital room, arm in a sling, flirting shamelessly with a cute little nurse. This is when I remember that Stan is single. I offer sympathy, thank him for his help and warn him in no uncertain terms to keep his mouth shut about our presence here, lest we both find ourselves out of a job the following morning. He vows silence and satisfied, I leave the room. The nurse does not.

I drive back to the studio but even as I do, I feel my adrenalin supply quickly being exhausted. It's nearly midnight and I'm exhausted. I would like to collect my things and head for home but by the time I stumble into my office, all I can think of is sleep. I manage to get the sofa bed open in record time—eight minutes punctuated by a variety of four-letter words—and after kicking off my shoes, I flop down on the mattress fully clothed and pull the skimpy blanket around me. I succumb to sleep in a matter of minutes.

CHAPTER FIFTEEN

I awaken to the sound of typing coming from the next room and then the ringing of a phone. The typing stops. I stare at the ceiling and orient myself. I'm afraid to look at my watch. The little hand will be past the nine. Maybe even the ten. I swing my legs to the floor and slip on my shoes, then stand and fumble my way into the bathroom. I look in the mirror. An old man with matted hair, bloodshot eyes and five o'clock shadow stares back at me. I would not buy a used car from this man. In fact I wouldn't even give him the time of day. Speaking of that, I peek at my wrist. Nine-fifteen. It could be worse.

I quickly brush my teeth, shave, splash water all over my face and hands, dab a little Brylcreem through my hair and comb it well enough to pass a cursory inspection. I'm lucky in that most days Jack Warner doesn't wander into the studio until ten o'clock. By that time I will give the illusion that I am working hard on studio business and have absolutely no interest what-soever in getting to the bottom of the so-called Wrigley Field murder. A lie, of course. Every time I talk to somebody about Nick's murder, the closer I get to the truth. Or at least it seems that way. Last night Fats McCoy confirmed to my satisfaction what I long suspected, that Andy Braverman and a couple of his buddies, probably with Eddie's blessing, worked Fats over in order to scare him off. The folks in Altadena seem very protective of their own and I wonder why and even more importantly, who am I going to get to tell me why?

I walk into the ante room and smile at Glenda Mae, giving the impression that I am functional. She smiles back and gets up to pour me a coffee. She also hands me a little white bag. I look inside. Mmmm. Two cheese danish.

"I didn't have the heart to wake you up, but I knew you'd be hungry. Tough night?"

"I was here all evening working," I say.

"Funny, she says, "I don't see anything that needs typing. Probably show up later today."

"Probably," I say.

"News item on my car radio on the way in this morning. Big shootout at County General last night. They caught up with that big guy who's been after you the past few days. Got him locked up. Guess you hadn't heard about that."

"I hadn't," I say.

"Good," she says. "Stick with that story. Mr. Berger wants to see you as soon as you're awake."

I come up short.

"You mean he----?"

"He stopped by the office. When he heard you snoring, he peeked in your door."

"Jesus," I mutter.

"He may assume you passed out drunk as a result of the party. You might want to encourage him in that hypothesis."

"Absolutely," I say heading out.

Charlie is amused.

"Had a little too much party last night, Joe?"

"Guess so," I say.

"I will say you've cleaned up pretty good. How's your head?"

"Functioning."

"Good," Charlie says. His smile fades. "Joe, J.L. told me about the conversation he had with you last night."

I nod. "Right."

"If it were up to me, I'd let you off the leash. I know how you feel about that man's death. I know you blame yourself even though it wasn't your fault but J.L. is right. We have a studio to run and you get paid a good salary to do your job. No one quarrels with your ability but you are not a policeman and you have no business getting embroiled in this investigation."

"Mr. Warner made that clear."

"And now I'm making it clear. J.L. is making me personally responsible for your behavior and I will not take the fall for you. Are we clear about that?"

"I understand, Charlie."

"The cops will sort this out, believe me."

"I'm sure they will," I say.

"Good man," he says. Then he adds, "Two aspirin and a glass of V-8."

"What?"

"Try it. You'll like it," he smiles.

As I head back to my office I think about the politically ambitious Harlow Quinn who is not going to let anything be sorted out until he is good and ready. Aaron's the lead investigator on this case and while he may gripe loudly about my participation, he has an open mind. and if you have something cogent to say, he'll listen. Not so Harlow Quinn and therein lies the rub.

There are just too many unanswered questions to sit quietly by and do nothing. There is a sizable amount of money unaccounted for and I'd like to know where it is. There's a so-called "widow" in Altadena who has been hoping to sell the sports bar but never could. At least not until now. And there's an officer of the law with a selective agenda about which laws he'll enforce and which he won't. And finally the town boasts a bookmaker who apparently likes everyone and is well liked in return and who operates openly without impediment.

Do I think that Nick Scalese has been murdered by someone from his past? Yes. Most likely. But there's a small piece of me that is beginning to suspect that maybe his past ties in Chicago have nothing to do with his death and the answer lies much closer to home.

I enter my office anteroom and breeze past Glenda Mae. "Grab a pad and pencil," I say to her as I step into my private office.

A few moments later she follows me in, armed for dictation. Before I can speak Glenda Mae beats me to it.

"As I was saying before you stomped out of here, its a funny thing but a couple of people swear some lunatic was there at the hospital and actually talked the big guy into giving up. Walked right up to him, hands raised, and talked him down. Cops are denying it, of course."

"Lunatic?" I say.

"He'd have to be, don't you think?" she asks sweetly as she sits down across the desk from me and modestly crosses her legs, pad in lap and pencil poised. I glare at her. She keeps smiling.

"First, I need Ray Giordano. Second, get me Warren Giles, he's the President of the National League. Probably in New York. I'm not sure. Third, find out the name of the biggest and best hotel in Milwaukee."

"Reservation?"

"No, just the name."

"That it?" she asks.

"That's it," I say.

A few minutes later I'm on the phone with Ray.

"How is Madison doing?" I ask him.

"Well enough, I guess. I got her a room at a little motel a few blocks from my place."

"You picking up the tab?" I ask.

"Why? Would you like to volunteer?" he asks.

"Sure," I say.

"Forget it," Ray says. "Next time you need my help I'll over-charge you outrageously."

"Fair enough. Has she seen Tom yet?"

"I got her in last night for about fifteen minutes."

"What do you think?"

"About her? True love hath no greater champion."

"Who said that?" I ask.

"I did. The two of them, one ditzier than the other. Was I really like that when I was twenty?"

"I don't know. Give me the name of your college sweetheart and I'll let you know."

"My wife," he says gruffly.

"Sorry. In that case, forget it. What's the outlook?"

"Grim," he says. "Quinn's got no case. Even so, he's puffing himself up to anyone who'll listen and making a lot of press friends in the bargain. I suspect in a few weeks he'll quietly dismiss the charges after he's milked the situation dry."

"Just what I thought," I say. "Meanwhile, two young people are miserable and the actual killer remains free and the trail gets cold."

"That's about it," Ray says.

"Anybody representing Gordo Gagliano?"

"Not that I know of, and don't look at me That's called conflict of interest."

"I feel sorry for the guy."

"Hey, if not for you, he could be dead," Ray says. "And remember, Joe, he did shoot someone."

"I know. Well, if you know a halfway decent young lawyer who needs work and who'll represent him for rock bottom dollars, I'll pick up the tab."

"Sucker," he jibes me.

"Always have been," I say and hang up.

Next up is Warren Giles but first Glenda Mae comes in with my mail and the trade papers and several early editions of out-of-town newspapers. She gives me the name of the Milwaukee hotel which is old and revered and has a five star reputation. She also tells me that Giles is out of town. Would I like to speak to his assistant? Absolutely, I say.

Elliott Pomeroy is Giles' aide-de-camp and talks through his nose. He also is saddled with a Boston accent which makes it hard for me to take him seriously. Nonetheless I will try. If I am lucky Elliott will be from a wealthy and privileged family which normally means he won't be too bright, Back Bay'ers not being known for indulging in hard work or challenging studies.

"So sorry you missed him," Elliott is saying. "I'm sure he'll be disappointed."

"My mistake, Elliott, I say. I was sure Warren said he wouldn't be leaving for Boston until Friday evening."

"Actually he left at noon yesterday, but perhaps there is some way I can help you, Mr. Bernardi."

"Perhaps so. In case you weren't aware, we are filming the life story of one of the National League's greatest pitchers, Grover Cleveland Alexander."

"No, I hadn't heard," Elliott says.

"Oh, yes," I say, "and that very popular actor, Mr. Ronald Reagan is portraying Mr. Alexander."

"Reagan. Yes. Wonderful choice."

"And Doris Day plays his wife Aimee."

"Delightful. I adore her."

"The release date for the film is June 20th and by the first week in July, the picture-- it's called 'The Winning Team'-- will be in nationwide release and it occured to me that wouldn't it be terrific if Mr. Reagan were to appear at the All Star Game in Shibe Park on July 8th to throw out a ceremonial first pitch?"

I sense a slight hesitation.

"Of course, he'd be wearing his outfit from the movie, the St. Louis Cards uniform that Alexander wore when he won three Series games and singlehandedly humbled the mighty New York Yankees."

"Yes," he says slowly. "I think I see it---"

"And naturally Miss Day will be on hand to lead the crowd in the singing of 'Take Me Out to the Ball Game."

"Yes!" Elliott says with enthusiasm. "A marvelous idea. I'm sure Mr. Giles will approve wholeheartedly. I expect him to check in later today and I will bring it to his attention."

"Would it be better if I talked to Warren personally? He's still in Boston, isn't he?"

"Yes, but he's traveling west tonight by train. I don't know his exact schedule. It's pretty fluid,"

Here's where I gamble.

"I guess he'll be staying at the Pfister Hotel then."

"Of course," Elliott says.

"Yes, I thought that was what he told me. And that's where they're going to make the announcement?"

There is a momentary silence on the other end.

"What announcement?" Ellliott asks, his voice more wary now.

"About moving the Braves to Milwaukee."

"What are you talking about?" Elliott says. "No such announcement is planned. Who gave you such an idea?"

I play dumb.

"I don't know. I'm sure I heard it from someone. I thought it was Warren. I may be wrong."

"You are wrong, Mr. Bernardi. There are no plans to move the Boston franchise anywhere."

"But I keep reading in the papers----"

"The papers are wrong," Elliott says. "Now if there is nothing else--"

"No, no. And you will speak to Mr Giles."

"At my first opportunity," Elliott says and hangs up.

I immediately tell Glenda Mae to get me Chick Fullmer at the Times.

"Who's this?" he growls.

"Your best friend," I say.

"Haven't got any friends," he says.

"That doesn't surprise me."

"Joe Bernardi?" he asks coming alive.

"The same. I tried to nail down the Boston story for you. I couldn't."

"Did you get anything?" he asks.

"Not much. Warren Giles is in Boston. Tonight he's taking the train to Milwaukee. He'll be there for several days."

"Wow. Anything else?"

"Just denials," I say.

He perks up.

"Denials. That's good. That means they're hiding something."

"Maybe they're denying because it isn't true."

"Don't be naive," Chick says. "When it's true, they deny. When it's false, they say they'll get back to you."

"Who's on first?"

"What?"

"I was just thinking, I feel like I'm in the middle of an Abbott and Costello routine."

"You're not and thanks for the tip."

"What tip?"

"If you ever need anything, call me."

He hangs up like he can't wait to get to his typewriter. I wonder what the hell he's going to write. What he's got is cotton candy, no umbrella and it's raining. I think I have made a mistake in trying to help him out.

I pick up the out of town papers, the Chronicle and the Examiner from San Francisco and the Union and the Tribune from San Diego. All four have printed stories about the Reagan nuptials with a smattering of good press for the film. Two have even printed a silly picture of Bob O'Farrell squatting in a catcher's stance wearing his mitt while Reagan stands behind him leaning forward and peering over his shoulder as if waiting for a pitch. The Reporter's story was right on message but unfortunately, Mildred Owens wrote the story for Variety. Mildred knows nothing about baseball but she's a sucker for weddings. Every paragraph but one is about Ron and Nancy and the bright future that awaits them. Only the last paragraph mentions the film and she gets it wrong. She calls it 'The Winning Game'.

I decide I have enough to show Jack Warner so I go looking for him. I find him in the parking lot getting ready to drive over to the Lakeside Country Club for a round of golf. I tell him about the marvelous coverage we've gotten as a result of our press conference. He's impressed. I dazzle him with my brilliant idea of having Reagan at the All Star game tossing out the first pitch. He's even more impressed. Here I am, manning my post, giving my all for the studio. In comradely fashion he claps me on the shoulder with a big smile and I suspect that all thoughts of firing me have vanished into the ether.

"Incidentally, Joe, I'm flying to New York tomorrow morning and I may not be back until late Wednesday. We're working on something special and it's so good, even Harry likes it. If we green light it, it'll be yours if you want it."

"Hint?" I ask hopefully.

"3D," Warner says. "It's a remake of an oldie, 'The Mystery of the Wax Museum.' We've got a damned good script and I think it's a potential blockbuster."

I've heard about the process and the need to wear special glasses so I'm not as keen on it as J.L. but one doesn't argue with the boss, particularly this boss, about anything including the weather.

"Sounds great, J.L.," I say. "Can't wait."

Warner grins. "Yeah. Three dimensions. Let's see those television people beat that."

He drives off and I head back to my office. I'm relieved to hear that he's going to be out of town for several days because I have places to go and people to see and if Jack Warner and Charlie Berger and Harlow Quinn and Floyd Willard think they are going to get in my way, they are woefully mistaken.

In the second floor corridor of the office building I pass the clock that reads 12:04. This is going to be a long, long day.

Glenda Mae hasn't left for lunch yet and when I enter, she says to me, "I need a check."

"What for?" I ask.

"March of Dimes. You pledged two hundred dollars. Cheap at the price considering they're giving you a pair of freebies for tomorrow night's benefit."

I remember. Tomorrow night. Me and Jillian at the Shrine. I also remember the pledge. I can't afford five hundred dollars each for tickets but it's a good cause and I can afford two bills.

Glenda Mae scoops up her purse and heads for the door. "I left the checkbook on your desk," she says as she goes out.

I go into my office and sit down at my desk. The checkbook is there. It's an account I use only for personal expenditures that are tax deductible. Mostly these are charities. It helps when tax time rolls around to keep things separated.

I grab a pen and write the check. I am about to close the book when an idea hits me. I lean back and give it some thought. I kick it around and the more I do, the better I like it. I pick up the phone and call the Los Angeles Times. I ask for Lou Cioffi, their ace crime reporter.

"You forgot to invite me to the party," he says when he comes on the line.

"You'd have hated it, Lou. No dead bodies."

"Really? I was sure I heard that Reagan was there."

"Funny. Since when did you become a movie critic?"

"Since I had to sit through 'The Girl from Jones Beach'. What can I do for you, my friend?"

"Harlow Quinn."

"That idiot."

"That's the guy," I say. "I'm told he's planning to run for D.A. this fall."

"You were told right," Lou says.

"Who's his biggest competition?" I ask.

"Everybody."

"I mean, if you had to name one person who could sink his candidacy."

"Harlow Quinn."

"One laugh after another. I'll try again."

"Chester Mulholland," Lou says.

"Famous name," I observe.

"Fourth cousin or something. Got the name, don't got the money, but he's sharp as hell and everybody likes him."

"Unlike Quinn."

"Amen to that," Lou says.

"Thanks, Lou," I say. "I owe you one."

I hang up and flop open the checkbook. Meticulously, I write out a check. I tear it out. I write the amount on the stub but I don't identify what it's for. I look at the check long and hard. Should I? Should I not? Finally prudence gets the better of me and with a sigh I tear up the check into eighths and toss the pieces into the wastebasket. I close the checkbook and get up from my desk. Lunch time and I'm hungry.

I am halfway out the door when I stop. I look back at the checkbook closed on my desk. I swear it is whispering to me, 'Come back, come back!' I hesitate and then with a rashness I may soon come to regret I return to the desk, whip open the checkbook and write another check for the identical amount. I fold it up and slip it into my shirt pocket. If and when Jack Warner finds out about this, I will be out on Barham Boulevard, my typewriter under one arm and my shiny desk name plate under the other. The hell with it. I can always go back to the oil fields of Oklahoma where the only dead things are played out wells. I'm almost looking forward to it.

It's two-thirty. I'm at City Hall sitting in a chair at third floor reception right outside the office of Assistant District Attorney

Harlow Quinn. Even though I have no appointment his secretary is sure he will find time to see me as I have identified myself as a political supporter anxious to make a donation to his upcoming run for District Attorney. For legal reasons I do not give my name but I do wink at her. She gets it. I would bet that she gets a lot of winks for the same reason.

I don't have to wait long. At two-thirty eight she tells me Mr. Quinn can see me and I enter his sanctum. Even before I close the door behind me he is on his feet with a smile and coming around the desk. His hand is outstretched. We shake.

"So nice to see you," he says. "Please sit down." He gestures me to the chair opposite his desk as he resumes his place behind the desk. A look crosses his face and his brow furrows as he leans forward.

"I know you," he says.

"Joe Bernardi," I say. "We met a couple of years ago. The Virginia Jenks murder. You were romantically involved with Emma Schroeder."

"Oh, that one." I can tell he has a sour taste in his mouth.

"No longer together?"

"Happily, no. A lovely woman in many ways but, uh, delusional."

"Yes, that's how I remember her."

"So, Mr. Bernardi, my secretary mentioned something about a contribution."

"Indeed," I say. I reach in my pocket and take out the folded check and hand it to him. He takes it with a smile and unfolds it. The smile morphs into a full fledged grin.

"Fifty thousand dollars. Extremely generous, Mr. Bernardi."

Then the grin fades and he looks at me, confused.

"This check is made out to Chester Mulholland," he says.

I rise from my chair and reach across the desk, taking it from him. "Is it? I'm very sorry. My mistake."

"What's this all about?" he says with some annoyance.

"I apologize, sir. I had a check for you made out for five hundred dollars and I obviously put the wrong one in my pocket. I'll have my girl put the proper check in the mail to you first thing Monday morning. At the same time I'll be mailing this check to Mr. Mulholland."

I turn on my heel and head for the door.

"Hold it!" he says loudly and I turn back to face him. "First of all, you can't make that size contribution. It's against the law."

"Really? Then I'll just chop it up among my friends and co-workers. Thanks for the tip. I sure wouldn't want to break the law. Especially if you ever got to be District Attorney."

"What's that supposed to mean?"

I move back to the desk and stare him down.

"It means, Mr. Quinn, that I don't want someone running law enforcement in this city who makes every decision based on his personal political ambition and not on reality."

"Such as?"

"Such as the incarceration of Thomas Scalese who you have charged with first degree murder on the flimsiest of---- I was about to say evidence but you don't actually have any of that--- on the flimsiest of suppositions. This isn't Moscow, Mr. Quinn, it's Los Angeles though I seriously think the distinction escapes you."

"You can't tell me how to run my office," he fumes.

"I'm not. Run it any way you please. I can't stop you. Not until November. So let me leave you with two thoughts. I can chop this check up into fifty little pieces and the next check into fifty more and the next into fifty more. There is no end to the amount of checks my friends and co-workers at Warner Brothers can write over the next several months. And we will. That's one thought. Here's the second one. It doesn't have to be this way if you decide to step back and operate evenhandedly according to the dictates of your office. I will hold off for 72 hours before I personally deliver this check to Mr. Mulholland. That should give you plenty of time to reevaluate your position on Thomas Scalese. Need I remind you that your campaign will benefit by fifty thousand dollars?"

I head for the door again. This time I do not stop. I hear Quinn shouting after me. "I will not be blackmailed!" I ignore him as I walk out of his office slamming the door behind me. I feel good about myself, damned fool that I am. I am no closer to finding out who really killed Nick Scalese but I may have pushed a button that will allow Tom to go free and for he and Madison to scoot back to Chicago and resume their lives. I sure hope so.

CHAPTER SIXTEEN

anta Anita racetrack is a Southern California landmark and even those who have never dropped a buck or two at its windows have certainly heard of it. It's been around for nearly twenty years and through its turnstiles have passed dozens of Hollywood legends like Crosby and Gable and Jolson. Some just came to bet and to socialize, others were actually owners including Harry Warner, J.L.'s older brother. It sprawls across three hundred acres and can accommodate up to 60,000 people on any given day. The infield area is peppered with picnic tables and features trees of every sort in an idyllic park like setting. In 1942 racing was suspended and the facility was converted into an internment camp for thousands of Japanese-Americans. Not its finest hour. Reopened in 1945 it resumed its place as one of the premier entertainment getaway sites in the Southern California area. Today it caters to the rich and famous as well as to auto mechanics and plumbers and other blue collar Americans looking to spend a leisurely day with their families away from the pressures of everyday life they left behind at home.

I drive through the main gate, find my way to clubhouse parking and entrust my car to an eager valet. I purchase a ticket, loop its string through my jacket lapel, and push my way through the turnstile. There's an elevator to the clubhouse but I choose to take the stairs. It's a gorgeous day, sunny with clear blue skies and even clearer air unpolluted by downtown L.A.s smog.

At the top of the stairs, the banks of individual seats and private boxes are off to my right. To my left is the covered area which features dozens of tellers who sell tickets in every denomination and cashiers who parcel out money to the lucky winners. There are several refreshment stands which feature burgers and franks and beer and soda and an upscale sit-down restaurant for those who prefer to eat in style.

I have not come to bet. Playing the horses is a sucker's game. All the so-called research available in the past performance charts is no guarantee of what a horse is going to feel like doing on any given afternoon. Even if he's frisky and ready to go, the trainer may not be. Maybe the price isn't good enough. Maybe they're holding him back for a huge payday at big odds a few weeks down the road. Or maybe they'll breeze him for a mile but are really looking to set him up for six furlongs next Wednesday. Is this something I want to risk my money on? I don't think so.

I stroll around in search of Eddie Braverman. After about ten minutes of fruitless searching it occurs to me that on this day, Eddie may not have any large bets to lay off in which case I am here on a fool's errand.

I pass by a table with the remnants of a hamburger and french fries as well as a copy of this morning's Los Angeles Times folded open to the sports section. I stop as I read the headline: BRAVES HEADED FOR MILWAUKEE. I pick up the paper and scan Chick Fullmer's article. I am identified as a reliable source close to the situation. The rest of it's there. Pfister Hotel. The gathering of baseball's nabobs. Ford Frick and Warren Giles unreachable. Lou Perini, no comment. Everything that Chick has written is carefully worded with phrases like "rumored to be", "allegedly", "thought to have", "unconfirmed", "highly likely", "off the record". It is a masterpiece of non-news and speculative hyperbole and even though there are no hard facts, Boston's mayor throws around words like 'treacherous', 'despicable', 'lawsuit' and 'boycott'. Not a happy man, the mayor.

I put the paper back and resume my search for Eddie Braverman. Almost immediately I spot him. He's sitting at a small table away from the crowd, munching on a burger and drinking a beer while he studiously goes over a batch of papers in a three-ring binder.

I approach him.

"Hi," I say.

He looks up. If he recognizes me he gives no sign.

"Hi," he says in return.

"We haven't actually met. I was in Altadena a couple of days ago chatting with Minerva."

"Yeah, your face is sort of familiar. I'm good at faces. Names not so hot."

I put out my hand.

"Joe Bernardi."

"Eddie Braverman."

We shake.

"Pull up a chair," Eddie says.

"Thanks," I say. "Guess you have at least one big bet."

He laughs.

"Yeah, we got this kid in town, Dave Grimes, works at Hovack's Bar and Grill, thinks he has all the answers. Today it's a filly in the third named Gay Godiva. If I was on crutches I could outrun her. I'll be stunned if she goes off at less than fifty to one. But the kid thinks she's a sure thing so he gives my boy,

Andy, fifty bucks. That's like two days pay. On the nose, he says. I told Andy, if the guy's a friend, don't book his bets but Andy says, a bet's a bet and business is business."

"If the horse is that bad, why not just keep the fifty and take your chances?"

Eddie laughs. "Please, Joe, this is the horse business. A pregnant mare could jump out of the gate dead last, fall down and give birth at the second pole, get up and finish first." I give him an amused look. He shrugs. "Unlikely, I admit," he says, "but I take no chances. Fifty bucks at fifty to one is twenty five hundred simoleons which I do not care to pay out. So here I am. Better safe than sorry."

"I understand Nick wasn't much of a bettor either," I say.

He looks at me curiously. I quickly put his mind at ease.

"Nick, Ned, whatever name he happened to be using at the time. I know all about him."

Eddie nods and smiles again.

"Yeah, in addition to being a lousy handicapper, Nick was also unlucky. He couldn't pick flowers in a field of daisies. I finally stopped taking his bets. He was too good a friend. I don't steal from friends."

I nod. "That's how Minerva described it. So when the fat man came around asking questions about Nick, you weren't about to tell him a thing."

Eddie suddenly becomes wary. "That's right. What do you know about the fat man?"

"I know that if he had found Nick, he probably would have killed him."

"Is that right? Joe? Is that your name? Joe?"

"Joe Bernardi."

"Are you a cop, Joe?"

I shake my head.

"An interested party. It's a long story, Eddie, but the bottom line is, they have Nick's son locked up in County Jail facing a murder charge."

"Tom?" Eddie says. "They're holding Tom?"

"You know him?" I ask.

"Know of him. Nick and I had no secrets from one another. He really loved that kid. It was the hardest thing Nick ever had to do was to walk out without a word. Well, you know what the situation was in Chicago."

"Yeah, I do."

"So what's the extent of your interest, Mister Interested Party?"

I shrug. "I'm going to find out who really killed your friend Nick because aside from you, I may be the only one who cared about him."

"What's that supposed to mean?"

"For one thing, it means the autopsy's complete and Nick's body is still in the County Morgue, unclaimed."

He frowns. "I didn't know. I thought Minerva had made arrangements."

"She hasn't."

"I'll talk to her," Eddie says.

"Do that," I say as I stand. "Good talking to you, Eddie."

"Same here."

We shake and I walk away and leave him to his paperwork. I don't know much more about Eddie Braverman than I did when I sat down. He comes off as an open book without guile or artifice but that may be just a skill honed over the years. I have one more thing to do and then I can leave. I look around for a security guard and spot one near the $50 window. I walk over to him.

"Excuse me," I say.

He smiles. "Can I help you, sir?"

"I hope so. A friend bet a horse a week ago Thursday and forgot to check whether he won or lost. Is there any way I can find that out?"

He nods, pointing. "Take that set of stairs down to the next level. There's a room with tables and chairs for the convenience of the handicappers. You'll also find copies of the Daily Racing Form or The Morning Telegraph going back a month."

I thank him and head for the stairs.

The room is crowded but it is quiet. I hear a little murmuring, a lot of newspaper pages being turned but that's about all. These are the pros, the ones who make their living at it and while it may ultimately be a meager living at best, they are self-employed and take lip from no one. There are, I suppose, worse ways to survive.

I find a copy of The Racing Form dated Friday, March 3rd. I look for and find the results for Santa Anita and run my finger down to the chart for the seventh race. There he is at the top of heap. Base on Balls finishing first by a neck and paying $128.00 for a two dollar bet. I do the math. The odds were 63-1. A thousand dollar bet at 63-1 is---- The enormity of it hits me. No wonder bookies like Eddie Braverman lay off big bets at the track. $63,000. Did poor unlucky Nick Scalese defy the odds and finally hit the jackpot? And then I think, if he did, he didn't have long to enjoy it. If he made the bet and if he collected and if he was walking around with $63,000 on his person. this could fundamentally change the dynamic of his death.

I head for valet parking, debating whether Aaron needs to know all this and I decide he does. As I approach, Eddie is already standing there waiting for his car to be delivered. The third race must be over.

"What happened to the longshot?" I say as I sidle up next to him. "Where'd she finish?"

"I don't know," Eddie says. "I think she's still out on the track trying to find the finish line." He shakes his head smiling. "I just love guys with sure things," he says.

At that moment the valet drives up in Eddie's car. Or at least the car that Eddie is driving.

"Nick's Studebaker," I say.

"How'd you know?"

"He drove it to the ball park last week."

"Minerva lent it to me," Eddie says. "My car's in the shop. Alternator's shot. They have to send for the part."

"Generous lady," I say.

He shrugs. "Good friend. Besides, she doesn't drive much. Never has. The car just sits there. Well, see ya around, Joe." He slips the valet a buck and takes off. I hand the valet my stub.

When I get home, I call Aaron at his house. No answer. I try Metro headquarters. No one's seen him all day. Then I remember that last week he was working which means that this weekend he has his son Josh. Chances are they're on a father-son outing. I'll call him late tomorrow or Monday. Meanwhile I have a date to get ready for.

Jillian has a great laugh and it's uninhibited. Martin and Lewis are on stage breaking up the bandstand and the auditorium is in stitches. We've already been treated to Doris singing 'It's Magic' and her new single 'A Guy is a Guy'. Gene Kelly reprised the ballet sequence from 'An American in Paris' with Cyd Charisse standing in for Leslie Caron and Nat King Cole did a medley of his hits. I have one eye on the stage and one eye on Jillian who is having the time of her life. Eighth row center for the show of the year. She must think I'm a real sport. At least I hope so.

On the way back to her place she can't stop talking about the show and I have to admit, it was all star entertainment with a capital E. I had suggested going to the Coconut Grove for a couple of drinks and dancing but she said no. She was anxious to get home and I suddenly realized that Martin and Lewis were an aphrodisiac. Who knew?

An hour later we are snuggling on her bed after an energetic go around. I am spent. She seems ready to go again. If anything, the sex was better than last time and in my opinion, last time was a world beater. Maybe it was because this time I wasn't fumbling for protection. Jillian let me know that she had taken care of things and so, relieved of even that tiny smidgen of caution, we were able to enjoy one another with wild abandon.

I wander off in search of libations and return with a cold Coors and a room temperature cabernet sauvignon. She's sitting up and I slip under the covers beside her. We both drink. The beer tastes good. I don't know why but sex makes me thirsty.

"Tell me about Bunny," she says.

I look at her sharply. No preamble. No edging into it. There it was, flat out and bald faced. I almost said, none of your damned business.

"I'm trying not to pry, Joe, but I need to know what I'm up against. I like you a lot but if Bunny is still a part of who you are and always will be, I think it only fair that I know that now."

I stare off into space for a few moments and then I choose my words carefully.

"Bunny's gone and I don't think she's coming back," I say.

"And if she did?"

Again I hesitate.

"I could lie to you and tell you it wouldn't make any difference but the truth is, I don't know. First of all, it isn't going to happen. She wants a career and she's got one, a good one, and she's not going to throw it over to play house with me."

"You seem pretty certain of that," she says.

"I am. At the end we were sliding into a break up and she didn't know how to tell me. Of course, she didn't have to. I knew what was happening but I didn't want to hear it."

She nods. "I like you, Joe. I like you a lot and I'm willing to fight for you but I can only do battle with flesh and blood. I can't do battle with idealized memories."

"I understand," I say. "Bunny's not like you, Jill. You're together, sure of yourself, able to cope in any situation. Bunny is frail and often afraid. She wants to measure up but is certain that she doesn't. She wants to thrive but doesn't really know how. She thinks she needs a protector and hates herself for thinking it."

"Do you see yourself as her protector?" Jillian asks.

"No. I mean, God, I hope not. I need someone I can deal with on equal terms."

"Someone like me," she says.

I nod. "Someone like you." I hesitate. Caution reins me in. "I think, though, that we shouldn't get ahead of ourselves."

"Agreed. Believe me, Joe, I'm not looking for a lifelong commitment. I have other plans." She reaches up and brushes some hair away from my eyes. "I'm in this for the laughs, the companionship and the wild and woolly sex. Anything else and I'm liable to jump ship without notice. How's that sound to you?"

"Couldn't have said it better myself." I slip my arm around her and pull her toward me.

It's past one o'clock when I leave Jillian's and start for home. We have an arrangement. I don't sleep over. Neither does she. We sleep in our own beds. She may not need the beauty rest but

195

I do. The traffic is moderate going back over the hill toward the Valley. No question it was a great evening so why am I put off by her questions about Bunny? I shouldn't be. She had a perfect right to query me. I don't know her long range plans. Maybe they include me, maybe not, but at 37 she is running out of options. Possibly I'm annoyed that she dredged Bunny up from the dark recesses of my mind where I had consigned her, not knowing how else to deal with her. Bunny's not coming back, I'm convinced of it, but if she did? I know what I told Jillian. What, in stark honesty, do I tell myself? I don't know and what's more I don't want to think about it. It hurts too much.

I turn onto my street. It's quiet. It always is, even on a Saturday night. These are working class folks with families. Burgers at the diner and a movie is a wild night out. The street lamps are lit, all but one, and I find this strange because I recall it working fine last night. It's a couple of doors down from my house on the opposite side of the street and I realize there is a car parked beneath it. As I draw near I can feel my skin suddenly get clammy. As I pass it by, I see that it is a white 1950 Studebaker Starlight and I don't need to see the registration to know that it is Nick Scalese's car. There is a man behind the wheel but he is slouched down and I can't see his face. I start to turn into my driveway, then think better of it, back out and start to drive quickly down the street.

In an instant the Studebaker has made a U-Turn and is hot on my tail. My engine's a 6. His is apparently an 8 because he's on top of me before I know it. I still can't see his face but I do see the pistol in his hand and I wrench the wheel to the right, ducking down just as he fires. At that speed I lose control of the car and look up in horror as I smash into a utility pole. My head snaps back and forth and I am totally disoriented. Groggily

I look up and see him pull up to the curb in front of me. He starts to get out of the car. I am seeing two of everything and my mouth is dry and I cannot turn my head. Just then a pick up truck comes up the street and frames the scene in his headlights. The man with the gun, whose back is to me, doesn't hesitate and dives back into the Studebaker and drives off, leaving rubber on the pavement.

I find the door handle and manage to stumble out of the car as the driver of the pickup truck hurries to my side. By now my vision is back to normal and while my neck hurts I can turn my head. My Good Samaritan asks if I'm okay and I tell him I am. He thinks maybe I need a hospital and I say I don't. He wants to know what was going on and I tell him I think the guy was trying to rob me. Should we call the police? Too late now, I say. I thank him profusely for coming along when he did and then I get back in my car and turn the key. The engine turns over. I throw the car into reverse and it backs away from the utility pole. I'm ambulatory. The pick up guy is still worried but I convince him I'm fine and after a minute or two he drives away.

Quickly I drive to my house and hurry inside. I grab the overnight bag which I have not yet unpacked and slip my .25 Beretta into my pocket. Back in my car I make a beeline for the studio. Gordo Gagliano may be in jail but there is somebody out there that doesn't want me to see Sunday morning and I am going to do my level best to make sure he is disappointed.

CHAPTER SEVENTEEN

Sunday morning and I have no hubbub outside my office window nor a Glenda Mae to wake me so it's with some annoyance that I peer at the clock sitting on the top shelf of my bookcase and discover it is quarter to ten. I have been sleeping soundly in my skivvies for almost seven hours on a narrow sofa bed with a thin unyielding mattress and a paper thin blanket that couldn't keep Shadrach warm in the fiery furnace. Every muscle and tendon in my body aches as if I have been pummeled by a light-heavyweight in need of a workout. My neck is worst of all. Now I know what they mean by whiplash.

I sit up, then stand and hobble over to my window and raise the venetian blinds that have been lowered all night. I squint in self-defense. The sun is up and the air is clear with no sign of rain. My poor wreck of a Ford is parked in all its ugliness in my parking spot, the bullet-nose front end dented in and one headlight smashed to smithereens.

Even before I brush my teeth I sit down at my desk and call Aaron Kleinschmidt, hoping that whatever he might have had going with his boy was merely a one day adventure.

He picks up on the third ring.

"It's me. Joe," I say.

"It's Sunday," Aaron says.

"I know but this won't keep. I got jumped outside my house last night."

"Are you all right?"

I say I am and then give him the abridged version of what went down.

"Where are you?"

"The studio and I'm staying put."

"Wise decision," Aaron says.

"The shot that flew by my head, I think it's embedded in the passenger seat upholstery."

"Are you sure?"

"Pretty sure. I spotted the hole before I got out of the car last night."

There's a pause and then he says, "I'm on my way over. Leave a pass at the gate."

"Will do."

"I'm bringing Josh."

"Fine," I say and hang up.

I leave a pass at the gate and thirty minutes later Aaron drives up to my building and parks next to the Ford. I leave my office and go down the outside steps to join him. His son Josh has come with him and I almost don't recognize him. The last time I saw him was at the ball field at Pierce College where Jimmy Cagney was umpiring a Little League game for charity. Josh was ten and maybe five-five. Now he's thirteen, almost six feet tall with a zits here and there that mar his good looks only slightly. We shake hands. He really doesn't remember me despite coaching from his Dad. It's okay. Teenagers live in a world of their own. Who am I to interfere?

The car is open and Aaron slides in and starts to examine the bullet hole jn the upholstery. He digs around with his finger but can't get a grip so he takes out a pen knife and widens the hole substantially. He digs in again and this time extracts the bullet. He holds it up admiringly.

"A real beauty, Joe," he says. "Unmarred. And best of all, a .32 caliber."

"Best of all?"

"Same caliber as killed Scalese. Not your ordinary gun. Someone may have tried to kill you with the murder weapon."

I suddenly realize I am hungry.

"Have you two had breakfast?" I ask.

"We were just going out for brunch when you called," Aaron says.

"Let's eat. There's a swell Mom and Pop cafe around the corner. Food's great."

"Sounds good." Aaron eyes the front end of my car. "I'll drive," he says.

Shirley & Sam's is already getting crowded at this hour of the day but my pal Shirley finds us a good table and before long we're downing waffles and eggs and sausages and really, really good coffee. We chat about family, Aaron's and my lack of one. I don't mention Jillian. If I did I wouldn't know quite what to say. We're in it for the sex and not much more. Even if Josh weren't sitting next to his Dad, it's not a proper topic for discussion.

Aaron and I order more coffee while Josh heads for the back room where they have a trio of pinball machines. Now we can get down to business.

"Any chance Tom Scalese snuck out of jail last night and then was able to sneak back in undetected early this morning?" I ask.

Aaron raises his hands defensively.

"Okay, I get it. Don't rub it in. I'll talk to Quinn first thing in the morning. Even he can't escape the fact that he's locked up the wrong man."

"You may not have to argue very hard," I say. I tell him about the little charade involving the fifty thousand dollar check. Aaron looks at me in awe.

"Jesus, Joe. You have balls of brass," he says.

"Not really. Quinn's greedy, self-serving and a coward. If he's ever heard the expression 'equal justice under the law', I'm sure he has no idea what it means. I presented him with an unpleasant situation. He'll do what he has to do to avoid it."

"And if he goes whining to Warner?"

"He'd better not. I know how Jack feels about gun ownership, illegal immigration, confiscatory taxes, and personal privacy laws. I also know what Quinn thinks. Better he keeps his mouth shut."

Aaron nods. He, too, is aware that Harlow Quinn is a hack politician for whom incompetent is too kind a description.

"So let's say Quinn drops the charges against Scalese," Aaron says. "That still leaves us with a problem."

"That's right," I say, "and Chicago is not at the root of it."

"Altadena?"

"Has to be," I say. "The white Studebaker clinches it. The problem is, who was driving? And how do we find out since everyone in town seems hell bent on protecting everyone else's ass."

"Everyone?"

"Including your pal Floyd Willard, the town's on again, off again enforcer of the law."

"You don't know that," Aaron says.

"No, but I can guess. He leaves Eddie Braverman alone and he seems to be in tight with Jesse Hovack. What's more his wife died two years ago and even though he's eligible for retirement, he not only won't retire, he won't even accept a promotion and transfer to CHP headquarters."

"Meaning what?" Aaron asks.

"Meaning Minerva is a reasonably attractive woman who seems to have two swains hovering around her in the persons of Braverman and Hovack so why not a third?"

"Like I said, you don't know that?"

"No, not for sure," I say, "but it's a lovely thing to contemplate. Brings out the romantic in me."

Aaron just shakes his head.

"So what do you suggest?" he asks.

"What time does your ex pick up Josh?"

"Five o'clock."

"I'm thinking about going home and spending the night because the same guy who tried last night might try again if he thought I was an easy target."

Aaron nods thoughtfully. "Not knowing that you would be sitting up in the dark, your tiny cap pistol clenched in your hand and your faithful pal, Aaron Kleinschmidt, at your side, actually armed with a lethal weapon."

"Something like that," I say, "and it's not a cap pistol."

"It couldn't stop a charging housecat."

"Bring one along and we'll see," I say.

"It's a stupid idea," Aaron says.

"How bright do you think our killer is, driving around in Nick's Studebaker?"

Aaron starts to respond, then thinks better of it. The wise non-cop in the room has actually come up with a half decent idea.

"I'll be at your place by six o'clock," he says. "Meanwhile I'll take this slug to ballistics and see if we've got a match."

"Til six, then," I say, draining the last of my coffee.

The clock says 9:40 and Aaron and I are sitting in the dark in my living room, back in the shadows, staring out of my front window at the street. He arrived at six as promised with a bag of groceries. Hamburger meat, buns, frozen potatoes, corn on the cob, apple pie. I cooked. We ate. The forensics guys confirmed that the slug in my car seat matches the one taken from Nick's skull. Aaron's stlll not sure this vigil will amount to anything but he's willing to give up some sleep to find out. There's beer in the refrigerator but we don't go near it. I have a pot of coffee on the stove and when that runs out I'll make another one.

At least one of us has to be awake at all times.

In addition to a view of the street, we also have a clear angle on my front door. In the kitchen, Aaron has placed a water glass at the base of the kitchen door and atop the glass he has stacked a half dozen forks and spoons. Anyone trying to push the door open will upset the glass and the flatware will raise a clatter. My beat up car is parked conspicuously in my driveway. We are ready.

We have sat sipping coffee, conversing easily, watching the sun go down. Relaxed and unguarded, Aaron talks about himself more this evening than ever before. Inately a private person, he seems to trust me enough to let me peek into his life.

He joined the force in '39 but when Pearl Harbor was hit, he enlisted in the Marines. By late '42 he found himself on Guadalcanal where a machine gun bullet found him. He was shipped back to Hawaii for surgery but the bullet was imbedded too close to his spinal cord and couldn't be removed without risking permanent paralysis. So they left it in and handed him his Honorable Discharge papers. Despite his wound the LAPD took him back amidst a flurry of waivers. They had to. The force was becoming a department of 35+ greybeards as more and more of the younger officers either enlisted or were drafted. By war's end he'd already made detective and months later he was promoted to sergeant. He should have been proud. He wasn't. The department, under Chief Clement Horrell, had become a cesspool of corruption. To get along, you went along and he did. No evidence? Create it. Suspect won't talk? A rubber hose in a basement room solved that problem. And finally one day he'd had enough and he rebelled against the system. He started playing the game honestly and when Bill Parker took over as Chief of Police, Aaron found himself on the right side. Why the epiphany? Simple. I remember him telling me he could no longer look his son in the face.

I look over at him. He is staring out at the street, absorbed in thought. I am thinking, despite all that has gone before, despite the fact that he once tried to frame me for murder, this is the person I would most trust to watch my back in a tight spot.

The hours pass slowly. I doze for a short time, then Aaron grabs a little sleep while I keep vigilant. Shortly after six the sun starts to appear. My assailant from the night before has not appeared. Aaron and I are grungy, achy and in bad need of sleep. I try to conjure up our next move. I can't think of one.

We hear a thud as something hits the front door. It's the kid from the next block delivering my L.A. Times. He has a helluvan arm. Never misses.

"Morning paper," I say, getting to my feet. "You get it while I fix another pot of coffee."

Aaron rises. "You get the paper. I've been drinking your lousy coffee for ten hours. Enough is enough."

He heads for the kitchen while I get the paper. He prepares coffee while I rummage around for breakfast fare. We've got toast. butter and grape jelly. No juice, no eggs, no bacon. Aaron doesn't care. We'll make do.

I open the paper, flip through the sports pages looking for news about the Braves. Nothing official. Not yet. I turn back to the front page and my blood turns cold. There are two photos. One of a woman's body lying on a bathroom floor. The other is a head shot of an attractive, well groomed woman in her late fifties. The headline reads: PASADENA SOCIALITE FOUND DEAD. Vivian Phelps has come to a bad end.

"Jesus," I mutter softly.

Aaron has heard me.

"What?" he asks.

"Someone's dead who shouldn't be," I say.

I scan the article. A half empty glassine envelope of cocaine was found on the bathroom floor. At her bedside was a near empty bottle of scotch and a glass. She was found shortly before midnight by the live-in housekeeper who was bringing her her nighttime assortment of medicines. The preliminary time of death has been pegged between ten and eleven. There were no signs of a struggle. When asked Sergeant Ellis Forrester of the LAPD refused to speculate about the cause of death but someone else close to the scene suggested an accidental death. "Drugs and booze. She needed them both. Some people never learn," he said.

I recap the story for Aaron, then lay the paper down and sit back. my mind whirling. Aaron slides a mug of coffee in front of me, watching me closely.

"Spit it out," he says.

"What?"

"Whatever you're thinking. Let's hear it."

I look at him. "It crossed my mind but it seemed insane---"

I stop, still trying to fathom it.

Aaron sits down opposite me.

"I'll wait," he says.

Then I tell him everything I can remember about that afternoon encounter at Hovack's bar. And as I narrate it, aloud and uncensored, I realize my instincts that afternoon were correct.

Aaron has listened in silence, sipping his coffee thoughtfully. When I'm finished he looks at me curiously.

"Chula Vista. That phone call. You're sure the bartender said Chula Vista?

"Positive. Why?"

"Two nights ago the Staties working with the Chula Vista Police Department broke up a local drug ring that had been supplying half of Southern California with heroin, cocaine and marijuana. They were a hair too late. They grabbed three of the nobodies and all of the drugs but the big fish got away."

"I guess now we know what Hovack's other sources of income were," I say.

"We do. But what's it got to do with Nick Scalese's death? Or doesn't it?"

"I think maybe it does," I say. "Hovack wants to buy The End Zone, makes a huge offer, but Nick apparently isn't intertested in sellng at any price. Do you seriously think someone like Hovack won't resort to other means to get what he wants? Not only that but is smart enough to kill Nick in such a way that it points directly to a Chicago hit."

Aaron nods. "If we could only search the damned bar."

"Need a warrant," I say.

"Need probable cause to get it."

"What we have isn't enough?" I ask.

"Not even close," he says.

He leans back in his chair, lacing his fingers behind his neck and staring up at the ceiling.

"What about this chauffeur?"

"What about him?"

"Maybe he knows something."

"Maybe."

"You think he'd chat with us?"

"Might. Seemed like a pretty good guy."

Aaron smiles. The Cheshire Cat licking his lips.

"Let's you and me take a little trip to Pasadena," he says.

CHAPTER EIGHTEEN

n Pasadena they spell culture with a capital C and society with a capital S. There's the famous Pasadena Playhouse and the symphony orchestra and the Community Theater and a slew of colleges and universities. For the most part the power structure in this elegant city is driven not by old money but by older money. Old money is still scratching at the door. The nouveau riche are not tolerated but are permitted to live in nearby Glendale.

Aaron and I drive down a beautiful tree lined street in the most elegant section of town. Each house is either two or three stories. Ranch homes need not apply. One-half acre is the minimum lot. Most houses stand on an acre or two. The lawns are green and manicured. The trees are tall and stately. The gardens are well tended and profuse with color. All driveways are empty as all cars are stowed away in garages of the 2-3-or-4 door variety. There are no abandoned washing machines lying around the side of the house, rusting away. No pre-war cars up on blocks waiting to become antiques. All is pristine. All is quiet. Such is the ethos of Pasadena.

The Phelps mansion is dead ahead on the left hand side of the road. Two LAPD squad cars are parked at curbside. A police van is in the driveway and it appears that some sort of official activity is being conducted inside the house. Two uniformed cops have been posted in the street in both directions to prevent rubbernecking or parking. I doubt they're busy. Pasadenans have too much class to hang around a crime scene like voyeurs. More likely they are hiding behind ivied fences and rustic gates, too ashamed to show their faces. Drugs are for the teeming rabble of L.A.'s seedier neighborhoods, not for the favored gentry of Pasadena.

Aaron flashes the tin and we skate past the street sentinel and park. At the front door we repeat the process. We learn that Sgt. Ellis Forrester, whom Aaron knows well, has left for the day. We also learn that the chauffeur is around back in a small apartment above the garage where he's been ordered to stay for the time being. The cop sees no reason why we can't talk to him.

Hamilton, the chauffeur, opens the door wearing a terry cloth robe and slippers. His hair's a mess, his eyes are bleary and I think we've awakened him.

"Hi. Remember me?" I say.

"No," he says. He starts to close the door but Aaron shoves his badge in Hamilton's face. He reconsiders and opens the door wide. "Sure, why not?" he says. "Who needs sleep anyway?"

He plops down on the sofa and reaches for a pack of cigarettes on the coffee table and lights up.

"Up all night?"

He nods. "They rousted me out of bed around one o'clock. They let me go about an hour ago."

"Did you talk to any reporters?"

"Yeah. One. From the Times, I think." He inhales deeply and blows it out through his nose.

"I think you were quoted. Did you say something like 'drugs and booze, she needed them both.'"

"Yeah, I think so."

Aaron's sitting a few feet away in an upholstered chair, just taking it in. We'd agreed that I'd do the questioning since I knew the guy. He's ready to jump in if things stall.

"So you knew about the drugs?" I say.

Now he looks over at me and his eyes aren't so bleary any more. He glances toward Aaron and then back to me.

"And if I did?"

"Nobody's here to bust your balls, Mr. Hamilton," Aaron says. "Nobody's going to arrest you, nobody's going to put you in jail. We're interested in Jesse Hovack. "

"Miserable bastard," Hamilton says. "I liked the old lady, I really did. Sober she was very kind and a lot of fun. Drunk not so much and when she started with the coke, her moods went up and down like a yo-yo. It was sort of there while her husband was dying. After he went, she just bottomed out and Jesse Hovack was right there to help her stay there."

"So Hovack supplied her with the cocaine."

"I just said that, didn't I?" Hamilton says edgily.

"I needed to hear it for the record," Aaron says. "So you and Mrs. Phelps would drive to Altadena to make the purchases."

"No."

"No?" I say.

"Most the time the kid delivered it. The one they call Andy. Once or twice it was the other one. Davey. Twice I drove there when the kids couldn't deliver and made the pickup."

"Did you know what you were picking up?"

"Sure I knew. Do I look stupid?"

"The other day. Why did Mrs. Phelps come with you?"

"Because she was wasted. They'd missed a delivery and she was going out of her mind. She said she couldn't even wait for me to drive back with it."

Aaron and I share a look and then Aaron says to Hamilton, "I'd like you to come back to headquarters with me and fill out an affidavit recounting what you've just told us. We'll present it to a judge and I'm almost positive we'll get a warrant to search Hovack's premises."

Hamilton looks at us nervously. "I don't know---," he mumbles.

"The only people who will see or know about this affidavit will be me, Mr Bernardi, and the judge. It won't be used to arrest you or implicate you in any way and if you are eventually required to testify, I will see that you get immunity."

Hamilton hesitates for a moment, then stubs out his cigarette and gets up from the sofa.

"Let's do it," he says.

Forty five minutes later Hamilton is sitting at Aaron's desk filing out the paperwork. I am on the phone to Glenda Mae, feigning great pain, and telling her that I am at my dentist's office, victim of a sudden and excrutiating toothache. It's so bad I may have to lose a tooth. Don't expect me in the rest of the day, I tell her. All of this is for the benefit of Jack Warner who, while in New York, still has the ability to call in and check on his minions. I am a minion on a tight leash.

At 2:18 that afternoon, all hell breaks loose in Altadena. A crack drug enforcement unit headed by Lt. Victor Ricci walks into Hovack's bar and grill. The warrant is served and a half dozen experienced officers start to tear the place apart. Aaron and I are there as onlookers and the instant Hovack has the warrant in his hand, Aaron is on the phone to Floyd Willard notifying him of the raid. He was not forewarned because, frankly, Aaron and I both had misgivings about where his loyalties resided.

In less than thirty minutes Hovack's stash of drugs is discovered in wine crates in a back room. The haul is significant.

Besides cocaine they've turned up heroin and marijuana. Ricci has been carrying arrest warrants with him and as soon as the cache is discovered, Hovack is put in handcuffs and two officers are sent to pick up Andy Braverman and Davey Grimes.

Aaron and I go outside to get some fresh air and a substantial percentage of Altadena's population has crowded onto the street and sidewalks taking in the spectacle. Four LAPD squad cars are parked haphazardly in the street in front of the bar. Traffic can't get through not even the Greyhounds which are loading and discharging passengers two blocks away. When Hovack is dragged roughly from indoors and perp-walked to one of the cars, a loud murmur arises from the crowd. I suspect that some are in awe of the proceedings while others may be nervously wondering where they will be able to go to replenish their supply of happy powder or cannibis.

I look up the street. Willard has parked a couple of blocks away and is approaching on foot along the sidewalk. He catches my eye and walks toward us. He is not a happy looking man.

Willard stops next to us taking in the scene and then looks at Aaron.

"A heads up would have been nice," he says.

"I wasn't sure which team you were playing for, Floyd."

Willard nods. "Yeah. Guess in your shoes I'd have done the same." He reaches in his shirt pocket and takes out a cheroot and lights up. I have this urge to move upwind of him but I stay put.

"I've been watching him for a couple of months now," Willard says. "Got lucky about three days ago. Caught the Grimes kid joyriding north of town. He's got a souped up Model T, cut down, big tires. She'll do a hundred and fifteen on a straightaway. I know. I clocked her. "

"Guess he wasn't interested in getting a ticket," I say.

"Worse than that. He's got three violations in the last six months. This would have made four. They'd have taken his license. I put a little pressure on him. It was like cracking an egg. He gave up Chula Vista."

"Chula Vista? The drug bust?" Aaron says. "That was you phoned in the tip?"

"It's on the record, Aaron," Willard says. "Don't blame you fellas for being suspicious, especially you, Bernardi. I played it close to the vest. Had to. Couldn't let on what I was doing."

"But you were on his pad," I say.

"Yep," Willard says. "A hundred bucks a week. Each Saturday night he'd slip me five twenties. Next morning I'd put a check for a hundred into the plate at St. Dominick's, the checks being my way of proving I wasn't a crooked cop."

I nod. "Sorry I misjudged you, Captain," I say.

He grins. "Don't be sorry. You're a pesky devil, Bernardi. Good citizen, too. We need more like you."

Aaron just shakes his head.

"Jesus, Floyd. Do you have to encourage him?"

Willard smiles. "Sorry. Aaron. Anyway, comes a trial and I'll be testifying. You want to lock it up tight, go after the Grimes kid. He'll turn to Jello if you frown at him and I think he's got a lot to tell."

Aaron nods.

"Don't suppose you've got anything on Andy Braverman," Aaron says.

Willard shakes his head.

"Other than shooting squirrels with his target pistol, I got nothin'. Don't mean he's clean, only that he's careful."

By four-fifteen Aaron and I are on the way back to head-quarters where I've left my car. Well, not exactly my car. Since the Ford's a wreck I'm puttering around in Bunny's wheezy old Plymouth. Hovack, Andy Braverman and Davey Grimes are on their way to County Jail where they will be held pending formal charges. It's been a good days work. Now the question is, can we hook Hovack into Nick Scalese's death? If either Andy or Davey knows something concrete that will tie him in, I have no doubt they will chirp like nightingales.

I check the news stations on Aaron's car radio. The sports shows are previewing pre-season games, pontificating about the basketball playoffs and mostly lauding the American team's second place showing at the Winter Olympics in Oslo. There's some concern about our chances in the Summer Olympics in Helsinki, now that the USSR has announced they will compete. Experts say it will be very close for medal count. As for the mysterious summit meeting in Milwaukee of baseball's ruling elite, not a word. Either they are laying low for an announcement at a later date or there's been a snag in the negotiations. Either way I feel bad for Chick Fullmer.

It's just before five when I place a courtesy call to Glenda Mae at the office just to see if anything interesting is going on, like maybe a fire that needs to be put out. I subtly alter my speaking voice to approximate tooth pain. I think of everything.

No, she says, everything is quiet.

Were there any calls from Mr. Warner?

No, she says, although Mr. Berger dropped in and said to tell you to feel better soon.

So, that's it? I ask her.

That's it, she says, and then quickly reverses herself. One thing she forgot to mention. My dentist called to remind me that I had an appointment tomorrow afternoon at four o'clock for my semi-annual cleaning and checkup.

Busted.

I head for home, bring in some Chinese, watch a little news and then get caught up watching "Angels WIth Dirty Faces" for the hundredth time and for the hundredth time, I get choked up when Pat O'Brien as Father Jerry begs Rocky (Cagney) to die like a coward when he goes the chair so the neighborhood kids won't idolize him. Fade out. The end. I sigh, get up and take my trash into the kitchen. That's when the phone rings. No, I scream to myself, everything is taken care of. Whatever's left is out of my hands. Just leave me alone. But still I answer the phone.

"Joe?"

I'd know her voice anywhere but still I ask, disbelieving.

"Bunny?"

"Did I wake you? Were you in bed?"

"No, just straightening up the kitchen. How are you, Bunny? Are you okay?"

"I'm fine," she says. She doesn't sound fine. I glance at the clock. It reads 11:05. If she's in New York it's 2:05 in the morning.

"Couldn't sleep?" I ask.

"What? No, not that. No. I'm okay. I just wanted to hear your voice."

"Here I am," I say.

"There you are," she says and giggles. There's a long silence.

"Are you sure you're all right? Do you need anything?" I ask.

"No, we're okay, really."

What's this 'we' stuff?

"Are you with someone?"

"I'm with Jacob. We're in Utica. That's in New York."

"Yes, I know. What about the magazine?" She's been working in Manhattan for Collier's Magazine for the past couple of years.

"Oh, I'm not with them any more. I quit."

There's a quavering timber to her voice that I don't like. She sounds disconnected. Maybe it's booze. God, I hope not. Whatever it is I'm worried.

"We were supposed to stay with Jacob's parents for a while but they don't want him so we came here to Utica. Jacob's going to get a job. He's going to start looking first thing in the morning. Joe, I went to meetings. I went to a lot of them."

"That's good, Bunny. Do you need money?"

"Oh, no, We have plenty of money. Jacob also knows someone in Pennsylvania who might give him a job. We might go there next week. I don't know." There's another long pause. "I was thinking about Monterey. Do you remember Monterey, Joe?"

"Sure, I do."

"Remember the fish. You helped me catch it."

"I remember."

"It was the biggest fish I ever saw. Did we throw it back in the water, Joe? I'm pretty sure we did."

"Yes, we let him go," I say.

Suddenly I hear a man's voice in the background. It is sharp and demanding and angry. I hear Bunny say, "A friend." More background. Bunny cries out. "Let go of me, I'm talking." More of the man's voice and then a click and we are disconnected. I stare at the handset. I want to throw up. For the longest time I just stand there and then slowly, I hang up.

I go into the bedroom and undress. I set the alarm for 7:15. I could have saved myself the trouble. I don't really sleep and when it goes off, I trudge into the kitchen in my skivvies and robe. I ask for New York City information and when they give me the number for Colliers I ask to be connected. It's 10:30 in the city. Plenty of time for Walter Davenport to be behind his desk at Collier's and too early for him to have left for lunch. He's the editor in chief and the one who hired Bunny away from me. I have questions. He had better have answers.

His secretary answers the phone. She wants to know the nature of my call. I say, tell him my name. He'll talk to me. Sure enough, a few seconds later he's on the phone.

"Joe, my God, man, it's been a long time," he says.

"At least a year," I say.

"Where are you? In town?"

"L.A.," I say. "Walt, I got a call from Bunny late last night."

There's a long pause before he speaks.

"How is she?"

"I don't know, Walt. You tell me."

"I had to let her go, Joe. I just couldn't keep her any longer."

"Booze?"

"That was part of it," he says. "Lots of late night parties, coming in late or calling in sick. I couldn't depend on her any more, Joe, and her work was second rate."

"I get the picture. When?"

"A couple of months ago. I gave her ten week's severance. I think she ran through it pretty fast."

"What do you know about a guy named Jacob?" I ask.

"Is she with him? Jesus," Walt mutters.

"Bad news?"

"The worst. She met him at an A.A. meeting. She went for a while. It never took hold. He's a 40 year old, no talent bullshit artist. Fancies himself a painter. I wouldn't hire him to paint a barn door. Gets part time work as a bartender but those gigs don't last long. He can't stay away from the merchandise."

I sag down onto a kitchen chair. My worst fears are confirmed.

"Joe?" Walt says.

"I'm here," I say.

"I'm sorry. I wish it were otherwise."

"I know. We both do."

We chat for another minute or two. Aimless talk, Meaningless words. Finally we hang up, both of us relieved that the ordeal of disclosure is over. I sit for the longest time trying to figure out what I can do and I finally realize there's nothing I can do.

I get to my feet and head for the bathroom.

I walk into my office at five after nine. I force a smile and a cheery hello but there's no fooling Glenda Mae and she knows instinctively that I'm mired in the bottom of the barrel. I sit at my desk, peruse the mail and glance at the front pages of the trades. Glenda Mae brings in my coffee.

She looks down at me.

"You want to talk, you know where to find me," she says.

I smile and give her a mini-salute. She smiles back and returns to her desk. I make a courtesy call to Bill Kuehl, the producer, to see if there's anything I can do for him. He says all is well and we chat amiably. Charlie stops by. I throw him a grimace of pain to fortify the fiction of my dental appointment the day before. He commiserates. I thank him for his concern. Problems? None. Jack Warner? Still in New York. Peace and quiet, ain't it grand? All I have to worry about is Bunny on her way to a life of hell on earth.

At ten-fifteen I hear from Aaron and I'm grateful to have my brain pointed in a new direction.

"I have good news and bad news," he says. "Which do you want first?"

I opt for the good news.

"Floyd Willard was right about the Grimes kid. When he was brought into the interrogation room, I thought he'd crap his pants. He couldn't tell us fast enough and believe me, Joe, he told us plenty. Names, dates, places. Hovack is looking at five minimum, probably more like ten."

I can feel myself frown.

"What about the murder?"

"That's the bad news. The night of the 2nd, that Thursday, the Grimes kid drives Hovack in the delivery van to Chula Vista for a pickup. Hovack usually makes the run on his own but he had some kind of foot problem, ingrown toe nail or something and his foot was all bandaged and he couldn't drive. The kid was with him until four o'clock in the morning. The coroner puts the time of death between one and two a.m."

"You think the kid's telling the truth?'"

"Does a rooster say cockle-doodle-doo?"

"What's Andy Braverman say?"

"Nothing. Tough little bastard. Surly, too. Kept his mouth shut until he was bailed out about an hour ago. Hovack's lawyer arranged it. Andy and Davey are out on bail. Hovack's still in custody but his lawyer's working all the angles to get him sprung."

"I thought we had something, Aaron."

"Me, too, Joe. Catch you later."

He hangs up and I lean back in my chair. At that moment Ray Giordano appears in my open doorway.

"Glenda Mae wants to know if you want more coffee," he says.

I shake my head. "My kidneys are already at high tide."

"No on the coffee," he calls to Glenda Mae in the other room and then comes in and sits down.

"Well, buddy, if I were wearing a hat, It'd be off to you right now."

"For what?"

"The play of the year. Quinn's running for cover. He's releasing Tom Scalese at noon. No press conference, no explanation. Just out the door, here's your hat and goodbye."

"But he'll have to say something," I say.

"One at a time. If a reporter calls, he'll be told that the evidence, although substantial, was not enough in the eyes of the D.A. to proceed. If it were his choice, he'd go to trial but he's not in charge. Not yet."

I have to chuckle. "That slimy toad. If it turns out Scalese was involved his ass is covered. If not he gets credit for releasing him."

"Not to mention that huge donation he thinks you're going to hand him."

"He'll have a long wait," I say.

Ray grins. "Oh? Reneging on a promise are we?"

"Certainly not," I say. "I told Quinn his campaign would benefit by fifty thousand dollars. That would be the fifty thousand I am NOT going to give to Chester Mulholland."

Ray stares at me for a moment and then smiles.

"Have you ever thought about becoming a lawyer?" he asks. "You'd be good at it."

I smile back at him.

"Ray, my dear buddy, haven't you figured out that you and I are in the same business, namely trying to turn chicken feathers into coq au vin. Except when I get it wrong, nobody goes to jail."

He laughs. I laugh right along with him. If there's one thing he and I really enjoy it's lawyer jokes.

CHAPTER NINETEEN

fter Ray leaves I lean back in my chair and stare at the wall. This particular wall has mystical powers because whenever I stare at it for any length of time, brilliant thoughts pop into my mind. This morning I do this for about ten minutes and nothing happens. Perhaps this is one of those days when the wall fails me. Too bad because I have a lot to think about.

For one thing Tom Scalese is not flying back to Chicago even though Ray has offered to put him and Madison on the four p.m. flight. Tom has learned that his father's body is still being held in the county morgue, unclaimed by Minerva, and he is determined to see that Nick gets a proper burial. How he plans to do this I do not know. Minerva is the so-called next of kin according to police paperwork. If she doesn't act soon, Nick will end up in an unmarked grave in a county dumping ground. To make matters worse, I doubt Tom has two sticks to rub together, parochial schools being notoriously low paying. And it's unlikely that Madison, the copy editor, is much better off. But youth does not recognize obstacles of a practical nature and I think Tom may be stubborn enough to prevail, some way, somehow.

I recognize that it may take a visit by someone to Minerva to make it happen. I also recognize that that someone is probably me.

Jack Warner is still out of town and not due back until tomorrow evening. Dare I tempt fate one more time and if I do, what's today's excuse? I decide to worry about that later and check the contents of my wallet as I think I am running low on cash. I have two twenties, a ten, two fives and three singles along with a folded piece of paper. I unfold it. It's my betting slip from the horse I booked with Andy Braverman. I wonder how the nag did. At 1-5, how could she have lost? I shake my head and replace the slip. Next time I see Eddie or Andy I'll check it out. My ten dollar slip may actually be worth eleven dollars. Wow.

I tell Glenda Mae my tooth is starting to hurt again and I am off to the dentist. She is to stick to that story until the moment she is backed up to the wall facing the firing squad. At that point she has my permission to rat me out.

It's 11:45 when I pull up in front of The End Zone. There are plenty of parking spots at this hour of the morning. Business is slow if not actually stopped. I go in and my suspicions are confirmed. A solitary drinker at the end of the bar is reading the Morning Telegraph. The bartender, whose name I recall is Ralph, is watching an exercise show on television. He looks to be about a 46 around the middle and maybe he thinks he can lose weight by osmosis.

I rap on the bar to get his attention.

"I'm looking for Minerva," I say.

"Not here," Ralph says.

"Where?" I say.

He jabs a finger skyward.

"Upstairs."

"What's upstairs?"

He looks at me tolerantly and speaks slowly as if to a four year old.

"It's where she lives."

I nod in understanding.

"Will you please tell her I'm here. Joe Bernardi. Warner Brothers."

"I know who you are," Ralph says.

"Tell her I bring news from the LAPD."

He stares at me for a moment, then goes down to the end of the bar, picks up the phone and starts talking. When he's finished he returns to me.

"She'll be down in ten minutes."

I thank him and order a cold Coors. No sense letting a good bar stool go to waste.

True to her word, ten minutes later I spot her coming down a staircase at the end of a hallway at the rear of the building. As she comes close, I see that she seems a little bleary eyed and her makeup has been applied haphazardly and her blouse is not quite tucked in all the way.

"Hi, Joe," she says.

"Hi, Minerva," I respond.

"What's all this about the cops?"

"They want to know when you're going to claim Nick's body?"

She glowers. "Is that it? I already told 'em I don't give a damn what they do. He's not my problem."

I nod. "Well, he IS his kid's problem, Minerva, and that makes you also his kid's problem."

"Kid? What are you talking about?"

"The police were holding Nick's son, Tom, on murder charges. They just let him go for lack of evidence. Instead of going back to Chicago he's staying here in L.A. until he can give his father a proper burial."

"His kid? Here? I didn't know."

"And he can't have the body released to him unless you sign some sort of paper."

She nods. "Paper? Sure, I'll do that." She shakes her head sadly. "Nick loved that kid. Talked about him all the time."

"He's a nice young man, Minerva," I say. "You'd like him."

She snaps out of her thoughts.

"Yeah, well, who's got time for that?" she says roughly.

"Sorry about Jesse Hovack," I say.

"What about him?" she asks sharply.

"Well, there goes your million dollar offer."

"Yeah, well, there'll be other offers. Besides I've decided not to sell."

I look past her to my left as Eddie Braverman appears at the bottom of the staircase. He's tucking in his shirt and as he approaches he runs his hands through his damp hair.

"Any particular reason," I ask, "aside from Eddie?"

I head nod in his direction and Minerva looks, then looks back at me. I think she reddens slightly. I'm not sure.

"We were doing business," she says.

"I'll bet," I say.

Now she really reddens.

"Hi, Joe," Eddie says as he sits in the stool beside me.

"Eddie," I say.

Minerva pipes up. "I was just telling Joe that we were upstairs going over some paperwork."

Eddie laughs.

"Dear sweet girl," he says, "my friend Joe was not born in the back of a pickup truck late yesterday afternoon. Give him a little credit."

"You give it to him," she snarls as she grabs a glass from the shelf behind her and fills it halfway with Johnnie Walker blue label.

"Minerva and I are in love, Joe. Have been for a long time."

I nod. "I thought something like that. Why didn't you just get married? "

Eddie shrugs. "It's complicated."

Minerva shakes her head. "Nothing complicated about it. I owned a piece of the bar. I didn't want to lose it. Besides I didn't want to hurt Nick. He picked me up out of the gutter five years ago and gave me a decent life. I owed him a lot."

"Did he know? About you two?"

"I don't know," Minerva says. "He might have. He never said anything."

I nod thoughtfully.

"Tell me about the night he was killed," I say.

"Tell you what? I don't know anything about that night."

"Where were you?"

"None of your business," Minerva says. "You're not a cop."

"Funny, Jesse said the same thing to me so I called a cop to help me out. Well, you saw what happened to Jesse."

I smile at her. I smile at Eddie, too.

"We were here in Altadena," Eddie says.

"Together?"

"Yes, together."

"When you say together, do you mean----?"

"That's exactly what I mean," Eddie says.

"Weren't you both taking a chance? Suppose Nick had come home?"

"He hadn't been home in three nights. Not with his baseball buddies in town. Anyway, so what? Nick was killed at the ball park."

"Actually, the police don't believe that. In fact they think he was killed here in Altadena and his body driven to L.A. and dumped on the pitcher's mound."

"That's crazy," Minerva says.

"Not really. The police found his car parked a block from here in town that Friday morning so they knew he'd come home Thursday night. Someone here in Altadena killed him and then drove him to L.A. in an attempt to make it seem as if he'd been killed by someone from Chicago."

"Jesse Hovack," Minerva says.

"No, he has an alibi."

"You're saying one of us?" Minerva says, becoming very edgy.

"I'm not saying anything," I tell her. "I'm just asking questions. Like who drove the Studebaker to L.A. last Saturday evening?"

"What the hell are you asking that for, Joe?" Minerva demands to know going from edgy to irritated.

"Because whoever was driving it tried to kill me," I say sharply.

Minerva and Eddie share a look.

"The car's out back," Eddie says, "parked next to the rear door. The keys are in it. Minerva's made it clear anybody who needs wheels can borrow it any time they wish."

"Meaning anyone could have taken it."

"Meaning just that," Eddie says. "But it wasn't me."

"Don't look at me," Minerva says.

"Could Jesse have taken it?"

"Could have" Minerva says. "Don't know why he would. He had his own car."

"Maybe to cloud the issue," I say. I pause thoughtfully. "Look,

Minerva, you're right. I'm not a cop but for a minute I'm going to think and act like one. Let's say you two are upstairs playing house and Nick comes busting through the door. He's furious. He attacks one or both of you. There's a fight. Somebody grabs for a gun. Bang. Nick is dead."

"Suppose all you like, Joe. It never happened and never would have. That wasn't Nick's style."

"All right. Instead, let's suppose he comes charging through the door waving a parimutuel ticket worth over sixty thousand dollars. That's a lot of motive."

Eddie snorts. "Sixty thousand dollars? Nick? You're out of your mind."

"Am I?"

"Yeah, you are," Eddie says coldly. "Nick couldn't pick a sixty thousand dollar winner if his life depended on it."

"I disagree. Nick was precisely the kind of lousy handicapper that could stumble onto a sixty to one shot that a good bettor wouldn't look at twice."

"I didn't kill him," Eddie says. "Neither did Minerva."

"Would you tell that to the police?"

"Hell, yes. Bring 'em on," Eddie says. "Look, Joe, you can suppose and theorize and postulate all you want but there's nothing mysterious or evil about me or Minerva. I lost my wife many years ago and I've been lonely ever since. Minerva's been grateful to Nick for five years but gratitude isn't love. We found each other and made what we could of it. I expect that maybe in a few months we may get married and I'll be moving in upstairs. I'll keep making book and she'll keep running the bar with my help. That's how it is and if you want to bring in the entire L.A. police force to prove otherwise, well, you go right ahead. But for the moment I'd appreciate it if you'd leave us alone."

I look from one to the other and then slide off my stool.

"I'll be going then. Minerva, I expect Tom Scalese will be showing up with the paperwork for the release of his father's body."

"I'll be looking for him," she says.

"All right, then," I say and I turn and walk out.

It's a long ride back to the Valley, not so much in mileage but in time, because I get caught in a Caltrans work zone. Widening, new pavement, I don't know which and I don't care. Caltrans must be under orders from a higher power to work only at peak traffic times and to make sure that there are sufficient workers on hand so that one can work for every two that stand around leaning on their shovels. Bumper to bumper. One car at a time. It's maddening.

I flip on the radio for amusement and catch the latest sports news. The reporter is flipping out because the Daily Double at Santa Anita was a shade over five thousand dollars and six lucky bettors are going to leave the track with their pockets bulging with cash. I ask myself, do you really want to walk around with that much money in your pocket, especially at a place like Santa Anita which likely attracts all sorts of hustlers, thieves and con men? No, with that much money, they must give you a check. And then I think of Nick and his big score and I wonder if he scored at all. I realize I know nothing about racetracks and horses and parimutuel betting and it occurs to me that maybe I had better learn.

I skip the studio and drive directly to the massive L.A. Times Building downtown. It's only three o'clock and I'm pretty sure I'll catch Chick Fullmer at his desk. And I do.

I raise my hands in surrender as I approach his desk where he is folding a blank sheet of paper into an airplane.

"Mea culpa, mea culpa," I say as I reach him.

He smiles up at me, a crooked grin with a devilish twist. He's a hefty guy, over six feet, early 40's, looks like a one-time-athlete gone to seed which he is. His nose is a mess and there's a hint of scar tissue around the eyes. I'm told he was a pro heavyweight for about four years before he got tired of ending up on his back most of the time. His last fight lasted forty-six seconds. That's when he hung 'em up and got into sports writing.

"Joe, my man! Welcome," he says. "And none of that apology crap. You were onto those guys. They just hit a snag, that's all. Boston to Milwaukee, guaranteed to happen. I'd bet my next paycheck on it."

"Then no hard feelings?"

"Are you kidding?"

He lets fly with the paper airplane.

"There she goes! Navy Hellcat, got a MIG in his sights, on his tail. Ratatatatat. Got him!"

The plane lands harmlessly on a desk halfway across the city room.

"What can I do for you? Want a drink?"

He reaches in his desk and pulls out a pint of Early Times.

"No, no thanks, Chick. I'm here for instruction. How much do you know about horse racing?"

"Everything!" he crows, pouring himself two fingers into a dirty drinking glass. "I used to be a jockey!" And then he laughs and I laugh along with him. "No, seriously, Joe, that was one of my first jobs, covering Golden Gate Fields when it first opened in '41. Lasted a year until Pearl Harbor and then the Navy took the place over until the end of the war. So, what do you want to know?"

"Okay, for openers, say you bet a couple of hundred on a

longshot and all of a sudden you're looking at a payoff of, say, five thousand bucks. How do you collect?"

"Present the ticket, take the cash or take a check. Simple as that."

I nod. "So if you hit a really big winner, the check would be the answer."

He smiles. "Anything else would be dumb. What else?"

"I know there's a figure for the total amount bet on any horse---"

"The handle."

"But is there any way to get a breakdown of that number, that is, how many bets of a certain denomination were made."

Chick leans back in his chair and studies me.

"Why don't you stop yanking my chain, Joe, and tell me what you want to know."

I nod.

"Sure, why not? A friend of mine allegedly—and I emphasize allegedly—bet a horse at Santa Anita on the second of the month. He said he wagered a thousand dollars. The horse won and paid $126.40."

Chick's eyes widen for a moment, then narrow.

"Feature race? Big handle?"

"I don't know. It was the seventh race. The horse was named Base on Balls. That's all I know."

"Hold on," Chick says as he gets up from his desk and walks into a small room adjoining the city room. After a minute or so, he emerges leafing through a copy of the Racing Form. He sits down and then folds back the paper.

"Here it is," he says. "Seventh Santa Anita. Maiden claimer for colts. Winner Base on Balls. Pays one-twenty-six-forty to win, thirty-two-ten to place and twenty-three-eighty to show." He pauses and shakes his head. "No way," he says.

"No way what?" I say.

"No way your friend bet this horse," he says. He gets up and comes around the desk and lays the paper in front of me. He points. "You see this figure here. This is the total amount bet on your friend's horse to win. Nine hundred and forty four dollars. I think your pal was pulling your leg." Chick says.

"So Nick doesn't bet the horse. And I guess a bookie laying off a bet didn't bet either," I say.

Chick shakes his head.

"There's no separate window for bookies, Joe."

I stare at the paper. So, either Nick was a blowhard who was walking around with a thousand dollars in his pocket and lost his nerve at the last minute and later that evening lost both the thousand and his life or----

A shadowy, ill-formed scenario is beginning to take shape in my mind.

CHAPTER TWENTY

Wednesday. My last chance. Jack Warner is still in New York but returning on a noon flight and landing in L.A. late tonight. Tomorrow I will be under his personal microscope and whatever doesn't get done today won't get done. At least not by me.

I was busy last night with Aaron and a man named Vladimir. No last name. Just Vladimir. Sixtyish and bald with wispy fringes of grey hair sprouting around his ears and the back of his neck, he wore thick lensed glasses and spoke a mixture of Armenian and English. Aaron described him as a genius and fun to be around when he wasn't in jail which wasn't often. His specialty, I was told, was the ten dollar bill although throughout his career he had had some luck with stock certificates and British pound notes. Basically, Aaron said, there wasn't anything Vladimir couldn't do with paper, pen and ink in his hands.

I read my mail, skim the trades and drink coffee but I am just marking time. Finally at 10:15, Ray shows up with Tom and Madison in tow. I get up to greet them as Tom strides toward me, hand extended.

"Just want to thank you, sir. Mr. Giordano told me what you did," Tom says.

"Forget it," I say, the self-effacing hero.

"Won't ever be able to do that, sir," he says.

"And forget that 'sir' business. Just Joe is fine," I say.

Madison comes to my side and puts her arms around me and squeezes me tight.

"Thank you so much," she murmurs quietly.

"Okay, okay," I say, a little embarrassed. I wonder if the Lone Ranger ever had moments like this. "Grab a chair. We have to talk."

Ray gets a couple of spare chairs from Glenda Mae's anteroom and in a few moments we're all seated.

"Tom, you were able to claim your Dad's body?"

"Yes, sir. I mean, Joe. The lady was very nice about signing the paper. We must have talked for fifteen or twenty minutes about my father. I think she liked him very much."

"I'm sure she did," I say. I notice that he isn't stammering and seems very much at ease. "And you also got your Dad's personal effects."

"There wasn't anything except his clothes," Tom says.

I nod.

Ray chimes in. "Forest Lawn picked up Nick's remains about an hour ago, Joe. We're working out something simple and respectful at a decent price."

"When's the service?" I ask.

"We think Saturday morning," Ray says.

I turn to Tom.

"Has Ray explained to you what we're going to try to do?"

"Yes, he has," Tom says.

"You realize there's an element of danger."

"I know that. I don't care."

I look at Madison.

"What about you, Madison? Do you care?"

"It's Tom's decision," she says. "I want what he wants."

I nod.

"All right, then. I've already talked to Captain Willard of the County Sheriff's office. He's ready to go." I get up from my chair. "Let's get to it."

Madison hugs Tom. I shake Ray's hand and then Tom and I are gone. I am still driving the rickety Plymouth and though it is highly unlikely I hope I do not get involved in a car chase unless the other "car" is actually a bicycle. On the way Tom and I rehash the scenario and he's dialed in. Smart kid. His students at that Catholic high school are damned lucky to have him.

It's eleven-thirty when we pull up in front of The End Zone. We park next to the Sheriff Department's cruiser. Floyd Willard is already here. We go inside. They are all assembled, Minerva behind the bar and Eddie and Willard sitting on bar stools. Minerva looks from me to Tom but says nothing. Eddie gets up and confronts me, eyes flashing with anger.

"What the hell's going on, Bernardi? Floyd here says you've got a problem. What kind of a problem takes me away from my business and has me sitting around here with my thumb up my nose?"

Willard steps between us.

"Take it easy, Eddie. This isn't going to take long. Now sit down."

He says it sharply and Eddie, grumbling, complies.

Willard turns to me.

"Okay, Mr. Bernardi, you wanted 'em here together. You got 'em. Get to it."

"I'll let Tom take it from here," I say.

Tom nods with a smile. "First off, ma'am," he says to Minerva, "I want to thank you for allowing me to claim my father's body. We've already arranged for the burial."

Minerva nods.

"I also was able to claim his effects which were the clothes he was wearing and nothing more. But when I went through his pants pocket, I found this and I believe it's worth a great deal of money. Captain Willard agrees with me." He takes out the folded bookmaker's betting receipt and hands it to Eddie. "I checked," he says. "This is a winning ticket."

Eddie looks at it and frowns. It's all there. March 2. Santa Anita. 7th Race. $1000 to win. A capital A written in the lower left hand corner of the ticket which, unknown to Eddie, has been carefully altered from a ten dollar betting ticket written several days later on a 1-5 favorite.

"A thousand dollars," he says, confused. "No, I don't think---"

"It's your ticket, sir," Tom says.

"It sure is, Eddie. Knew it the minute the youngster showed it to me," Willard says.

Eddie looks at Willard and there is anger in his eyes. Anger mixed with confusion and maybe disillusionment.

"The horse went off at 63 to 1," Tom says.

Eddie's eyes widen for a moment and he starts to shake his head. "I didn't write this ticket," he says.

"Maybe Andy," I suggest.

"Yes. Andy," he says. "I have to talk to Andy about this."

"Maybe you should, Eddie," Willard says. "You know where to find him?"

"He's home."

Eddie gets up and starts toward the door carrying the ticket.

"I think maybe I'd better come with you," Willard says.

Eddie looks at Willard, then at the ticket in his hand and he nods in undertstanding.

"Yes. Absolutely," Eddie says.

Willard nods to me and Tom and we tag along.

Outside, Eddie and Willard start up the street on foot. Eddie and his son live in a one story two bedroom ranch about a block from The End Zone. It's been Eddie's home since the day he was first married.

We open the gate to the walkway that leads to the front door. Eddie enters and calls out Andy's name as we step inside behind him. The living room is small but neatly furnished with a stuffed sofa, an easy chair and an old fashioned rocker in the corner. On a table in front of the sofa is a 10" TV set with rabbit ears. A bookcase is half filled, mostly with paperbacks. Atop it are a half dozen family photos in frames. Eddie, his deceased wife, Andy at different ages. On a far wall over a small writing desk is a large framed formal photo, Eddie in morning clothes, his wife in her wedding gown, standing side by side facing the camera. Except for the television set, everything in this room is old and reeks of days gone by.

"Andy!" Eddie calls out again.

"Here, Pop!" we hear him call out and he appears from the back of the house. He's wearing jeans, no shirt, his feet are bare, his hair is wet and he's carrying a towel which he uses to dry his hair.

"Just taking a shower," he says and then stops short when he sees that Eddie is not alone.

"You got a girl back there, son?" Eddie asks.

"No, sir," Andy says adamantly.

"You want me to go look?" Eddie asks.

Andy looks away and then down at the floor.

"You go tell her to leave by the kitchen door. I don't want to see her and I got a feeling she sure doesn't want to see Floyd."

"Yes, sir," Andy says and goes back where he came from. In a minute he reappears. He's embarrassed as well as puzzled. He has no idea what's going on. He starts to sit.

"Stand up!" Eddie barks.

Andy stiffens and stands.

"This young man here is Nick's son from Chicago," Eddie says. "He just claimed Nick's body and his personal effects from the coroner's office." Andy says nothing, his eyes flitting nervously around the room, settling on me and then Tom and then looking down at the floor. "When he was going through his father's trouser pockets, he found this." He hands Andy the betting slip. "You want to explain this."

Andy looks at it like it was a hand grenade without a pin and quickly tries to hand it back.

"I don't know nothin' about this, Pop."

"You didn't take this bet?"

"Hell, no."

"That's your initial A in the corner."

"Well, I didn't write it! Damned thing's a phony."

"Why do you think that, Andy? Because you tore up the ticket or maybe thought you did. Maybe you tore up a losing betting slip from months ago that he'd forgotten to throw away."

"No, no! Hell, Pop, didn't you warn me about takin' bets like this. I mean, Jesus, a thousand bucks. I wouldn't do it, Pop. I swear. Especially not on a longshot like this one."

"Who said it was a longshot, Andy?"

That brings the kid up short.

"What?"

"Who said it was written on a longshot? There's no odds listed on this ticket."

He flounders and looks at Tom.

"Well, didn't he say--uh---?"

"Nobody said anything, Andy."

Eddie moves very close to his son and he speaks quietly.

"Did you kill him, son?"

"No!" Andy screams shaking his head.

"Why didn't you go to the track and lay it off?"

"Pop, please----"

"All you had to do was lay it off, Andy. Just lay it off."

Andy shakes his head violently and I think he's crying.

"Jesus Christ, Pop. It was a thousand dollars. You spend all day taking nickel and dime bets from these local pikers and here a thousand bucks falls in my lap bet on a milk horse, a stiff with no chance. No chance! What would you have done?"

Eddie looks at him sadly.

"I'd have laid it off," he says quietly.

Willard moves forward.

"Come on, son. I gotta take you in," he says.

Again, Andy shakes his head. "You stay away from me, old man. You ain't takin' me nowhere." He's backed up to the small writing desk and now he reaches in a side drawer and pulls out his .32 caliber target pistol, the one he uses to shoot rabbits.

Willard stops in his tracks.

Eddie steps closer to his son, glaring.

"Put down the gun, Andy," he says.

"I can't, Pop," the boy wails.

Eddie steps forward again and puts out his hand.

"Give it to me!"

Floyd Willard has the flap of his holster unsnapped and is gripping the handle of his firearm.

"I can't!"

Eddie reaches out and slaps his son hard across the face. Once, twice, three times. The gun falls to the floor. Andy begins to sob. He starts to sag toward the floor. Eddie catches him and holds him close.

Willard moves forward and cuffs Andy and leads him away. Eddie stands stock still staring off into space and then he turns and looks at Tom.

"It appears I owe you some money, young man," he says.

Tom shakes his head.

"No, sir," he says.

"That ticket is a phony, Eddie," I tell him. "Your son really did destroy the original."

Eddie nods.

"Doesn't change the fact that your Dad had a winning ticket that my son booked and what he booked, I booked."

"No, sir," Tom says. "I don't see it that way. There's been enough hurt around here today. Let's just leave it be."

Eddie looks at him and then nods. He turns and goes out the door. I follow and watch him as he walks down the street. I look across the street to the unmarked police car. Aaron's sitting behind the wheel. Unneeded back up. He throws me a thumbs up. I nod.

I turn and look again at the receding figure of Eddie Braverman. His shoulders are hunched and he's staring at the ground as he walks. I'm sure he is crying. I know I would be.

CHAPTER TWENTY ONE

The air is heavy and the sun overhead is playing hide and seek with grey water laden clouds. Rain is expected but not until this afternoon and it's only five after eleven. We have walked from the chapel to this serene section of Forest Lawn to say a final goodbye to Nick Scalese.

Jillian, who had been away for two days at a book fair in San Diego, is at my side, appropriately dressed in grey and black. A few others emulate her. Most don't. There was a time when a funeral called for somber colors but in Southern California tradition is falling into disrepair. People attend the theater in chinos and golf shirts, wear business suits to black tie affairs and think nothing of wearing pink and red and orange to funerals. The dead don't mind. The survivors seem to mind less and less. There may come a day when office people will come to work in blue jeans and sweat shirts. The thought depresses me.

Ray and his wife Trudy are there, of course, along with my friend Mick Clausen and my ex-wife Lydia. Jillian and Lydia were chattering like magpies before the memorial service. I think I was the main topic of conversation. Also on hand is a large contingent from Altadena who may not like strangers but know how to honor their own. I spot Floyd Willard in civvies and off to one side, standing close together, Eddie and Minerva. Eddie is ashen and his expression is blank. He is going through the motions because I suspect his thoughts are mainly with his son who is being held without bail and faces a charge of first degree murder. The priest is intoning the words of a prayer which I barely hear because my thoughts are elsewhere.

God, our father, Your Power brings us to birth, Your providence guides our lives and by Your command we return to dust.

Andy has made a full confession. His account is tragic. At eighteen, he is half man and half boy and he was not mature enough to act intelligently. He should not have taken the bet. Having taken it, he should have gone to the track and laid it off. He did neither. The sight of Nick's thousand dollars in cash muddied his senses. Greed took him by the throat. He was so certain the horse had no chance he didn't even check the race results so that when Nick came pounding on the door just before midnight that Thursday evening he was totally unprepared. Money. Nick was demanding money, a lot of more than Andy could comprehend, And Eddie? Where was Eddie? When Andy refused to go get him, Nick became unfuriated. He could guess where Eddie was, in his bed with Minerva. Where else? And so he turned and started from the house. That was when Andy took the gun from the desk drawer and shot him in the back of the head.

Lord, those who die will live in Your presence, their lives change but do not end. I pray in hope for the family, friend and relatives of Nicholas Scalese and for all the dead known to You alone.

Andy knew of Nick's troubles with Chicago. All his close friends did. He knew of the reward. If only he could divert suspicion and make it look as if an out of towner had killed Nick. Yes, that was the answer. Nick had been spending all that time at the ball park making himself more and more visible. If he could shift blame to a revenge killing no one would ever think of looking in Altadena. And so Andy put Nick in the back of his car and drove him to Wrigley Field and put him where he would surely be found. He took his rings and watch and wallet and the damned betting slip which he burned as soon as he was away from the ball park. His father must never know what he did. Never. No matter what.

In company with Christ who died and now lives, may they rejoice in Your kingdom, where all our tears are wiped away. Unite us together again in one family to sing Your praise forever and ever. Amen.

At the forefront of the mourners sits Tom Scalese with Madison beside him. He stands now and picks a rose from a nearby basket and lays it atop the shiny mahogany casket. Madison follows suit. One by one others approach and pay their final respects. I am among them. Jillian and I walk away from the grave site joining the others who are milling about and talking quietly. The last to approach the casket are Eddie and Minerva. She places her rose and steps away. Eddie stands for the longest time staring at the casket, then he kisses his fingers and leans forward and presses his fingers to the wood. He blesses himself with the sign of the cross and then he and Minerva walk away.

Tom is under the impression that I called Peanuts Lowery at the Cardinals training camp and that the ball players passed the hat to pay for Nick's internment. Not true. Eddie wrote a check for everything. In addition, he gave me an envelope containing ten thousand dollars which I will slip to Madison just before she and Tom board the plane back to Milwaukee. He wished it could have been more but now he is practically wiped out. I sense that he has promised himself he will make good on that sixty-three thousand dollars if it takes him the rest of his life to do it.

The mourners are heading for their cars. The show is over. The curtain has been lowered. Instead of heading for my car, newly repaired by the body shop, I stroll along a pathway with Jillian on my arm, looking at the various headstones. Regardless of how we spend our lives, this is the last stop, whether it comes tomorrow or decades from now. I feel a twinge each time I see a family grave. Husband and wife, side by side in death. Loving husband, precious wife, adored father, beloved mother. I have known a lot of loneliness in my life and I am sick of it. I want to belong somewhere.

I look over at Jillian, bright, attractive, kind and attentive. She is everything I could ever hope for.

And yet, even as I look at her, I think of Bunny.

THE END

AUTHOR'S NOTE

As usual, this book is a fanciful mixture of fact and fiction. All of the dialogue has been invented including all the exchanges involving Ronald Reagan and Doris Day and Jack Warner. Nothing here has been written with the intention of demeaning or minimizing the real life personalities who are part of the narrative. As for fact, it is true that Ron and Nancy Reagan were married on March 4, 1952, at the Little Brown Chapel in the San Fernando Valley in a very private ceremony with William Holden acting as Best Man and Brenda Marshall as Matron of Honor. "The Winning Team" was released to mixed reviews from the critics but was well received by the public and it is generally agreed that Reagan gave one of the best performances of his career as Grover Cleveland Alexander. The picture did indeed include cameo roles by a dozen real-life ball players including Peanuts Lowery who, at age 35, was coming to the end of his career. However, 1952 proved to be a banner year for Lowery who set a major league record with seven consecutive at bats where he successfully pinch hit. The following year he came up one shy of the major league record with 21 pinch hits over the season. The Boston Braves, as rumored, made the move to Milwaukee the following season opening the floodgates of carpetbaggerism throughout both leagues. Ronald Reagan did, indeed, vote for Dwight Eisenhower that year and continued to embrace conservatism, culminating in his election as our 40th President in 1980. Doris Day moved on from frothy musicals to straight drama and then found a new career in light comedy playing opposite the major leading men of her generation. She had two brushes with Oscar: the nomination she received for "Pillow Talk" and the nomination she should have received, but didn't, for "Love Me or Leave Me".

MISSING SOMETHING?

The first five books in the Hollywood Murder Mystery series are still available from Grove Point Press. All copies will be personally signed and dated by the author. If you purchase ANY THREE for $29.85, you automatically become a member of "the club". This means that you will be able to buy any and all volumes in any quantity at the $9.95 price, a savings of $3.00 over the regular cover price of $12.95. This offer is confined to direct purchases from The Grove Point Press and does not apply to other on-line sites which may carry the series.

Book One—1947
JEZEBEL IN BLUE SATIN

WWII is over and Joe Bernardi has just returned home after three years as a war correspondent in Europe. Married in the heat of passion three weeks before he shipped out, he has come home to find his wife Lydia a complete stranger.  It's not long before Lydia is off to Reno for a quickie divorce which Joe won't accept. Meanwhile he's been hired as a publicist by third rate movie studio, Continental Pictures. One night he enters a darkened sound stage only to discover the dead body of ambitious, would-be actress Maggie Baumann. When the police investigate, they immediately zero in on Joe as the perp. Short on evidence they attempt to frame him and almost succeed. Who really killed Maggie? Was it the over-the-hill actress trying for a comeback? Or the talentless director with delusions of grandeur? Or maybe it was the hapless leading man whose career is headed nowhere now that the "real stars" are coming back from the war. There is no shortage of suspects as the story speeds along to its exciting and unexpected conclusion.

$12.95 (9.95 to Club Members)

Book Two—1948
WE DON'T NEED NO STINKING BADGES

Joe Bernardi is the new guy in Warner Brothers' Press Department so it's no surprise when Joe is given the unenviable task of flying to Tampico, Mexico, to bail Humphrey Bogart out of jail without the world learning about it. When he arrives he discovers that Bogie isn't the problem. So-called accidents are occurring daily on the set, slowing down the filming of "The Treasure of the Sierra Madre" and putting tempers on edge. Everyone knows who's behind the sabotage. It's the local Jefe who has a finger in every illegal pie. But suddenly the intrigue widens and the murder of one of the actors throws the company into turmoil. Day by day, Joe finds himself drawn into a dangerous web of deceit, dupliciity and blackmail that nearly costs him his life.

$12.95 (9.95 to Club Members)

Book Three—1949
LOVE HAS NOTHING TO DO WITH IT

Joe Bernardi's ex-wife Lydia is in big, big trouble. On a Sunday evening around midnight she is seen running from the plush offices of her one- time lover, Tyler Banks. She disappears into the night leaving Banks behind, dead on the car-pet with a bullet in his head. Convinced that she is innocent, Joe enlists the help of his pal, lawyer Ray Giordano, and bail bondsman Mick Clausen, to prove Lydia's innocence, even as his assign-ment to publicize Jimmy Cagney's comeback movie for Warner's threatens to take up all of his time. Who really pulled the trigger that night? Was it the millionaire whose influence reached into City Hall? Or the not so grieving widow finally freed from a loveless marriage. Maybe it was the partner who wanted the business all to himself as well as the new widow. And what about the mysterious envelope, the one that disappeared and every-one claims never existed? Is it the key to the killer's identity and what is the secret that has been kept hidden for the past forty years? *$12.95 (9.95 to Club Members)*

Book Four—1950
EVERYBODY WANTS AN OSCAR

After six long years Joe Bernardi's novel is at last finished and has been shipped to a publisher. But even as he awaits news, fingers crossed for luck, things are heating up at the studio. Soon production will begin on Tennessee Williams' "The Glass Menagerie" and Jane Wyman has her sights set on a second consecutive Academy Award. Jack Warner has just signed Gertrude Lawrence for the pivotal role of Amanda and is positive that the Oscar will go to Gertie. And meanwhile Eleanor Parker, who has gotten rave reviews for a prison picture called "Caged" is sure that 1950 is her year to take home the trophy. Faced with three very talented ladies all vying for his best efforts, Joe is resigned to performing a monumental juggling act. Thank God

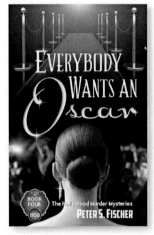

he has nothing else to worry about or at least that was the case until his agent informed him that a screenplay is floating around Hollywood that is a dead ringer for his newly completed novel. Will the ladies be forced to take a back seat as Joe goes after the thief that has stolen his work, his good name and six years of his life? *$12.95 (9.95 to Club Members)*

Book Five—1951

THE UNKINDNESS OF STRANGERS

Warner Brothers is getting it from all sides and Joe Bernardi seems to be everybody's favorite target. "A Streetcar Named Desire" is unproducible, they say. Too violent, too seedy, too sexy, too controversial and what's worse, it's being directed by that well-known pinko, Elia Kazan. To make matters worse, the country's number one hate monger, newspaper columnist Bryce Tremayne, is coming after Kazan with a vengeance and nothing Joe can do or say will stop him. A vicious expose column is set to run in every Hearst paper in the nation on the upcoming Sunday but a funny thing happens Friday night. Tremayne is found in a compromising condition behind the wheel of his car, a bullet hole between his eyes. Come Sunday and the

scurrilous attack on Kazan does not appear. Rumors fly. Kazan is suspected but he's not the only one with a motive. Consider:

Elvira Tremayne, the unloved widow. Did Tremayne slug her one time too many?

Hubbell Cox, the flunky whose homosexuality made him a target of derision.

Willie Babbitt, the muscle. He does what he's told and what he's told to do is often unpleasant.

Jenny Coughlin, Tremayne's private secretary. But how private and what was her secret agenda?

Jed Tompkins, Elvira's father, a rich Texas cattle baron who had only contempt for his son-in-law.

Boyd Larabee, the bookkeeper, hired by Tompkins to win Cox's confidence and report back anything he's learned.

Annie Petrakis, studio makeup artist. Tremayne destroyed her lover. Has she returned the favor?

$12.95 (9.95 to Club Members)

250

COMING SOON!

Book Seven—1953
PRAY FOR US SINNERS

Joe finds himself in Quebec but it's no vacation. Alfred Hitchcock is shooting a suspenseful thriller called "I Confess" and Montgomery Clift is playing a priest accused of murder. A marriage made in heaven? Hardly. They have been at loggerheads since Day One and to make matters worse their feud is spilling out into the newspapers. When vivacious Jeanne d'Arcy, the director of the Quebec Film Commisssion volunteers to help calm the troubled waters, Joe thinks his troubles are over but that was before Jeanne got into a violent spat with a former lover and suddenly found herself under arrest on a charge of first degree murder. Guilty or not guilty? Half the clues say she did it, the other half say she is being brilliantly framed. But by who? Fingers point to the crooked Gonsalvo brothers who have ties to the Buffalo mafia family and when Joe gets too close to the truth, someone tries to shut him up...permanently. With the Archbishop threatening to shut down the production in the wake of the scandal, Joe finds himself torn between two loyalties.

TO PURCHASE COPIES OF THE HOLLYWOOD MURDER MYSTERIES...

Check first with your local book seller. If he is out of stock or is unable to order copies for you, go online to Amazon Books where every volume in the series is available either as a paperback or in the Kindle format.

Alternatively, you may wish to order paperback editions direct from the publisher, The Grove Point Press, P.O. Box 873, Pacific Grove, CA 93950. Each copy purchased directly will be signed by the author and personalized, if desired. If your initial order is for three or more different titles, your price per copy drops to $9.95 and you automatically become a member of the "club." Club members may purchase any or all titles in any quantity, all for the same low price of $9.95 each. In addition, all those ordering direct from the publisher will receive a FREE "Murder, She Wrote" bookmark personally autographed by the author.

TURN TO THE NEXT PAGE

for the easy-to-use order form.

Want to know more about

THE HOLLYWOOD MURDER MYSTERIES?

click on

THEGROVEPOINTPRESS.COM

ORDER FORM

To
THE GROVE POINT PRESS
P.O. Box 873
Pacific Grove, CA 93950

☐ Please send the volume(s), either one or two, checked below at $12.95 each. I understand each copy will be signed personally by the author. Also include my FREE "Murder, She Wrote" keepsake bookmark, also autographed by the author.

☐ Please send the volumes checked below (three or more) at the low price of $9.95 each. I understand this entitles me to any and all future purchases at this same low price. I also understand that each volume will be personally signed by the author. Also include my FREE "Murder, She Wrote" keepsake bookmark, also autographed by the author.

QTY

_____ *Book One—1947* **Jezebel in Blue Satin**

_____ *Book Two—1948* **We Don't Need No Stinking Badges**

_____ *Book Three—1949* **Love Has Nothing to Do With It**

_____ *Book Four—1950* **Everybody Wants An Oscar**

_____ *Book Five—1951* **The Unkindess of Strangers**

_____ *Book Six—1952* **Nice Guys Finish Dead**

_____ *Book Seven—1953* **Pray For Us Sinners**

NAME _____

STREET ADDRESS _____

CITY _____

STATE _____ **ZIP** _____

Enclosed find in the amount of _____ for a total of _____ volumes. I understand there are no shipping and handling charges and that any taxes will be paid by the publisher.

ORDER FORM

To
THE GROVE POINT PRESS
P.O. Box 873
Pacific Grove, CA 93950

☐ Please send the volume(s), either one or two, checked below at $12.95 each. I understand each copy will be signed personally by the author. Also include my FREE "Murder, She Wrote" keepsake bookmark, also autographed by the author.

☐ Please send the volumed checked below (three or more) at the low price of $9.95 each. I understand this entitles me to any and all future purchases at this same low price. I also understand that each volume will be personally signed by the author. Also include my FREE "Murder, She Wrote" keepsake bookmark, also autographed by the author.

QTY

_____ *Book One—1947* **Jezebel in Blue Satin**

_____ *Book Two—1948* **We Don't Need No Stinking Badges**

_____ *Book Three—1949* **Love Has Nothing to Do With It**

_____ *Book Four—1950* **Everybody Wants An Oscar**

_____ *Book Five—1951* **The Unkindess of Strangers**

_____ *Book Six—1952* **Nice Guys Finish Dead**

_____ *Book Seven—1953* **Pray For Us Sinners**

NAME _____

STREET ADDRESS _____

CITY _____

STATE _____ **ZIP** _____

Enclosed find in the amount of _____ for a total of _____ volumes. I understand there are no shipping and handling charges and that any taxes will be paid by the publisher.

ORDER FORM

To
THE GROVE POINT PRESS
P.O. Box 873
Pacific Grove, CA 93950

☐ Please send the volume(s), either one or two, checked below at $12.95 each. I understand each copy will be signed personally by the author. Also include my FREE "Murder, She Wrote" keepsake bookmark, also autographed by the author.

☐ Please send the volumed checked below (three or more) at the low price of $9.95 each. I understand this entitles me to any and all future purchases at this same low price. I also understand that each volume will be personally signed by the author. Also include my FREE "Murder, She Wrote" keepsake bookmark, also autographed by the author.

QTY

_____ *Book One—1947* **Jezebel in Blue Satin**

_____ *Book Two—1948* **We Don't Need No Stinking Badges**

_____ *Book Three—1949* **Love Has Nothing to Do With It**

_____ *Book Four—1950* **Everybody Wants An Oscar**

_____ *Book Five—1951* **The Unkindess of Strangers**

_____ *Book Six—1952* **Nice Guys Finish Dead**

_____ *Book Seven—1953* **Pray For Us Sinners**

NAME _____

STREET ADDRESS _____

CITY _____

STATE _____ **ZIP** _____

Enclosed find in the amount of _____ for a total of _____ volumes. I understand there are no shipping and handling charges and that any taxes will be paid by the publisher.

ABOUT THE AUTHOR

Peter S. Fischer is a former television writer-producer who currently lives with his wife Lucille in the Monterey Bay area of Central California. He is a co-creator of "Murder, She Wrote" for which he wrote over 40 scripts. Among his other credits are a dozen "Columbo" episodes and a season helming "Ellery Queen". He has also written and produced several TV miniseries and Movies of the Week. In 1985 he was awarded an Edgar by the Mystery Writers of America. "Nice Guys Finish Dead" is the sixth in a series of murder mysteries set in post WWII Hollywood and featuring publicist and would-be novelist, Joe Bernardi.